MW01485161

during the last few years.
Robin Helm
Phil. 4:13

Guardian

The Guardian Trilogy, Book 1

ROBIN HELM

Copyright © 2011 Robin Helm

All rights reserved. No part of this publication may be reproduced, stored in a retrieval system, or transmitted in any form or bay any means, electronic, mechanical, photocopying, recording or otherwise, with the prior written permission of the publisher.

The characters and events portrayed in this book are fictitious or are used fictitiously. Any similarity to real persons, living or dead, is purely coincidental and not intended by the author.

ISBN-10: 0615528481
ISBN-13: 978-615528489
All rights reserved. No part of this publication may be reproduced, stored in a retrieval system, or transmitted in any form or by any means, electronic, mechanical, photocopying, recording, or otherwise, without the prior written permission of the publisher.

The characters and events portrayed in this book are fictitious or are used fictitiously. Any similarity to real persons, living or dead, is purely coincidental and not intended by the author.

Scripture quotations taken from the New American Standard Bible®, Copyright © 1960, 1962, 1963, 1968, 1971, 1972, 1973,1975, 1977, 1995 by The Lockman Foundation.
Used by permission (www.Lockman.org).

DEDICATION

In loving memory of my mother,

Norma Lynne Griffin Mills,

a Proverbs 31 lady who led me to faith,
encouraged me to write,
and instilled in me a love of reading.

To my husband Larry,
and my daughters, Mandy and Melanie,
who supported me wholeheartedly.

ACKNOWLEDGEMENTS

My heartfelt thanks is extended to Gayle Mills and Stephanie Hamm, who edited *Guardian*; to Julianne Martin and Rosemarie Spitaleri, who gave suggestions, corrected errors, and encouraged me; to Brenda Webb, who created a friendly place for me to publish my first work in progress; to Katie Baxley, who helped me to develop my writing style and served as my cold reader; to my daughter Melanie, who corrected my teen speech, texting, behavior, and clothing; to my daughter Mandy, who helped me to choose realistic details and inspired me by writing her first book; to Kelsey Farnham who contributed design ideas for the cover; to Wendi Sotis, Larry Helm, and Barbara Anderson, who helped me with formatting and publishing; and to Grace, who gave me invaluable advice in staging fighting scenes correctly. I also appreciate the input of all my readers who commented as this work was being posted, and especially those who gave me constructive criticism and support when I needed it.

PROLOGUE

"In the beginning, God created the heaven and the earth. And the earth was formless and void; and darkness was over the surface of the deep."
Genesis 1:1-2

The Rebellion

Just after the dawn of time, there was an unheard of disturbance in heaven. There was the feel of an approaching storm signaling something ominous on the horizon, as if heaven itself might be ripped asunder by the mighty rush of millions of wings beating at once in fierce battle.

During the time between the first and second verses recorded in the book of Genesis, great and awful events took place that shook the foundations of the universes and forever altered the course of human history. Before humans were ever created, choices were made that would greatly influence them and all other created beings.

The beautiful archangel Lucifer, the light bearer, glorious in his appearance, strode confidently through the majestic halls. His white robe fluttered, trailing in his wake as he approached Michael and Gabriel, the two other archangels, who stood with Xander, the highest ranking of all guardians.

"My brothers," he said to them in a silken voice, his amber eyes flashing his excitement. "Why should we be content to be servants? We are the highest and most powerful of the angels, yet we are expected to bow before God with the lowest of our kind. Let us join together. Even God Himself cannot stop us if we are united. Join me, and we will rule the universes."

Michael, the great warrior, the one who resembled his master, Jehovah God, faced Lucifer with a scowl marring his countenance. His green eyes flashed a warning as his jaw tensed. From his towering height of seven feet, the largest of all angels glared at the most beautiful.

"Your pathetic sycophants have puffed you up with conceit, Lucifer. Do not let your followers lead you into rebellion. We are honored to serve our Master, Yahweh. There is no higher calling. What is the purpose of attaining more power than He has already granted to us?"

Gabriel, God's able-bodied one, the hero of God, turned his azure eyes to Lucifer and Michael with unconcealed concern. His gentle demeanor belied his great strength in battle. Though Gabriel desired to be a peacemaker and would not take up arms against another angel easily, he was assured of victory if he did so. The flowing sleeves of his white robe fell back from his strong arms as he laid his hands on the shoulders of Lucifer and Michael.

Xander, chief among legions of protectors, spoke his carefully chosen words in a deliberately moderated tone, "Lucifer, you are already powerful beyond all angels except for those in this group. Must you rule us as well? Only Elohim has more authority than do we. Do not force His hand. Do not sever our bonds. Once you choose this path against our Master, you cannot untravel it. It is an irrevocable choice."

"Lucifer, Michael, Xander, let us not argue. Jehovah desires for us to live together in unity and harmony. We have but one purpose – to glorify the Almighty Creator," Gabriel said reasonably.

Lucifer sneered openly at them, his brawny arms crossed tightly over his broad chest. He shook his head in derision, and his glossy black hair fell across his shoulders.

"I thought as much. You are too cowardly to confront the One who holds us captive to His will. I do not need you to accomplish my plans. You are correct in one thing, Michael. I do have many followers, and they will die for me if necessary."

Michael, the strongest of them all, quickly unsheathed his sword and brandished it with two strong hands above his golden head. "Then let it be so! I will slay those who oppose my Master! First I will smite you, and then your groveling hordes."

A deep, sonorous voice spoke silence and stilled all of heaven as a brilliant light appeared before the four. All of heaven except Lucifer bowed to one knee and lowered their heads in gestures of submission. As Michael saw Lucifer openly defy the Creator of All Things, he jumped to his feet and called the Host to battle. As suddenly as lightning strikes, the angelic forces from all of heaven met as the two sides engaged in war. Swords clashed with a thunderous roar, and heaven shook with the fierceness of it, until God spoke His judgment, as recorded in Isaiah chapter 14.

"How you have fallen from heaven, O Lucifer, star of the morning, son of the dawn! You have been cut down to the earth, you who have weakened the nations!" The Father of All spoke a brief mourning for the loss of His brightest angel before consigning him to everlasting darkness. His voice invoked awe in the heavenly ranks as He continued, "But you said in your heart, 'I will ascend to heaven; I will raise my throne above the stars of God, and I will sit on the mount of the assembly in the recesses of the north. I will ascend above the heights of the clouds; I will make myself like the Most High.' Nevertheless, you will be thrust down to Sheol, to the recesses of the pit. Those who see you will gaze at you."

At God's word and through His power, with the rest of the host as witnesses, the pretender was cast out of heaven to the earth. Lucifer was no longer light. He was now the essence of darkness, and his very name mocked him. He became the god of this world, the ruler of the earth, for a season.

When Lucifer, the most cunning of all angels, was expelled from the presence of the Master, the rest of the angels chose sides for eternity. Xander, along with millions of others, elected to stay with their Creator and serve

Him. Lucifer managed to convince many hundreds of thousands of their kind to desert all good things and their places in the ranks in order to follow him. After humans were created, the sole reason for Lucifer's existence became to prevent humans from believing in God; failing that, the dark ones hoped to rob believers of their joy and their usefulness to the Master. Lucifer was constantly watching for any opportunity to accuse believers and to point out their sins to God. He and those who chose to be with him sought to thwart the plans of Jehovah at every opportunity. The fallen were totally destructive and continuously evil. Whereas the light beings were pure souls, the dark ones had given up their souls at the moment they had chosen their common destiny. Those of the light never sinned, and those of the darkness never stopped sinning. Salvation was not needed for the holy angels, and it was not possible for the fallen.

Eventually, in God's chosen time, the dark ones would be defeated once and for all and condemned to the abyss. Of course, Lucifer had convinced his forces that he would be ultimately victorious, and they believed his lie. He was the Father of Lies. Lucifer's demonic forces were divided into hierarchies and ranks just as light beings were, but they held their positions through threats and abuse. There was no loyalty among them. They could achieve only a perverted sort of happiness through causing others misery.

Chapter 1

"For Thou didst form my inward parts; Thou didst weave me in my mother's womb. I will give thanks to Thee, for I am fearfully and wonderfully made; wonderful are Thy works, and my soul knows itvery well." Psalm 139:13-14

His ancient eyes impassively observed the birth of the tiny girl as he tried to discern what made her different from the thousands of other children born on that day. Her family seemed ordinary enough, and the guardians with her parents were of the middle ranks. He knew that there was a divine reason for his selection as the girl's protector, and he did not question the decision that put him in that place on that day. But he was curious. He had been the guardian of hundreds of apostles, rulers, patriarchs, and pivotal humans in history for thousands of years. He had been with Noah as he built the ark; with Abraham as he had made his trek through the desert toward Ur; with Jacob as he had fathered the twelve tribes of Israel; with Moses as his mother had set his basket afloat in the Nile; with David as he had slain the giant Goliath; with Daniel as he had faced the lions; with G. F. Handel as he had composed beautiful music, including *The Messiah*, to the glory of The One; and with Dwight L. Moody, and other evangelists who had brought the Light to the world. He had guarded kings, Presidents, Prime Ministers, and military heroes. He was the principal guardian from the highest order; servant to Elohim, the Most High Master, Lord of Lords, King of Kings,

Almighty Creator of the universe. What made this tiny baby special enough for his assignment as her guardian?

He thought back to the summons he had received in the previous year upon the completion of his assignment. There had been nothing unusual about the manner of Asim, the scheduler, when he had communicated the identity and location of Xander's next charge. However, Xander had been surprised that he was being sent to guard the offspring of such an unremarkable family in an unimportant place. Normally, guardians of his rank and record were given to those who would change history, those who would hold positions of power, and those who would be extremely important in the work of his Master. But Xander asked no questions. He accepted the assignment immediately and without betraying any hint of his thoughts. He had confidence that there was a reason for this dispatch, and that he would be told what he needed to know when it was necessary. In the meantime, he would do his job from the moment of her conception. No one, nothing would harm this child until the appointed hour of her death.

Elohim, in His omniscience, had heard Xander's confusion concerning his charge and had summoned him to the throne room as he was leaving Asim. Xander had removed his sandals and bowed on his knees before the pure, holy light that was his Master, the King of the Ages.

"Xander, chief of all my guardians, do you wish to ask anything of me?" God asked his servant in a gentle voice.

"No, my Lord. Whatever you command is good in my sight. I am pleased to obey," Xander had answered quietly without lifting his head.

"I know your heart, Xander, and I know that what you say is true; however, I will answer what you will not ask. Had my own Son needed a guardian, I would have chosen you. As He could command the legions Himself, I instead charged you with guarding His mother. Just as you kept her safe from the evil plans against her life and His while she carried Him, I need for you to guard this human girl who will be born. I have an important design for her life, Xander. She will be the means of turning the earth world back to Me, and she will also provide the way to defeat Lucifer's champion for this age. Her influence will be felt for many generations. Of course, she will have free will in this. She could refuse Me, but she will not. Xander, I will ask more of you when the time is full, and what I will ask will not be easy for you. I know that you can protect her, and I know that you will do anything that I ask of you, but I wish for you to accept this willingly. You can decline this, if you wish, and continue as you have always been. Do you wish to have a different charge?"

Xander had never heard of any angel being given a choice. Humans had free will; angels did as they were commanded. However, he carefully considered what the Father of All had said to him before he answered, though his head remained bowed.

"My Lord, You chose me for this, and I am humbled that I was selected. You know all things, and You seek only what is good for all that You have created. The only reason I exist is to serve You, and I would no longer wish to live if I did not do my best to please You in all things. Please allow me to protect this special child."

God spoke. "Your request is granted."

~~~~~~~~~~

Xander was somewhat acquainted with the protectors assigned to his charge's parents and older sister. If the other three were surprised at his presence with them, they were too well trained to betray it. As guardians of the same family, the team shared their own minds as well as knowing those of their charges and other people who were in close proximity. Within a few seconds of joining the team, he knew the entire history of the small group consisting of the humans and those assigned to guard them. All guardians and others of their ranks with different responsibilities could communicate with each other telepathically, but the complete knowledge of another's mind was limited to those who shared guardianship of a family within the confines of a few miles of distance.

Only the servants of his Master, along with children too young to have made a decision, had guardians. This human family had been guarded throughout their lifetimes. The mother of his charge, Lynne Bennet, had made her decision early in her life, as had her parents and grandparents. The father, David, though born into a non-servant family, had become a follower when he was sixteen and had first heard the story. Janna, the older sister, had been a believer from early childhood and was now nine and a half years old. They were faithful followers, but they were not unusual. Suddenly, a startling thought occurred to Xander. *The Son had been born to an ordinary family in a humble place.* Perhaps there was more to this family than he had seen thus far. The Master had a way of using the humble to confound the mighty.

Xander, was the largest of the four protectors, with a sharp intelligence and a massive strength. Though humans could not see them unless the light beings chose to be seen, Xander's appearance and towering height were intimidating even to others of his own kind. He was known to be fierce in the execution of his duties, and he was one of the few guardians who had battled the dark forces with an unblemished record. Xander had never been defeated. He had never lost a battle. His charges were his first priority, and he had kept all of them safe until their appointed times.

He had seen all the good and the bad of the human race, and felt some comfort that he would be with a family of believers who loved and respected each other. He and the others had been created for a purpose. He never had doubted that his purpose was a lofty one, and that he was perfectly suited to it. From the beginning of time, he had been a protector, a guardian, as had the others with whom he would share this assignment. They had been part of the host who had witnessed the creation of the first humans, their separation from the Master, and their willful disregard for His plans. The guardians had been present at every major event in human history. As Mary's guardian, Xander had been present at the birth of the Lamb of God, and he had been by Mary in her grief at the crucifixion. Protectors had seen wars, violence, plagues, murders, and the effects of humanity's greed and lust for power. Though the human race had deserted the Master over and over, He had never turned His back on them. Xander was constantly amazed and awed by the One whom he served. The perfect love of the Master for human beings was an enigma for which he had no explanation.

Guardians, and others of their kind, existed in a frequency of the light spectrum invisible to human eyes, but they saw each other, and they could assume a visible human form if they wished to do so. As ancient beings, they were not overly concerned with appearance. They knew that many things were more important than how a being looked. Even so, Xander was arresting. Among beings all of whom were beautiful, his noble countenance was still remarkable. Whether he chose to appear in a human form or to remain in his natural state, he stood nearly seven feet tall with eyes the color of a cloudless summer sky. His gaze was intense and unwavering, never missing the smallest detail, sending fear through his enemies and a sense of safety to his charges. His dark brown, wavy hair meandered to his neck, falling carelessly in loose curls across his strong brow. Xander's broad, well-muscled shoulders, bronzed arms, and powerful legs hinted at his unparalleled speed and strength. His chiseled jaw, aristocratic nose, and full lips were perfect, and his rare smile was breathtaking. He appeared to shimmer in the simple, sleeveless, short white tunic he wore which was the garb of all protectors, as was the razor sharp sword which hung from the belt on his hip. A single swift blow from that sword had sent uncounted dark ones screaming and spiraling into the abyss.

His mind was incomparable. He was well-known for his ability to make difficult decisions quickly, and his good judgment ensured that his final choices were the correct ones. If he chose to speak, he was never ignored. His voice carried authority, yet it was never unkind. Though Xander's appearance and mind were those of a warrior, he was surprisingly gentle when he was not engaged in battle.

Xander had been bored, amused, surprised, and vexed, but he had never known the stronger emotions of anger, hatred, jealousy, or love. He had experienced the righteous anger every protector knew in guarding his charges from the dark ones, but never any anger on his own behalf. Those types of feelings were distinctly human. He had observed them but never experienced them. He did not desire to do so. He had seen the havoc wreaked by unchecked passions. Human empires had fallen because of jealousy and greed. People had murdered each other when they were ruled by the anger which was fueled by their hatred. Wars were fought in the name of every conceivable emotion. Even members of the host had been affected by allowing their emotions free reign; many of his kind had fallen from heaven and left the service of the Master because of their abominable pride and selfish lust for power. They had lost their light, and now served Beelzebub, Lord of the underworld, Prince of Darkness. No, Xander had no wish for emotions to interfere with his existence; he liked things as they were – orderly and uncomplicated.

Xander folded his arms over his chest and recalled the conversations of the family over the last few years that had led to this event occurring now in this delivery room. He narrowed his eyes as his thoughts drifted back in time, his perfect mind revisiting the thoughts of the other protectors he had heard upon joining the group.

The child was special to her family, of course. Xander had observed that her mother had wanted another baby two years after the birth of their daughter Janna, and had asked David if they could have another child, but he had not agreed. He had feared that his small income as a minister along with Lynne's teaching salary would not support two children, and he did not want to be unable to provide a good education and everything else that he felt was needed for his offspring. Lynne had not mentioned her desire again, but had prayed daily that if God wanted her to have another child, David would bring it up himself by the time she was thirty-five years old. As Janna grew, David had realized how much he enjoyed being a father. He had seen his wife holding the babies of her friends; he had seen her wistful expression as she had kissed the children and handed them back to their mothers. He loved her, and it had been difficult to bear her subtle sadness. His adored little Janna also had voiced her longing for a sister or brother.

During the earth year 1989, both David and Lynne had turned thirty-five. In July of that year, after returning from a summer retreat with the youth of the church, he had walked calmly into their house and made a life-altering statement.

Lynne and Janna had been watching TV when David had arrived. Lynne was lying comfortably on the couch when David had looked at her with a bemused expression and said, "If you still want to have another baby, I want to have one, too."

Because she had already accepted that she was now thirty-five and her desire for another child would go unfulfilled, she had nearly fallen off the couch in shock. "Are you serious, David? What brought about this change?" Her mind spinning, she was thinking, *Why didn't I pray that he would agree by the time I was thirty? Can I really do this at thirty-five?* Then, amused at her own inner response to David's capitulation, she chuckled softly as she thought, *This is no longer a choice. God has answered my prayers in a definite way. This is His will, and He will help me through it. I must not develop a lack of faith now.*

When his wife had questioned him a second time, David had avoided telling her what had caused him to change his mind. Lynne had known instinctively that God had dealt with him, and that He had answered her prayers; however, she wisely kept those thoughts to herself, not wishing to antagonize her husband. David had been sensitive to the Spirit's leading. It was enough.

In her extreme joy and excitement, Lynne had called her mother, Norma.

"Mom," she chattered, eager to share her news. "We're going to have another baby!"

"You're pregnant again?" asked Norma, a hint of surprise in her voice.

"Well, not yet. But David has finally agreed." Lynne paused, puzzled by her mother's lack of a congratulatory response.

"Honey, you've been on the pill for more than nine years now. You may not be able to get pregnant right away. It may take a while, and you're thirty-five years old now. Slow down a little, Sweetheart." Norma hated for Lynne to be disappointed.

"But, Mom, I've prayed for this child for all those years. I won't have any problem getting pregnant."

And she didn't have any problem at all. Now that David's mind was made up, he happily, even eagerly, joined with Lynne in her efforts to conceive. She stopped taking the birth control pills, and she and her husband explored alternate means to prevent conception until the time was right. Both David and Lynne seemed to wear perpetual smiles during those months.

"David," Lynne had whispered playfully to him one night, her green eyes twinkling in good humor. "I hope you don't mind all the extra work we've been putting into making a baby. You must be tired."

He had grinned lazily at her and replied in mock seriousness as he turned on his side to face her in their bed. "Not at all. I'm always ready to do my part for the cause." Then, in earnest, he had added tenderly, "You know that this is the best part of deciding to have another child. Maybe we could put a little more effort right now into realizing our goal." And they did.

Ever practical and thorough, Lynne had immediately added maternity coverage to their medical insurance, aware that it would have to be in place for ninety days in order for it to cover her pregnancy. Then she had counted down the days. She needed to conceive after the first day of October to be covered. Just as she had planned, by her estimation, she had become pregnant on October second. The child would be born in July after her teaching year ended, and she would be able to resume teaching when the new school term resumed in mid-August. The small Christian school at which she taught had a daycare, and the baby was already registered for the next year.

Xander nodded gravely. *Yes . . . This child was in God's design for their lives.* They could have no way of knowing, as he did, that their child was in God's design for the rest of the world as well.

Chapter 2

"We have become a spectacle to the world, both to angels and to men."I
Corinthians 4:9

As Xander thought back through the events that had brought this small group to Elizabeth's birth, his memories were as clear as if he were living the moments for the first time. He allowed his thoughts to wander again, this time remembering Mrs. Bennet's first doctor's appointment. Certainly he had not been pleased with the event, and Lynne Bennet had been even less so.

~~~~~~~~~

Xander's sharp eyes unrelentingly watched his enemy. He fixed the dark one with a piercing, intense stare as the demon grinned back wickedly at him from across the room.

Though the fallen ones had retained the beauty that had been bestowed on them in the beginning by their Creator, it had become twisted and evil. Whether they chose to be seen in human form, or, very rarely, in their true angelic forms, light beings and fallen angels were indistinguishable to humans. However, no one in either the light or dark angelic ranks would ever mistake one kind for the other. That was not possible. Holy angels radiated a gentle glow, while the fallen emitted no light at all. Xander did not question why Elohim had chosen to allow the evil ones to continue to exist; he simply accepted his Master's wisdom and knew that His ultimate purpose would be fulfilled.

Lynne's first visit to her OB-GYN had been frustrating in the extreme.

Dr. Gardner had rushed into the room and done a cursory examination. Without so much as a pretense at caring, he had scribbled on her chart, not even bothering to look up at her as he spoke in a voice laced with routine unconcern.

"Mrs. Bennet, I'm having the receptionist set you up with several tests," he said, writing hurriedly. "When my patients who are thirty-five or older are pregnant, I always perform an amniocentesis. There are higher percentages of babies with genetic abnormalities, such as Down syndrome and spina bifida, born to women in your age group. If the fetus is found to have either of those particular disorders or a range of other genetic defects, we want to be certain that you have time to make an informed decision. After the first trimester, abortions become riskier."

Xander and Lynne's guardian, the shorter, black-haired Niall, stiffened, taking protective stances, while the demon at Dr. Gardner's side smirked at them.

Lynne's eyes widened, and when she had sufficiently calmed herself to gather her thoughts, she replied, "Dr. Gardner, I have read that an amniocentesis can cause a miscarriage. Some studies say that the miscarriage rate is as high as one for every one hundred amniocenteses performed while Down syndrome occurs in about one in eight hundred babies. Even fewer babies have spina bifida. If what I have read is accurate, and I believe that it is, there is a far greater likelihood that the test will cause me to miscarry than that my baby could actually have either of those conditions. Furthermore, Doctor, out of every two hundred fifty tests showing positive results for Down, as many as five percent are false positives and forty-two percent of the Down babies are undetected. How many of those women that got false positives unknowingly chose to abort a perfectly healthy, 'normal' infant? In any event, I would not abort my child even if she did have Down, or any other genetic disorder. In fact, I wouldn't abort under any circumstances." Lynne absolutely refused to refer to her child as an "it," so "she" was her choice of pronoun, for now.

As Lynne voiced her challenge, Dr. Gardner stopped writing abruptly and looked up. He tossed Lynne's chart aside and glared at her impatiently, his dark brows nearly coming together as he furrowed them deeply. Clearly, he was angry. "You would not abort even if your fetus was anencephalic?" he asked in astonishment. "Even if it had no brain?"

Xander's hand moved reflexively to his sword as he narrowed his eyes. His enemy mirrored his movements.

Lynne held the doctor's gaze and did not flinch. She was not a woman to be so easily intimidated, especially by those who felt the need to play God with people's lives.

"Dr. Gardner," Lynne replied calmly, "I do know what the word means." It was with great effort that she maintained her unruffled demeanor.

"Then, Mrs. Bennet," he continued in a clipped voice, "you probably also know that a baby with anencephaly carried to full term could not live for more than two days."

"If that were the case, Dr. Gardner, my child would go to be with God," she said. "We are Christians. It would not be my decision. Don't be concerned. I can assure you that there is nothing wrong with my baby. She is an answer to prayer. Whatever God chooses to give us will be cherished."

Lynne stared at the doctor, wondering if she should tell him the human, or rather the humane side of the argument – that a couple in Lynne's church actually had parented a child with anencephaly who had lived two and a half years. Though she never learned to walk or talk, and most people may have thought that such a child had no purpose or value, she had given meaning to her parents' lives. They had loved her dearly. After her death, the couple had formed a nation-wide support group for parents of children with the disorder. Following a moment of silence, she simply shook her head. By the closed expression on his face, she knew it would be fruitless to argue with him. The doctor's mind was made up. Lynne broke their eye contact and held her counsel regarding the child of her friends. She knew that he would neither believe her story nor care about her friends.

He sighed at her ignorance and fixed his eyes on hers with barely concealed contempt. "You are very judgmental, Mrs. Bennet. Abortion is the main form of contraception in other countries," he said in a superior tone. *These self-righteous Christians grate on my nerves.*

"I am not judging anyone, Dr. Gardner. Every woman has to live with her own decisions. Though I will not have the test you mentioned as it could harm my child, I am perfectly willing to have any non-invasive tests that you suggest. That way, if my child does have a serious medical condition, there could be a team of specialists at the birth to take care of her."

"If you will not agree to an abortion, I see no need to perform any tests, Mrs. Bennet. Have a nice afternoon. Please set up your next appointment on your way out." He spoke brusquely and left the room without a backward glance.

Xander inwardly chuckled. His estimation of Lynne's strength of character had risen dramatically during that encounter. He had known that she was highly intelligent, but now he greatly admired her tenacity as well. From his experience in the last half century, he had found that most women accepted whatever a doctor advised without question. She, in contrast, had done her research and stood her ground, insisting on doing what she thought was best for her child. She was a woman worthy of his respect.

He turned his steely gaze to the enemy and took that opportunity to smile at the dark one, driving the evil angel to wrath. The first battle had been won without so much as a skirmish, though Xander's hand still twitched beside his sword, yearning to strike a blow at the imp, sending the fiend howling into the pit for eternity. But it was not yet time.

~~~~~~~~~~

In Xander's opinion, Lynne's next visit to the doctor's office went a little better. Fortunately, there was a woman, a servant, in the practice with the other two male doctors. She had taken a special interest in Lynne's pregnancy and had privately arranged to perform a sonogram on Lynne every month while charging her for only the first in the series. Dr. Neal's guardian, acutely aware of Xander, had watched with avid interest as the doctor carefully checked the baby's spine and rate of development each month so that, if necessary, she could have specialists present at the birth. Though these precautions had made Lynne more comfortable, they had proved to be unnecessary. Xander and Niall had nodded silently at Dr. Neal's protector in approval. As usual, the Master had provided for every contingency.

Her pregnancy was mostly uneventful. Niall, along with Xander, constantly watched her. There was never a moment when she was not protected. All guardians knew that the dark ones were especially alert whenever a believer was singled out for protection by the higher ranks. Xander's reputation was well-established, and his presence had already attracted their attention. The evil ones would do everything within their power to prevent the birth of this child. The OB-GYN was under their influence and had played a significant role in their first attempt toward this end.

Later, when Lynne was about six months into her pregnancy, she had tripped going through a doorway. Feeling herself falling, she had twisted her body to avoid landing face-forward on her stomach. Though she had not known it, both Niall and Xander had leapt under her to cushion her fall. She was of average height and build, about five foot six, but her bulky, pregnant form was as no weight to the guardians.

Lynne, to her great chagrin, had never been athletic or even well-coordinated, and both guardians had grimly tracked her every move. Xander was glad that she had two guardians with her at all times. She was a devout Christian who was musically talented and highly self-motivated. In addition, she was an excellent wife and mother. In fact, she did many things very well. Walking was not one of them. His favorite time of the day had been when Lynne was asleep. Even then, he had been vigilant. *She is clumsy enough to roll off of her bed in her sleep*, he had thought as he chuckled to himself.

Knowing Lynne's mind was extremely helpful to her protectors. She had been ecstatic to be pregnant, and she had done everything within her control to ensure a healthy baby and a safe delivery. She took every possible precaution, was careful to take her pre-natal vitamins, and did the recommended exercises. Any risky behaviors, even drinking her beloved coffee, were avoided totally. The safety and well-being of her pre-born child had been almost an obsession with her. David and their beautiful, brown-eyed Janna had also been thrilled that this child was to join their family. They had done all that they could to help Lynne – cooking meals, doing housework, and making sure that she had time to rest when she came home from teaching. David had also gone with Lynne to Lamaze classes, just as he had when Lynne was carrying Janna. Xander's charge had been well-loved before she had ever taken her first breath. He was pleased.

As Lynne and David had discussed names for their child, confirmed to be a daughter in the sixth month of Lynne's pregnancy, she had realized that a compromise would be necessary. Her husband liked short names and would not accept anything too formal. She insisted that a formal name was needed in case their daughter grew up to be a professional who needed more than a nickname. Finally, he had agreed to name the baby Elizabeth and call her El, but both of them had been undecided about her middle name. As Lynne had talked over their dilemma with Mary Collins, who was another pastor's wife, a perfect name had been suggested. Her friend had insisted that her second name should be Faith, because her mother had prayed for her for so long.

The comparison brought to Xander's mind the memory of another of his charges, the shepherd boy, David. Xander smiled as he recalled how Samuel's mother, Hannah, had pleaded with God for a child, and had promised to bring Samuel back to the temple after he was weaned and give him to Eli, the priest, to be trained for God's service. He had become a priest himself as well as a great judge who had been given the privilege of anointing David the second king of Israel. Was this child as beloved in the sight of the Father as David, a man after God's own heart?

And so it was that Elizabeth's name was a testament to her mother's constant petitions to the Almighty. Throughout her life, every time she heard or wrote her middle name, Elizabeth would remember how much she was loved and wanted.

~~~~~~~~~

Appropriately it was Halloween, a time when the veil separating the physical world from the spiritual realm was at its thinnest. It was the night when demons most easily slipped through the diaphanous curtain and came out to wreak havoc upon mankind.

The attention of the evil ones had indeed been drawn to Xander's presence with the Bennet family. The activity had been reported to the Prince of Darkness who had already felt that something was afoot. He had sensed faint waves of excitement in heaven. Contingency plans had been made, and within a month of Elizabeth's conception, another group of angels of a very different sort had been gathered to observe a major event in a different part of the country.

Holding court in utter pandemonium, the Dark Lord, the Prince of the Power of the Air, called his minions to order.

"Bring the girl to me," he ordered.

Two large demons roughly dragged the small, terrified teenager before their master.

The master, while still one of the most beautiful angels ever created, exuded the stench of pure wickedness. The girl was frightened beyond belief, nearly past the ability to speak.

"You have been chosen," he told her in falsely honeyed tones. "Are you ready?"

"Yes, my lord," she choked out, cowering before him, nearly incoherent and barely able to breathe.

"Good," he replied with a hideous smile that held no light or joy, knowing that his plan was being set into motion.

"Take her to the chamber," he thundered curtly at the two dark ones who held the girl.

The Dark Master turned on his heel and quickly strode through the curtains into the appointed place, his long black robes flowing about his feet as he strode confidently to the act that would achieve his purpose. Entering the room, he looked upon the altar on which the girl, almost unconscious from fear, was being laid as his minions prepared her for her destiny.

A demonic sentry drew the curtains aside so that all could view their lord's triumph.

The air of wickedness was nearly palpable in the abandoned warehouse as the dark ones watched, leering salaciously as their prince, Lucifer, the Day Star, took human form. This place was forbidden to the beings of light. It was within the realm of darkness and controlled by the dark forces.

The Dark Prince lay with the runaway, viciously impregnating the human girl who had been chosen and led to this desolate place for this heinous purpose. The teenager was disposable. A homeless prostitute would not be missed by anyone, and because she had been possessed by a dark one at a tender age, there had been none of the angelic guardians present to interfere with her abduction earlier on that fateful evening. Hope had abandoned her.

The vile act which had created the child she would carry was obscene – a parody of the act of love that had given life to Elizabeth. The girl had fought feebly, crying out piteously against the pain of the rape, but the dark one living within her had enjoyed her agony, feasted on her fear, and reveled in her torture. He knew that she had turned from God in her childhood, and now there was no one to help her, no one to hear her cries. After her purpose was completed and her child was born, the demon who possessed her would have to find a new body in which to live, but he was not concerned. Though the girl would not survive the birth of her son, she would be easily replaced from among multitudes of non-servants who would welcome the dark one, never knowing that it would cost them everything of any real value.

~~~~~~~~

On July 6, 1990, in the small, sleepy South Carolina town of Bethel, located in the thick of the Bible belt, Elizabeth Faith was born to David Thomas and Lynne Frances Bennet. As Dr. Gardner had finished his shift, Dr. Neal had rotated onto hers about four hours before the birth; consequently the delivery room was well fortified with five strong guardians who were heavily armed and ready for battle, but there were no dark ones present. Because of their visits to the doctor's office, Alexandra, Dr. Neal's golden-haired, Amazon-like guardian, was already aware of Xander and Niall. She knew them fairly well, and she had shared an assignment with David's guardian, Roark, some one hundred earth years previously, but she still had to repress a shock each time she encountered the powerfully built champion. She tried not to stare and willed her errant thoughts not to betray her awe, but Alexandra had never before met anyone of Xander's formidable reputation, overpowering beauty, and exalted position in the ranks.

Xander knew her thoughts, but it was nothing he had not heard before. He did not betray his knowledge by any change in his countenance. His thoughts were well-regulated, and Alexandra had no cause to be embarrassed. His total focus was on his charge.

While the stunningly beautiful Alexandra may not have been surprised, the labor nurse's guardian was totally unprepared for the sight of the imposing Xander. The sinewy, more slightly built Warner fought the urge to step back as he gazed at the small family with no little surprise and wonder. This tiny dark-haired girl being delivered with such an impressive audience was obviously someone important in the Master's plan, and both Alexandra and Warner were anxious for her to be safely born and in the unequaled care of Xander. They realized with a sense of reverence that they were part of a momentous occasion that could be a turning point in human history.

And with the current path humanity was choosing to travel, a turning point was desperately needed.

Chapter 3

"For it is written: 'He will command His angels concerning you to guard you.'" Luke 4:10

In the sterile delivery room of the local hospital in Bethel, Xander relaxed very slightly upon the safe delivery of Elizabeth and in the absence of any members of the demonic host in his immediate vicinity, but he maintained a vigilant watch on his charge just the same. The fiends had ample access to the facility because of all the non-servants who worked there, and Xander could almost smell them through the walls. He knew from the thoughts of Niall and Roark that they were uneasy as well. It would be so until they left this public place for the sanctity and relative safety of the Bennet home. He fully expected to see one of the dark ones floating through a wall at any time.

After she had taken her first breath and cried out, Elizabeth was laid on her mother's chest so that her parents could adore her properly, her eyes squeezed shut and her short brown curls still wet and matted. Her cries revealed a double-dimple in her right cheek.

Lynne tiredly joked, "Look, David. The angels kissed her before they sent our little El to us," producing a round of smiles from the invisible ones surrounding them.

David was too busy counting his daughter's tiny fingers and toes to give much of a reply other than a sigh of relief and a quick, silent prayer of thanksgiving that the ordeal was over. He kissed his wife as the nurses took Elizabeth to examine her and clean her up.

"She is perfect and beautiful, Sweetheart. God has blessed us again," David told his wife.

~~~~~~~~

In order to save money, Lynne had opted to stay in the hospital only eighteen hours, and she looked forward to going back to their modest home to introduce little Elizabeth to her big sister Janna. All of Janna's friends had siblings, and Janna had wanted a baby sister or brother more than anything else.

Lynne was delighted that David was such an involved father; having a baby at thirty-six was much more tiring than having one at twenty-seven had been. She was exhausted, and she went to take a nap soon after they arrived home.

"Can I hold El now, Daddy?" Janna asked plaintively, her arms outstretched and ready to receive her much loved little sister.

Xander, Roark, and Alexis, Janna's protector, hovered, smiling at the sweet scene. Niall listened from Lynne and David's room, enjoying the warmth of the moment.

"Yes, Janna. You *are* her big sister after all. Sit down and hold her head steady like this," David replied as he demonstrated the proper way to hold a newborn. "She isn't strong enough to hold her head up yet, so you have to support it for her."

Janna listened carefully to her father's instructions. She took her responsibilities as a big sister very seriously. David placed Elizabeth in Janna's arms, and she was thrilled to hold her baby sister for the first time. He looked at his two darling daughters and felt that his heart might burst with happiness.

Both Janna and David were ecstatic to have the care of Elizabeth left to them while Lynne slept. Janna had looked forward to her sister's birth more than she had ever anticipated anything before in her nine and a half years, and she was not disappointed. To her, Elizabeth was better than any toy, doll, or amusement. Janna and her father were both in love with their "little El."

Xander could see that his charge would be well looked after by her human family.

~~~~~~~~~

On the thirty-first of July, another family was forming in the suburban sprawl of Charlotte, North Carolina.

The pregnant girl had been running blindly since the rape in the warehouse. She had hitchhiked and jumped trains until she could run no more. She was terrified that they would find her again. But now, her time had come, and she was afraid of trying to have the baby alone. She stumbled into the ER of Mercy Hospital, already in labor.

"Can someone help me? Please?" she cried as she went to the admissions desk.

"My goodness, child. Do you have any family? Is there anyone I can call?" asked the kind lady, coming out from behind her desk. Another admissions clerk paged a nurse to the waiting area.

As the girl's water broke, a middle-aged couple stepped up beside her, each of them taking one of her arms.

"I'm her Aunt Cathy, and George here is her uncle," the woman replied.

The girl looked at them in astonishment. "What?" she began, as she tried feebly to shake her arms free.

"Don't worry about anything, honey. We'll take care of everything," the woman assured her, patting the girl's arm while handing an insurance card and identification to the admissions clerk. Cathy and George gave the requested information and filled out the paperwork.

The girl was too weary to argue. As she doubled over with another contraction, the nurse arrived, closely followed by two orderlies with a stretcher. The teen was caught by one of the men just as she fainted.

She had had no pre-natal care, no doctor's visits, no help at all. Her diet had been poor, and she was physically and mentally exhausted. In addition, she was very young. As the parasite within her had predicted, she did not survive, and no one mourned her passing. Within minutes, the demon had transferred to another host, having located a vulnerable human with no trouble at all.

The doctor cleaned himself up and came into the waiting area to speak with her "family."

"I'm sorry. We did everything we could, but your niece did not pull through." He spoke tiredly and sympathetically.

Cathy shed a few false tears while the dark one within her gloated. He loved controlling simple-minded humans, and he was very good at it.

"Did she suffer much?" Cathy asked with a show of concern.

"No, she did not fully regain consciousness after she left this area. She mumbled and muttered a bit, but she felt no pain. We delivered the baby by Caesarean section. Your niece was simply too weak and malnourished to fight for her life," the doctor replied. *Actually, she seemed to want to die. Where have you been while she was pregnant, and barely seventeen at that?*

"Oh, that's too bad. She ran away a couple of years ago, and we just found out that she was here in Charlotte. She called us from a pay phone on her way to the hospital. The rest of her family is dead; we were all she had left. We always wanted her to live with us. We had even added her to our insurance after her parents were killed in a car accident more than a year ago and left us as her legal guardians." The lies flowed easily from Cathy. She and George had the story well-rehearsed, and the Dark Lord had placed many of his servants in key positions to make the records agree with everything they said. Possessed humans were putty in the hands of his minions.

"How is the child?" asked George.

"He is fine. I want him to stay in the hospital nursery overnight, and you can take him home tomorrow," answered the doctor. He knew that there was something oddly convenient about Cathy and George appearing just at that particular time, but there were many other people in need of his attention, and he promptly dismissed his suspicions. *The child will have a home, and that is what really matters*, he thought.

~~~~~~~~

The following day, after spending the night in the waiting room on the maternity floor because they were unwilling to leave the baby unguarded, Cathy and George made arrangements with a local funeral home for the girl to be cremated, settled the remainder of the hospital bill not covered by insurance, and collected the baby boy to take him to their home. Everything was ready to receive the son of their master.

Upon arriving at their two-story colonial in an upscale neighborhood in the suburbs of Charlotte, they were greeted by a group of people who worshipped the same Dark Lord as they did. The living room was teeming with his followers and their companions – the vile fiends who possessed them and controlled their every thought and action. All of them, demon and human alike, bowed to the half-demon child in Cathy's arms.

Lucifer and his guards floated unhurriedly through the ceiling, and the Dark Lord took human form. He was magnificent. His long black hair flowed in waves across his powerful shoulders, his body was wonderfully proportioned, and the light amber of his eyes – ringed with thick, black lashes – was startling. His face was a study in sensuality – full lips, a strong chin and jaw line, and a perfect nose. He was glad that humans always pictured him as being ugly because it made it that much easier to trick them into trusting him. He laughed at the ridiculous caricatures which portrayed him as a goat with horns or a man in a red suit with a pitchfork and tail.

Fixing his eyes on the human couple, he asked, "What name did you tell them to place on the child's birth certificate?"

George kept his head bowed as he answered, "Gregory Drake Wickham, my lord, just as you commanded."

Lucifer bared his teeth in a semblance of a smile, "Very good. He will be my *Gregory*, my vigilante, who will right the wrongs that were done to me and will give me the power that should have been mine for millennia. He is also *Drake*, the dragon, my own son. He will thwart Jehovah's schemes. Whatever God has planned for the girl child will be stopped. She will die if she must. *Wickham* will identify his human origins. It is well done."

The assembly of humans and demons chanted Lucifer's name and worshipped him as he took his son from his adoptive mother and held him high for the assembly to see.

It was time to begin his training. Gregory Wickham would be taught to embrace his destiny.

~~~~~~~~~

The group of powerful demons waited in the warehouse for the arrival of Satan, the Dark Prince. All of them had arrived early from their different strongholds of power. To arrive after their master would be unthinkable – the penalty would be banishment.

They inclined their heads in submission as their master drifted unhurriedly through the rafters, his hooded group of guards clustered around him.

"Vega," said Lucifer menacingly, recognizing the huge demon who controlled the southeastern portion of the United States. Underprince Vega stepped forward and knelt before the Prince of This World, the Prince of the Power of the Air.

"Yes, my master?" he asked in a quiet, low voice, keeping his head bowed.

"I am entrusting a task to you. The human girl, Elizabeth Bennet, must die before she reaches adulthood. Do not fail me, Vega. It would be . . . *unpleasant* for you if you were to be unsuccessful in completing this assignment. Do you understand?" Lucifer's voice was quiet and threatening, silken. All in the circle of power shuddered at the sound. They had all heard that tone before.

Vega answered, keeping his voice carefully under control, "I understand, my Prince. It shall be done. I will not fail."

Lucifer sneered, exposing his white teeth as he looked at his cabal. "See that you do not." He gazed at the group of principalities with their captains and said, "You would all do well to remember that the death of this human is my, and therefore your, highest priority until it is accomplished. If she leaves Vega's area, you must be alert to continue the mission." *If she manages to reach adulthood, my own son will surely deal with her. Even the great Xander cannot defeat my own son,* he thought with satisfaction.

No one moved until Lucifer and his protectors glided back through the roof into the night. Then, as one, the underprinces and their captains released the breaths they had been holding, and silently flew through the walls in different directions, back to their dominions. All of them hoped for Vega's success, for none of the rest of them wished for the assignment if he failed. It was too horrible to contemplate.

~~~~~~~~

Xander, Niall, and Alexis glided effortlessly in formation alongside Lynne's Aerostar minivan as she and her daughters drove the familiar twenty minute drive home from school. It had been a normal day. Lynne had taught her high school classes while Janna had studied with her fifth grade classmates and three-month-old Elizabeth had stayed in the nursery. Janna was in the front passenger seat, and Elizabeth was strapped into her car seat behind her mother, gurgling contentedly. Lynne and Janna were chatting about the school day, as they usually did on the drive to and from school. Everything had been so calm and mundane, until it wasn't.

The dark ones had no intention of making Xander's assignment easy. They all knew that the word had been passed down from Lucifer himself, through the ranks to Vega, the underprince. The legions of dark angels were to do everything in their power to prevent Elizabeth from ever reaching adulthood. They knew too well the price of failure. More than one demon had paid the ultimate cost and had been sent to the pit by the Dark Lord.

Lynne's van picked up speed as she descended a steep hill. As she rounded a blind curve leading up to a bridge across Lynch's River, she was horrified to see one semi-truck passing another on the bridge and heading towards her. She knew that the truck now occupying her lane did not have time to completely pass the other truck before it would collide head-on with her. Her heart rate accelerated and she silently screamed a quick prayer in her mind as her eyes widened in fear. *Lord, help me!*

Lynne had always been a defensive driver, carefully watching everything around her as she drove, but she well knew that this situation was beyond her driving skills. A light rain was falling, making the grass on the shoulders of the road slippery. She was traveling at least fifty-five miles per hour when she glanced behind her to see yet another semi-truck following her closely. *I have no time to think! I can't do this, Lord!*

Quickly, Xander and Niall flew to the right of the minivan while Alexis took the left side.

Niall, help me hold the van! I'll stay on the right; you get behind it. We must stop it from rolling down the embankment! Alexis, protect the left side from the semis. Xander barked out orders, telepathing to the other guardians. Alexis flattened herself against the driver's side while Niall stabilized the rear. Xander took most of the weight on himself, muscles straining and rippling through his back and arms. As the van's tires left the road on the right, he flew under the vehicle, pulling his membranous wings tightly to his back. He would not lose his charge to the river or a collision.

Lynne took the narrow shoulder on her right and tried not to lose control of her van when she realized that the two trucks and she were all three across the road at the same time. It was over in a matter of seconds. She was shaking and her heart was pounding as she glanced in the rear-view mirror and saw the truck behind her jackknife. She then pulled completely off the road on the other side of the bridge to calm herself. When she turned and looked at where she'd just been, there were three semi-trucks, a couple of cars, and an Explorer lining the sides of the road, along with the semi that had jackknifed in the road rather than hit her when she had applied her brakes. She hadn't even seen the other semi or the cars at the time of the near-accident. As she looked at the situation and began to think more clearly, Lynne realized that she needed to go back and give her statement to the police. She didn't want the man who had risked his life and wrecked his truck rather than plow into the rear of her car to be in any trouble with the police or his employer.

"Is everyone all right?" she asked in a shaky voice. Janna nodded, unable to speak, her dark eyes huge. Lynne looked back at Elizabeth who smiled complacently at her. She prayed silently again, *Thank you, Father, for protecting my family.*

Carefully, she eased into a driveway and turned around to head back, unaware of her angelic escort. As she slowly passed the place where she and her daughters could have died, where her van was one of the three vehicles side-by-side on the road, she couldn't understand how she had made it through without wrecking or plunging down the twenty foot embankment into the river. There was a road sign in the place that her van had occupied only a few minutes before, and there was the river that she should be in right now. She knew that both of her passenger side tires had left the road and found no traction on the wet grass of the shoulder. How had she partially left the road at such a speed, avoided the sign, missed going into the river, and corrected the path of the van back onto the road? As she passed the two semis that had been directly beside her, she saw that their trailers were scratched where they had rubbed against each other. They had been that close together. Lynne had always believed in angels, but now she was sure that her guardian angel must be working overtime.

Xander smiled grimly at her thought. *Overtime, indeed.* He, Alexis, and Niall had flown on either side of her van and behind it, keeping it balanced and steady through the ordeal. Xander was certainly strong, but he was thankful that he had two others helping him during the near disaster. He looked at the driver of the semi whose illegal passing had nearly caused the catastrophe and saw that those on his team were not the only ones "working overtime." Perched on the seat beside the driver was a large, hulk of a demon, grinning evilly and snickering as he surveyed the wreckage. The dark one, Adrian, smirked at him with a promise – he and his cohorts would not be giving up anytime soon.

Humans are so easy to influence. Putting thoughts into people's minds is child's play for the dark ones, as long as they continue to reject the Master, thought Xander. He knew that the demon had used the truck driver for his wicked purpose, convincing the weak-minded man that he had plenty of time to pass safely.

~~~~~~~~~

In the run down mill hill area of Bethel, Vega called his meeting to order in an empty strip mall that reeked with the smells of homeless drug addicts, runaways, and prostitutes.

"Silence!" Vega commanded in a voice that brooked no opposition.

Immediately, the motley group of demons was quiet and motionless.

"Adrian, come before me!" Vega shouted angrily, his expression one of disgust.

"Yes, Vega?" the tall, gangly fiend asked, as he grimaced at the underprince.

"How do you dare to stand before me after your stupid, bungling attempt to kill the girl? Do you not comprehend, idiot, the price for failure?" Vega fixed his angry green eyes on the object of his contempt as he slapped Adrian with all his considerable might across the face, sending him flying backwards at the assembled group.

Adrian scrambled upright and threw himself at Vega's feet, groveling and begging. "Please, Prince Vega. Give me another chance. I have a better plan. I will not fail you again!" he cried piteously.

"No, you certainly will not!" Vega said emphatically, motioning to his captain. "Nyx, finish this," he ordered, glancing down at the dark one sprawled at his feet.

In one well-practiced motion, Nyx unsheathed his sword with an evil smile.

"For you, Prince Vega," Nyx murmured as he sliced Adrian in two neat halves, sending him screaming to the pit.

"Keiran," Vega called to a child-like demon.

"Yes, Prince Vega?" asked the small, black Keiran with confidence.

"I have a job for you," replied the underprince. "You will be allowed to use your special abilities for this mission. This is what I want you to do..."

Chapter 4

"See that you do not despise one of these little ones, for I say to you, that their angels in heaven continually behold the face of My Father who is in heaven." Matthew 18:10

Nearly four years later, 1994

In the humble home of the Bennets, Lynne watched her daughters as Janna held Elizabeth in her lap and read a book to her, pointing at the words and the pictures. Elizabeth's little hands rested on her sister's arms as she listened to Janna, engrossed in the story.

The Bennet sisters had the same deep brown eyes, olive skin, and thick, dark brown hair as did their father, but the three of them were not as much alike in temperament. David was very laid-back and friendly, and there were few people who did not like him. He was well-suited to the ministry as he was industrious and considerate of others. David nearly always thought before he spoke; therefore he rarely had to regret anything he said. He enjoyed his pastoral position and was a contented man. Janna was bright and happy, but her timidity made her a little more difficult to know than her father. Four-year-old Elizabeth's actions, facial expressions, and surprisingly mature speech showed that she was curious, precocious, and outgoing. She shared her mother's love of people; neither Lynne nor Elizabeth ever seemed to meet a stranger. Elizabeth and her mother were also more emotional than David or Janna, though Lynne was more expressive of her emotions than were the other three. Lynne's appearance differed from her husband and daughters' with her fair skin, green eyes, and light brown hair. The family shared a keen intelligence, however, and enjoyed a similar dry sense of humor. And they were all musically inclined. Lynne played the piano, flute, and organ, and David had a beautiful baritone voice. Lynne, who had double-majored in music and English and had her MAT, was teaching Janna to play the piano, and Janna had already sung solos in her children's choir and at school. Though they had similarities and differences, they were a unit. It was the way God had ordained families to be.

Because she received so much attention from her family, Elizabeth progressed rapidly. By the time she was three, she had learned to read by following the words her sister read to her. Her parents were also amazed at her ability to sing with clarity, amazingly accurate rhythm, and astonishing pitch control. She had been featured as an angel in the church's preschool Christmas program, and had sung her solo perfectly.

As Elizabeth aged, she grew bolder, Xander was glad that she was not as fearful and timid as was her sister Janna, who was gentle, loving, and loyal, but also shy and tentative about new experiences and strangers. Elizabeth was headstrong and tended to rush into situations without thinking about her personal safety. Compared to the rest of her family, Elizabeth was quicker to speak out and quicker to make enemies, but also quicker to show affection and quicker to forgive those she loved. She was also fiercely independent. Her parents fought a constant battle to teach her obedience.

~~~~~~~~~

Tabernacle, the Bennet family's church, was located within walking distance of their house on a commercial corner in Bethel. There was a fast food restaurant across the road from the church; Lynne often took Janna and Elizabeth there before Wednesday night services as a treat. The younger girl especially enjoyed the playground and the children's meals.

She disappeared after church services one Sunday morning just after she turned four, throwing her parents and the rest of the church members into a panic. Everyone had been looking all over the buildings and the grounds for her. Lynne was distraught. *What if El has crossed the road to go to the restaurant? I've seen some really sketchy characters in there. What if someone has taken her? Dear Lord, please protect my baby.*

Unknown to her parents, a small dark being had taken a human child's form and stepped in front of Elizabeth. He had been waiting for years for this moment, appearing to Elizabeth in parks, playgrounds, and other public places to lay the groundwork.

"Elizabeth! Come and play with me!" Keiran called, running before her. "Catch me!" he called back over his shoulder as he ran to her house. Recognizing him, Elizabeth laughed and followed, eager to join the game.

"Let's play hide and seek. You hide first," he teased as he led her away from the church and her family, into an ambush. Elizabeth hid in the bushes, giggling with delight as she waited for the boy to find her, unaware of the demons flying in to surround the area. Out of her sight, Keiran changed back into demonic form.

Xander, who had been watching the small demon for several years, followed closely after Elizabeth and sprang into action, sword flashing. The huge angel was immediately surrounded, but he took advantage of his position as he spun in a circle of light with his sword extended, quickly dispatching Keiran and five more of the filthy beings with a single swipe of his weapon, slicing them into pieces. They barely had time to scream as they hurtled to the depths.

Elizabeth saw the wind suddenly rise in the trees, and felt the bushes move about her. The howling sound of it was eerie and frightening. She huddled with her arms wound tightly around her knees and her face pressed against her legs, feeling very small and afraid. *I'm scared. I wish I had stayed at church.*

Her mighty protector unfurled his translucent wings and took flight at blinding speed after the others who had fled, screeching upon seeing him in full battle mode. In a matter of seconds, it was over. He quickly scanned the area from above for any more of the hellish ones, and, satisfied that they were gone, he flew back to the Bennet house. Xander could not leave

Elizabeth unprotected; she was his first priority. Furthermore, he was certain that he would have another chance to deal with the fiends later. Behind a tree, he took human form and returned to Elizabeth's side.

"Hi, there," Xander said playfully to Elizabeth, bending down to her eye level and being careful not to frighten her. He wore the casual garb of an earth male – khaki pants with a short-sleeved shirt and loafers. She lifted her head a little so that she could see him. Xander smiled and extended his hand to the child. He could hear her heart racing as she thought, *I don't know him. Mommy and Daddy said not to speak to people I don't know.*

Her fear touched him deeply. *I will always protect you, Elizabeth.*

"I'm not supposed to talk to strangers," Elizabeth replied, her eyes round. She was unsure of the situation. *Will he hurt me?* The young man seemed to be very pleasant, and he made her feel safe.

"I am not a stranger, Elizabeth. See? That is your name. You should never trust people you do not know, but you feel like you know me, right?" he asked gently, his large hand still extended. "You can trust me." *Please.*

Elizabeth deliberated a moment, her mouth puckered and her deep brown eyes squinted in concentration.

"What is my password?" Her mother and father had taught her never to go with anyone who did not know their secret code word.

He searched her mind and answered, "Music." He held his breath as she considered his answer, careful to keep smiling at her.

"That's right! I must know you." Relieved, she smiled back at Xander and took his hand. Elizabeth tilted her head and thought, *He is a pretty man. He is very tall and big. I like his blue eyes.* She believed him.

Xander smiled again, more broadly, flashing his dimples and his straight, white teeth as he heard her thoughts.

Feeling safe, Elizabeth giggled as if her escapade were a great joke, but Xander knew that she would be in trouble with her parents, for he was well-acquainted with the premium David and Lynne placed on obedience from their children.

He led her back to her mother with her small hand clasped in his, but stepped in front of her when her mother saw them. As Lynne reached for her errant daughter, her face changed from abject fear to irritation in a second. Elizabeth peeked out from behind her champion's legs. When she saw the expression on her mother's face, she realized that her mother was not laughing, and that she would be punished. Elizabeth began to sniffle and hold on to Xander's pants. *I'm going to get a spanking.*

"Promise me that you won't spank her, or I might have to take her home with me," Xander said, keeping his voice light. He managed to smile as he read Lynne's thoughts. He would allow, and even welcome, correction. However, he thought, *No one, not even her parents, will ever be allowed to strike Elizabeth in anger.*

Niall, standing beside Lynne, looked up at Xander with sudden interest. *There would surely be no need to protect Elizabeth from her loving parents.* Neither Lynne nor David had ever struck either child in anger. On the few occasions they had spanked their children, they had never hurt them. It was always the discipline of last resort, and in each instance had been discussed with the child beforehand.

"Thank you so much for finding her, young man, but she needs to be corrected." Lynne replied.

"Yes, but she did not know that she was doing anything wrong. She was hiding in the bushes at your house, playing a game. Now she knows not to do it again. I will need your promise," he said firmly.

"I really do appreciate what you've done for us, but exactly who are you?" Lynne asked the handsome young man.

Xander flashed her his best *you can trust me* smile, letting it reach his light blue eyes, and answered, "I have been visiting your church for quite a while now. You probably have not noticed me, but I have been there. Your husband is the minister, is he not?" *I have been here every Sunday. You just could not see me.*

Niall placed a hand on Lynne's shoulder to calm her, and she took a slow, deep breath, thinking, *How did I miss this tall, arresting young man? How did I not see Hercules in the congregation? I guess I'm always at the front playing the piano, and by the time I finish the postlude, most of the visitors are already gone.*

Niall rolled his eyes. *Hercules? Please.*

Xander smiled even wider, showing his dimples. *Watch and learn, Niall. Females trust the dimples.*

Lynne looked at him, her head tilted to one side, considering her answer. "Yes, David is my husband. I'm sorry for being suspicious, but a mom has to be careful these days." She smiled at him. "Okay, you win. I promise not to spank her. Come here, Elizabeth," Lynne said, holding out her arms to her small delinquent.

As her daughter tentatively approached her, Lynne grabbed her up in her arms and hugged her tightly. Through her tears of gratitude, she pushed aside Elizabeth's dark wavy hair and whispered in the little girl's ear, "I love you so much, my El. Don't ever frighten us like that again. You must always stay with me, Daddy, or Janna." *Thank you, Father.*

Xander finally allowed his relief to flood through him. He smiled at Niall, and nodded his approval. *All is well.*

Suddenly Lynne remembered her manners. She had not even asked the young hero his name, and she really should invite him to their home to eat lunch. Lynne looked up, but he was nowhere to be found. She asked a few of the other church members if they had seen him, describing him to them, but no one had seen him except for her and Elizabeth.

He had quickly ducked into a nearby open doorway, and, in a flash of light, he had changed back into angelic form.

Xander was beginning to realize that he would have quite a job keeping his adventurous charge from mishaps. Niall could not restrain a small grin at the thought, but he carefully averted his face from Xander's and struggled to control his mind. Xander had caught his fleeting thought, and grimaced, chagrined. Niall's charge was clumsy and accident-prone, it was true, but Elizabeth seemed to gravitate toward mischief.

~~~~~~~

Lucifer, the great Satan, materialized in the living room of the house in Charlotte. As he took human form, he issued a command to the human couple bowing before him. Four hulking demons began to take form on either side of him, flanking him protectively. The entire house was already filled and covered with imps – so many that the view of the house was blocked to light beings in the area. There was a complete absence of light.

"Bring my son to me," he said in a low, authoritative voice.

Cathy immediately went to the little boy's room where he was watching television. He looked up as she entered his room, and pushed the black, thick hair back from his amber eyes.

"Your father is here to see you again," she said quietly, taking him by the hand and leading him toward the place where the Dark Prince waited impatiently, pacing back and forth across the room.

As soon as he saw the boy, the Dark Lord took long strides to lift him into his arms. Lucifer laughed. "It's like looking into a mirror," he remarked to his grinning foot soldiers. "He is truly beautiful, is he not?" The question was rhetorical; no one would dare to disagree.

As the four-year-old looked evenly into his father's eyes, showing no fear, the Master of Confusion practically chortled. "Yes, my son. You will do quite well. I am pleased."

He looked at Cathy and George with a sardonic eye. "Have you arranged for his education as I instructed?"

Cathy averted her gaze and replied obsequiously, "Yes, My Lord. He is being taught by the best sorcerers and masters in each field that you named. Master Gregory will learn your ways as well as those of the enemy, and he has already begun to make significant steps toward achieving the goals you have set for him. He shows remarkable abilities and will exceed the skills of his teachers in a few years."

"When that time comes, I will finish my son's training myself. There are things that only Dark Spirit and I can teach him." A shudder rippled through the assembly at the mention of Dark Spirit. He was the most powerful and the vilest of all demons, except for Lucifer himself.

He looked into the eyes that were replicas of his own. "My son, you will be great and powerful. You will sit at my right hand when we rule the universes. All worlds will be beneath our feet after you join me in defeating my enemies. We will feast on them; we will draw their powers to ourselves. No one will stand against us."

Chapter 5

"So the Lord said to Satan, 'Behold Job is in your power, only spare his life.' Then Satan went out from the presence of the Lord, and smote Job with sore boils from the sole of his foot to the crown of his head." Job 2:6-7

Spring, 1995

Presiding in counterfeit glory from his throne on a platform in the old warehouse in which his son had been conceived, Lucifer called for order in the meeting. His highest ranking demons and their captains bowed low before him and awaited his words.

"Vega!" he said tersely, his beautiful face twisted in a scowl.

The huge demon stepped forward and lifted his eyes to the Dark Lord.

"Yes, my master?"

"Has the plan been set in motion?" Lucifer asked gruffly.

"As you have commanded, my lord, all has been done. Keegan has cast the dart at the human child."

Lucifer's face twisted in an evil grin.

"Excellent," he said. "I hope, for your sake, that this plan succeeds, unlike your last one."

~~~~~~~~

Xander leaned over Elizabeth as she slept, enjoying those last few childish dreams that fluttered through her mind. He saw her gracefully running, leaping, and turning as she imagined herself to be a world famous ballerina. Earlier, in another dream, she had been an Olympic gymnast, sticking a perfect landing to the cheers of the crowd. Then, she was a musician, holding the people enthralled with her skill at singing and playing the piano. Her dreams were always entertaining, and nearly always happy. This morning, she did not want to wake up. She wished to stay in her dreams, warm and contented.

At the usual time for a school day, her mother entered the girl's room and began their morning ritual, "kissing her up," as Elizabeth called it. Lynne wanted her daughters' first conscious thoughts each day to be joyful ones, so she sang to them and kissed their cheeks until they were awake. She had already been to Janna's room, laughing as she sang to the teenager.

Niall followed Lynne from room to room. The ritual never got old to him. *This is such a pleasant change from families in which the children are yelled at until they get out of bed.*

Lynne entered her room, sat on the edge of Elizabeth's bed, and sang softly, watching her daughter's face. *"You are my sunshine, my only sunshine. You make me happy when skies are gray. You'll never know, dear, how much I love you. Please don't take my sunshine away."* Then she began to place tiny soft kisses on her daughter's rosy cheeks.

Elizabeth, her eyes still closed and her lips puckered, reached up with her hands and began to rub her cheeks. She *really* wanted to dream some more.

Xander enjoyed the tableaux immensely. He looked at Niall and exchanged a smile with him.

Lynne drew back immediately, stopping a chortle before it could escape. "El, you're wiping off my kisses!"

Her eyes still closed, Elizabeth responded sleepily, "No, Mommy. I'm rubbing them in."

Xander's smile broadened at her quick response. *Elizabeth is always full of surprises – so witty and intelligent. She is wholly adorable.* Niall chuckled at the girl's antics.

Lynne laughed aloud. "Good save, El. Now it's time to get up for school. Today will be so much fun! And you can tell me everything as we ride home this afternoon."

~~~~~~~~

Lynne settled a still-sleepy Elizabeth into the van and buckled her into her car seat while Janna strapped herself into the front passenger side. Her morning had been busy, getting herself ready, dressing Elizabeth for preschool, making lunches, and grabbing book bags. Eighth-grader Janna was anxious about presenting her science fair project before the class in second period.

David had kissed them all goodbye at the door earlier. He and Roark had already walked to the church as Lynne made sure that nothing they needed was left behind.

As they started the drive to school, Lynne turned on the local Christian radio station to listen to the music.

Elizabeth let the music drift through her mind and began to wake up and sing along. *I love music. It's my favorite thing!*

As the song ended, the news report began.

"The death toll has reached six across the country. Doctors are warning parents to carefully monitor their children if they break out with chicken pox. Some children are developing a strep infection in the lesions, which, in some cases, has proven to be fatal. Look for swelling and spreading redness, along with a longer period of breaking out than the normal four days. Immediately take your children to a doctor if they begin to show these symptoms. There is a new vaccine available to prevent chickenpox.

However, if your child is already infected, the drug will be useless." The announcer went on to another subject.

Janna had already had the disease years earlier when she was four. Her case had not been severe, and she had recovered quickly with no scarring. Elizabeth, however, seemed to catch everything. Her pediatrician had postulated that her immune system was not as effective as that of other children, but there was nothing that could be done except to watch her carefully. He theorized that she would outgrow the problem eventually. Janna had rarely been sick and almost never needed to take an antibiotic. Elizabeth had been obliged to take several rounds of the medication each year of her young life. Ear infections, strep throat, upper respiratory infections, urinary tract infections – she had had them all in her four and a half years.

Lynne punched the button to turn off the radio as she glanced in the rearview mirror at her precious daughter. *This is not good*, she said to herself. *Not good at all. The chicken pox outbreak is sweeping through the country . . . Six young lives have already been claimed. I certainly hope my El doesn't come down with it, but . . .* Lynne sighed and shook her head as she pulled into the parking lot of Peniel Christian Academy.

Arriving at the school, early as usual, Lynne took her daughters to her classroom with her while she finished up a few last minute preparations for her teaching day.

As they walked down the hall together, Elizabeth was full of questions for Janna about her project.

"Are you scared? Will you be first? Will you tell me about it on the way home today, Janna?" Elizabeth's little face was turned up to her sister's in concern.

"I'm fine, El. I'm a little nervous, but it'll be okay. I don't know who will be first. She'll draw our names out of a bag. First would be great. Then it would be over with. I'll tell you all about it after school," Janna replied, looking down at Elizabeth's curious expression.

Janna looked up at Lynne. "Mom, can I leave my project here in your room and come back to get it before my second period science class? I'm afraid that if I take it with me to Mrs. Hammond's class, it might get messed up, and I want it to be perfect."

Lynne chuckled at her meticulous daughter. "Put it in the corner by the bookshelves. I'll take very good care of it, and you can come back and get it on your way to second period."

"Thanks, Mom!" Janna smiled at Lynne.

Lynne returned her smile and kissed her, wishing her luck as she watched her older daughter walk to the cafeteria to wait with her friends for the morning bell. Alexis nodded a brief goodbye at Niall and Xander as she followed Janna from the room.

Lynne glanced down to her bright-eyed four-year-old.

"Let's go, El. Time for class. I heard that Mrs. Williams has something fun planned for today," she said cheerfully.

Elizabeth looked up at her mother. "Oh, yes, we do! Today we get to finger paint, Mommy. I love finger painting!"

"I'm sure you do, Sweetheart. You are very creative, and perhaps Daddy will want to frame this one, too!"

Elizabeth giggled and sang as she skipped alongside her mother down the hall to the preschool wing. Xander matched his steps to Elizabeth's while his eyes constantly scanned the hallways.

While dropping her younger daughter off at her 4-K classroom, Lynne paused for a smile and a look at the roomful of chattering children. One of Lynne's favorite things about teaching at Peniel Christian was that the school housed nursery through high school on one large campus. She was never very far from either of her daughters, she knew their teachers, and she knew their friends. Her children were truly "a gift of the Lord," as the Bible said in Psalm 127:3. They were contented and happy, and she knew that as long as they were close by her, she would never worry for their safety.

Sighing with the fullness of her joy, she turned and made her way back to her class.

Lynne's first period class was a combined junior and senior Bible Doctrines class. Her students entered cheerfully and noisily, telling her good morning, chatting with each other, and taking their seats.

Niall stood with the other guardians circling the perimeter of the room. Most of the students were servants, and their protectors naturally came with them to school. There were a few non-servants in the group, but no demon would dare to enter a place so heavily guarded. The school glowed with the light of the large numbers of holy angels in and around it. Short of an actual possession of a student by a dark being which would give the demon a measure of protection, no fallen angel would be willing to face so many guardians.

The day continued in its normal pattern. Janna had stopped to retrieve her project between the first and second periods, and Niall had nodded to Alexis, trailing lightly behind Janna.

How do you think Xander's liking 4-K? Niall asked.

Alexis shook her auburn head, humor flashing in her hazel eyes. *I have no idea. You know how closed he is with his thoughts. I'm not worried about it. I've done my time at the kiddy pool with Janna. I should have a few more earth years before I'm back to square one.*

Actually, Xander's morning had been far from placid. It was obvious to him by third period that Elizabeth wasn't feeling well. All of them had heard the news report on the radio, and he had known of several preschoolers who had gone home with the chicken pox in the past few days. He remembered all of those nights that David and Lynne had been up with Elizabeth while she was sick with one thing and another. He knew how easily she succumbed to illness; she had already been exposed to this disease, and he was very concerned as he looked upon his small charge trying to complete her coloring before the break when she and her classmates would have their lunch.

He wrinkled his brow. *Something is not right. She's wiggling and squirming, and she looks unhappy.* Xander stroked his chin with his long fingers and tilted his head, fixing his gaze on the little girl.

Finally, Elizabeth could no longer ignore her itching and scratching, and she went to her teacher, Mrs. Delores Williams.

"Miss Lori, I don't feel good. What's this?" Elizabeth asked, pulling up her shirt and pointing to a spot on her abdomen. "It itches."

Both Xander and Mrs. Williams bent over to look at her tummy. There were five blisters on her red skin. *Chicken pox! There shouldn't be that many lesions in so short a time. A dart must have been thrown. How could I have missed it? Whoever threw it will certainly pay. Keegan! It must be his doing. Who else could have been so accurate from the distance he would have had to throw it to escape my notice?*

"Oh, my, Sweetie," said Mrs. Williams. "Why don't you sit here by my desk while we get someone from the office to come take a look?"

She really had no need for a second opinion, because she had seen lesions like Elizabeth's many times before, but Mrs. Williams called the office over the intercom, and Susan Canes, the daycare director, came to the room within a few minutes. Chicken pox was very contagious, and she wanted to get Elizabeth away from the other children as quickly as she could.

"Come, El. We're going to see your mother," Mrs. Canes told Elizabeth as she took her by the hand and led her down the hall to the high school wing. Xander walked on Elizabeth's other side with his fingers lightly touching the top of her head.

Elizabeth was afraid and upset. *I'm sick again! I hate being sick and missing school. I don't like medicine. I don't want a shot!*

As Lynne answered the knock at her door, she was filled with foreboding to see the daycare director and Elizabeth. She stood in the doorway so that she could still see her students and knelt down to look at her uncomfortable daughter. Mrs. Canes lifted Elizabeth's shirt so that Lynne could see her tummy.

"Chicken pox?" Lynne asked the older woman with a sigh.

"I think so, Lynne," came the soft reply. "I've already asked Mrs. Miles to call in a sub for you so that you can take El home. Until the sub gets here, I'll sit with your class. Janna will be waiting for you by the front entrance. Do they have an assignment to work on?" Susan asked, gesturing toward the students.

"Thanks for all your help, Susan. The homework assignment is on the board, and my lesson plans for the next two weeks are on my desk. Tests and quizzes are in the marked folders in my right top drawer. If you need anything, call me, and I'll tell you where to find it." Lynne was extremely organized, and it had served her well on more than one occasion.

Though she hated to miss teaching time, her children always came before her job. She was fortunate to work in a school that understood that.

Xander knelt rather impatiently by Elizabeth with one hand touching her arm and the other stroking her back. *Everything will be all right, Elizabeth,* he whispered to her. He was ready for Lynne to take her home and do whatever was necessary to relieve the child's discomfort.

Niall looked at him with concern. *We will be on our way in a moment. She shall be fine.*

She is not fine! Xander replied testily. Niall arched an eyebrow. Xander raised both of his brows and glared at him.

Lynne went back into the classroom to retrieve her handbag and other personal items, making sure that her plans, teacher's books, and grade book were plainly visible on her desk. Mrs. Canes stood at the door with Elizabeth who had begun to whine softly, waiting for Lynne to return.

Will this never end? thought Xander. Niall shook his head at Xander's impatience.

"Class, I want you to begin working on your homework assignment now. I'm taking El home. Mrs. Canes will sit with you until my substitute comes." Lynne hurried out the door to the sound of pages turning and backpacks being unzipped, and Mrs. Canes took her place at the desk.

"Let's go, El. We're going home to make the itching stop," Lynne said to Elizabeth as she took her hand and led her to the office. Janna met her there, and the group of humans and angels walked out of the building to the van.

Finally! thought Xander. Niall and Alexis glanced at him. *Surely there is no cause for such alarm. Everything is under control.* Xander read their minds and attempted to calm himself. They were right, and he knew it. He didn't fully understand his reactions himself. He concentrated on watching the area around the van as he glided smoothly above it.

The twenty minute drive seemed longer to Lynne as Elizabeth fretted, whined, and scratched. At her mother's suggestion, Janna had chosen to sit in the back seat beside Elizabeth to distract her and keep her from thinking about the itching. She read to her and played the games they usually played in the car, but was only partially successful. Elizabeth was miserable. And so was Xander.

Is she actually driving the speed limit for a change? Whatever happened to 'five miles over the limit is okay'?

Alexis and Niall were actually beginning to be amused at His Grumpiness.

As soon as they were home, Lynne called David to tell him about Elizabeth. He came right home, Roark following, after stopping by a drug store for an oatmeal bath and calamine lotion to soothe his daughter. By the time he walked in the door, Lynne had already dosed Elizabeth with a children's pain reliever, drawn the bathwater, and held Elizabeth, unclothed by the tub. He poured in the oatmeal preparation and put Elizabeth in, pouring the water over her.

"Isn't that better, El?" he asked gently. He was careful not to show any alarm. The blisters were far larger and more numerous than those he had seen with Janna. He had heard the same reports that Lynne had listened to that morning, and his "protective daddy" side was definitely taking over.

"Yes, Daddy," she answered, her sad eyes fixing on his. "Daddy, can we have ice cream?

"You can have whatever you want to eat, Sweetheart."

Though she was sick, she felt her power at that moment. She knew that her daddy would give her anything while she was ill.

"Daddy, does Jesus love me?"

"He sure does, El." Her father wore a perplexed expression. *Where is she going with this?*

Xander was puzzled as well.

"Did He give me to you?" Elizabeth asked the question, though she well knew the answer. Her father read the Bible and prayed with her and Janna every night. She already knew more about the Bible than many adults. Xander could nearly hear the little wheels turning in her head.

"Yes, El. You know that Jesus gave you to me and your mother."

"Daddy, Jesus isn't very happy when you spank me," Elizabeth said with great gravity.

Roark smiled, but Xander laughed aloud. It was good that he was in angelic form and was not using the sound frequency that humans could hear. She delighted him. Niall and Alexis heard his laughter from the other rooms in the house. *What was that? Was it Xander?* They had never heard Xander laugh before, and they were more than mildly surprised.

David laughed as well. *Maybe she isn't so sick if she can still think this well and be her sassy little self.*

"El, Jesus is very pleased with us when we discipline you. He told us to take care of you, teach you, and love you. One way that we show we love you is by teaching you to obey. You must learn to obey us so that you will know how to obey God."

She accepted his answer, though she wasn't entirely happy with it.

"I love you, Daddy."

"I love you more, El. I win!" he said, playing their game and bringing a smile to her little face that showed her dimples.

Xander truly liked David. Anyone who could make Elizabeth smile had his full approval.

~~~~~~~

After a restless night in which neither David, Lynne, nor Elizabeth got much rest, it was obvious to her parents that El's case of the chicken pox was not normal. She was covered all over her body with the lesions, she was feverish, and she was unable to urinate without extreme pain.

Xander was ready for somebody, anybody, to do something to help Elizabeth. He was considering taking human form and going for a doctor himself. He knelt by her bed and put his hand on her brow. Her unhappy dreams fluttered through his mind, and he worried.

Lynne called the pediatrician's office. They were swamped with chicken pox cases. Everyone had heard the reports, and every mother seemed to think that her child had the strep infection. The staff was overrun with anxious parents and unhappy children.

"Hello. This is Lynne Bennet. I need to see Dr. Childs today, please. El has the chicken pox, and I think it's serious."

From the sigh she heard over the phone, Lynne could almost picture Mrs. Glen's face, and how she must be rolling her eyes. Lynne tapped her fingernails on the counter as the scene played out in her mind.

Of course she thinks it's serious. Lynne Bennet thinks Elizabeth is the only child on the planet, thought Mrs. Glen sarcastically.

Finally, Mrs. Glen started to speak.

"We're very busy today, Mrs. Bennet. When did she start showing symptoms?" asked the receptionist with feigned courtesy, as the small demon on her shoulder whispered into her ear, his arm slung behind her neck companionably.

Lynne frowned. She knew that this woman would not take her concerns with any degree of sympathy.

Niall's jaw knotted as he clenched his teeth. *Mrs. Glen does not like the Bennets. It probably has something to do with her pet imp. That woman should not be allowed near small children.*

"Yesterday. But she is totally covered in lesions and cries every time she tries to urinate."

"Mrs. Bennet, chicken pox is very uncomfortable, that's true, but you really should give her a few more days before you become alarmed. I don't think we can fit you in today." Her demonic companion grinned and poured more doubt into her mind.

Xander paced back and forth in Elizabeth's small room, his frustration mounting.

"Fine. How early can we see Dr. Childs tomorrow?"

"Mrs. Bennet, you really should wait four days, until the breaking out stops, before you get worried about this." The demon wrapped his arms around her neck and strengthened his hold on her.

Unacceptable! thought Xander, frowning fiercely.

"Four days? I think that's too long. I would like an appointment tomorrow, please."

"I really don't see how we –"

"If you cannot see us, then I will take her to the emergency room. I am telling you that my daughter is sick – and not just a little sick. She is seriously ill."

Lynne could hear another deep sigh from the other woman, and it riled her. Niall placed a hand on her arm. *Relax. Control your speech.*

Xander was as close to anger as he had ever been. *Niall, can you not do something to help Lynne?*

"Very well, Mrs. Bennet. You may bring Elizabeth in at two o'clock tomorrow, and we'll *try* to fit you in." Mrs. Glen thought, *I said, 'We'll try.' I didn't promise anything.* The dark one hopped from her shoulder to the desk, smirking from ear to ear.

"Thank you. We'll be there at two." Lynne had to fight the uncharitable thoughts she was having toward the woman.

Xander's scowl softened. Once again, he admired the determination and sheer doggedness of Lynne Bennet. He could not have chosen a better mother for El had he selected her himself.

Niall leaned close to Lynne and whispered into her mind, *Remember Cindy.*

Xander also had growing respect for her guardian. *Good job, Niall. Calling Cindy is a great idea.*

Chapter 6

"In all circumstances take up the shield of faith, with which you can extinguish all the flaming darts of the wicked one." Ephesians 6:16

Vega met with a few of his most trusted goons in the strip mall. He called Keegan before him.

"You have done well, my little fiery one. Your dart was aimed true, and even now the girl sickens and approaches death. Our master will be pleased." Vega nearly smiled. Almost.

Keegan grinned, preening before the underprince. All they had to do now was wait and watch.

~~~~~~~~~

Xander knelt by Elizabeth's toddler bed throughout the long night, rubbing her back and trying to calm her. She had cried, moaned, and thrashed about in misery until the sheets were completely off, leaving her tangled in the disheveled linens. Lynne and David had slept very little – at least one of them was with Elizabeth at all times. All they could do was give her children's medicine for her fever and pain, and hold her as she sobbed.

Niall and Roark were in and out of the small room constantly as well. At one point they were surprised to hear Xander singing into Elizabeth's ear. *Jesus loves you, this I know, for the Bible tells me so. Little ones to Him belong. They are weak, but He is strong.*

Did you know that Xander could sing? asked Niall, grinning at Roark.

If he hears what you are saying, I might have to ask for a different assignment. I would not want to witness what he might do to you, was the whispered answer.

Xander studiously ignored them. He could bear the assault on his dignity if it made Elizabeth feel any better.

As soon as the sun was up, Lynne called her friend from church who was a nurse in Dr. Childs's office.

"Hello?"

"Hello, Cindy. This is Lynne. I hope I didn't wake you.

"No, that's fine, Lynne. Is there a problem? You sound upset."

"Yes . . .Oh, Cindy, I'm so worried. I wanted to catch you before you left for work. El has a severe case of the chicken pox, and I called Mrs. Glen to make an appointment yesterday." Lynne's voice broke. "She told us to come at two o'clock. From her attitude, I'm gathering that we'll wait, but we won't be called in. Cindy, I'm afraid for El. I've heard about the strep infection some children are developing, and you know how she seems to get everything that's going around."

"Don't worry about it, Lynne. Bring El to the office now. When I see you, I'll call you in myself. I know how Mrs. Glen can be." Cindy gave a small laugh.

"Thanks so much, Cindy. I owe you about a thousand now," Lynne replied with obvious relief. "I'll see you in about an hour."

"I'll be looking for you. 'Bye."

Xander appreciated Lynne's resourcefulness. *Good job. Now get ready, and let's go.*

David took Janna to school while Lynne took Elizabeth to the doctor. She promised to call him as soon as they were back home.

~~~~~~~~

Xander stalked through the unopened door to the doctor's office, seconds ahead of Lynne and Elizabeth, to scan the waiting room for enemies; he immediately spotted four of them in various postures around the people they accompanied. He put his hand to his sword, grasping the hilt, and fixed a threatening stare on each of them in turn. The dark ones glared back, eyes gleaming with hatred, but they did not move. They knew that any challenge to Xander would end badly for them. Xander did not look away from the evil ones as Lynne opened the door, carrying Elizabeth draped over her shoulder because she was too sick to walk. Niall followed closely behind them, his dark eyes searching the area and marking the location of each demon.

Lynne silently signed in with Mrs. Glen, sat down, and held Elizabeth on her lap, trying to amuse her by softly singing a favorite, familiar ditty in her ear. "I love you, a bushel and a peck, a bushel and a peck and a hug around the neck. Oh, a hug around the neck and a barrel and a heap, a barrel and a heap, and a-talking in my sleep about you!"

Xander allowed himself a fleeting expression of pleasure at the sweet scene, though he quickly resumed his scowl toward his enemies.

If Mrs. Glen was puzzled by Lynne's early arrival, she kept it to herself.

Cindy saw Lynne when she came out to call the first patient back and winked at her. Turning to the receptionist, Lynne's petite, red-haired friend said, "Mrs. Glen, we can't leave El out here. It's obvious that she has the chicken pox, and it's highly contagious. I'll isolate her in an examination room until Dr. Childs can see her."

Xander was pleased. *Good job, Niall.*

Niall nodded at his superior and smiled his thanks.

Xander and Niall walked to the exam room with their charges, raising their right hands to their shoulders, elbows bent, palms forward in recognition of Alessa, Cindy's dark-haired, brown-eyed guardian. Xander spoke, *You have done well, Alessa.*

Alessa inclined her head to the chief of all guardians, her countenance brightened by his praise.

Mrs. Glen grimaced, rolling her eyes, but there was nothing she could do. The imp on her shoulder frowned and cursed. He had to put up with Alessa every day. Now he had to witness the disruption of his plans by her and her cohorts.

It was to be the brightest spot in the week for Xander.

~~~~~~~~

Xander hovered over Elizabeth in the small room as Lynne pulled her daughter onto her lap to wait for the doctor. Lynne retrieved the books from her bag which she had brought to amuse Elizabeth. Though the child's throat was sore, she read her favorite stories aloud to her mother. When she started whining, Lynne read to her instead, pointing to the pictures and bringing the story to life by using different voices for the characters.

About thirty minutes later, a harried young man in a white lab coat opened the door and strode quickly in, reaching his hand out to Lynne. After they shook hands, Lynne set Elizabeth on the exam table, and he looked closely at his young patient.

Dr. Childs smiled tiredly at Elizabeth and spoke kindly to Lynne, "Yes, she definitely has the chicken pox. When did she first break out, Mrs. Bennet?"

"Yesterday at school. Her fever has been above 101° most of the night. Though we've been giving her a children's fever and pain reducer, she's hardly slept at all, and she screams every time she urinates. We've been using oatmeal baths and calamine lotion."

The doctor thoroughly examined Elizabeth, and he listened to her heart, talking to her in a conversational tone throughout the exam. Elizabeth liked

Dr. Childs because he never gave her shots. That was a job he left for the nurses so that the children wouldn't fear him.

Glancing into Lynne's weary eyes, he said, "I'm guessing you didn't sleep much either. She does have an aggressive case, and given her medical history, I'm not surprised that you are concerned. However, it's really too early to tell whether or not there will be complications. I'm going to write you a prescription for children's Motrin, to help keep her fever under control. I also want you to give her Benadryl for her itching. I'm writing the dosage down for you. The lesions are in her ears, nose, throat, hair, and on her body, including her genitals. Try to spread her legs widely apart while she urinates. Continue using the oatmeal baths and the lotion, and remember that a fever isn't always a bad thing. As long as it doesn't go any higher than 104 ° and stay that high for an extended period of time, she should be fine. It's a virus. It has to run its course."

Run its course? She has been hit by a dart, man! This is no ordinary case of the chicken pox! Xander thought, rather loudly. Embarrassed, he glanced at Niall who stared impassively at the wall.

Unwilling to end the visit with so little information, Lynne persisted, "At what point should I bring her back, Dr. Childs?" she asked.

"It probably won't be necessary, but if she continues to break out for more than five days, or the blisters don't dry up, bring her back in."

Niall was relieved, but Xander scowled and sniffed. *There did not seem to be much point in bringing her here.* In his opinion, the doctor had not helped Elizabeth. He was most seriously displeased.

~~~~~~~~

Five days later

Xander had grown increasingly anxious about Elizabeth, but, in his view, he seemed to be the only one who felt that way. He stalked back and forth, casting worried glances at her now and then. *She's getting worse, and they don't see it.*

Lynne thought Elizabeth was a little better, and she really needed to get a few things done at school. She had already missed a week, and most of the lesions were drying up, so Lynne called her sister. Grace Gardiner always had been there for Lynne whenever she needed to talk or to ask a special favor, and today was no different.

"Hello?"

"Hi, Grace. I need your help – again."

"Sure, Hon. I'll do whatever I can. How's my El?"

"Well, that's it. She's had a miserable time of it, but I think she's finally getting better. Most of her lesions seem to have dried up, but I can't take her back to daycare until they're all dry. Could you come watch her for a few hours while I go catch up a little at school? You know you're her favorite aunt," she wheedled.

"Yeah, I know," Grace laughed. "I'm her *only* aunt! I'll be there in half an hour."

Lynne left for the school as soon as Grace arrived. About four hours later, she got back home, bringing Janna with her, to find El lying limply on the couch and Grace leaning over her with a worried expression.

Lynne rushed to El. "What's wrong with her? Is she worse?"

Grace pulled up Elizabeth's shirt as the tiny, listless girl stared at her mom with blank eyes. "Look at this," said Grace. "I've taken her temp, and, Sis, it's 104°. She is seriously ill. I tried to call you twenty minutes ago, but you had already left the school."

Lynne was horrified. Elizabeth was burning up, her skin was red and swollen, there were new blisters everywhere, and some were filled with pus. They seemed to be meeting each other, playing connect-the-dots. It was exactly as the strep infection had been described on the newscasts. She gasped.

Xander had been pacing the small room the entire time Lynne had been gone. Now, reading Lynne's mind, he stormed over to the couch, crossed his arms with an exasperated sigh, and thought, *At last someone is getting it! She is not better – she's worse!*

Grace's guardian, Sigmund, regarded Xander with a puzzled expression. Niall, his face carefully blank, glanced quickly at Sigmund. *Don't think about it.* He kept his tone neutral.

Lynne quickly left for the kitchen and grabbed the phone there as it was the closest. When she called Dr. Child's office, she asked to speak with Cindy, not even bothering with Mrs. Glen.

As Cindy answered the phone, Lynne broke down into tears. "Cindy, El's fever is really high, she's covered everywhere, some of the places have pus in them, and I'm afraid she has that infection so many kids have died from. She's been breaking out for seven days! I've heard that the death toll is as high as a hundred now. Please talk to Dr. Childs."

Cindy was gone for only a few minutes when she came back on the line.

"Dr. Childs said to meet him at the hospital right away. I'll call David for you and tell him to meet you there."

"Thanks, Cindy. We're on our way."

Lynne hung up the phone, cradled Elizabeth in her arms, headed for the door, and called over her shoulder to Grace. "Could you get my purse for me?"

"Sure, Sis." Grace raced after Lynne and handed her sister her purse and keys.

"Grace, would you stay with Janna or take her to your house until I get back?"

"No problem. You just take care of El. Janna will go home with me and spend the night. Love you, Sis. Call me when you know something."

Xander's thoughts burst from his mind, *More than five days have passed, and she is only now on her way to the hospital! I have seen this disease many times, but never have I seen it continue to spread like this. It is very serious indeed. A dart was definitely thrown, and we all know that Keegan is the evil little fiend who is best at using that weapon. He will pay dearly when I find him.* Xander's voice had become low and threatening as his thoughts had progressed.

I only hope to be by your side when that time comes, Niall replied firmly.

Xander and Niall nodded to Grace's guardian and followed their charges.

~~~~~~~~

Xander flew just ahead of the van, looking carefully for dark angels as Lynne pulled into the hospital parking lot. He continued through the doors as Dr. Childs met Lynne in the emergency room, Niall following on her heels. The doctor took one look at Elizabeth and led them back to an exam room. David, with Roark close beside him, joined them a few minutes later while the doctor was examining his daughter.

After a cursory exam, Dr. Childs looked at them and then to the ER nurse, saying tersely, "I'm admitting her immediately. Let's go to the peds floor and get an IV on her."

"Will we be here overnight?" asked Lynne.

"You'll be here until she stops breaking out and the redness is gone," the doctor replied swiftly, running his hand through his hair. *She's really sick. It has to be the strep infection. I've never seen a chicken pox case like this.*

The doctor stopped to use the phone, sending El to the elevator on a gurney with an orderly. Lynne and David walked rapidly on either side of her, holding her hands and speaking softly to her. Elizabeth's eyes were huge as she looked from her mother to her father.

As Xander strode just in front of Lynne with his hand on Elizabeth's shoulder, he heard the fear in his charge's mind, and he thought, *I must tell her it will be all right. I wish she could hear my voice, and not just the thoughts I can put into her mind. If only I could take human form right now, but in this small hospital, I am sure everyone is well known to each other.*

Dr. Childs met them in the children's wing and directed them to a small room in which two nurses with their guardians waited by a table that held an odd looking board. As the nurses removed Elizabeth's clothing and helped her into a hospital gown, Lynne stared at the board. It was shaped like a cross with straps at places for the feet and the arms. Lynne had a very bad feeling about that board.

As Elizabeth fought to free herself, one nurse laid her on the board and the other quickly helped to secure the girl's flailing arms and legs with the bindings. Xander stood at the head of the bed and leaned over her, resting his face next to hers, his dark hair spilling over hers. He gently stroked her face with his large hands. Elizabeth began to scream and thrash as Dr. Childs approached her with the needle in his hands. Apparently, he would not leave this job for a nurse to do.

Xander bent even closer to the child and put his lips against her ear to whisper thoughts to her mind. *Elizabeth, everything will be all right. You are never alone. Try to hold still, and it will not hurt as much.*

Lynne felt like such a coward as she looked on the scene, but she knew that she would not help Elizabeth by crying in front of her, and she couldn't stop herself from sobbing.

"David," she pleaded, her voice cracking, "could you please stay with her? I can't do this."

Ever her rock, her husband replied in a tight voice, "I'll stay. You go out in the hall. This won't take long." He gave her a quick hug before she turned away. Roark stood behind David with his hands on David's shoulders to strengthen him.

As Lynne left the room to wait by the open door, she heard Elizabeth begging. It felt as if her heart were breaking into a thousand tiny pieces. Niall embraced her as she leaned against the wall and prayed. Lynne felt a strange peace settle over her as a still, small voice answered her prayer. *She will be fine.* Her faith strengthened, she thought, *God is watching over El. He loves her even more than David and I do.*

Xander used all his willpower and millennia of training, trying to hold his thoughts in check. He was more affected than he could believe was possible. He moved to stand by Elizabeth, across from David, with one strong hand on her shoulder, and the other softly stroking her dimpled cheek, struggling to present a face of stone to Roark, David's guardian. *She's so terrified that she cannot even think coherently,* Xander muttered.

"Daddy! Daddy! Please take me home! Please, Daddy! Don't let them! Don't let them!"

Her father had always taken care of everything for her. Xander knew that Elizabeth could not understand how her father could let them hurt her.

"No! No! Daddy, no!" she wailed in her high-pitched child's voice.

It was the hardest thing that he had ever done, but David took a few steps to stand at Elizabeth's head, gently stroking her face and hair, holding her eyes with his, and speaking softly to her as the nurses held her arm immobile so that the doctor could put the IV in place. Roark put his hands on David's arms. *You must be strong. This is what is best for Elizabeth. God will never allow you to suffer more than you can stand. His grace is sufficient for you, David.*

"It will be all right, my El. Everything will be fine. I love you so much," David crooned, holding her face between his hands as he leaned down over her.

Xander kept his hand on her arm while Dr. Childs finished his work. The mighty guardian leaned closer to her again, and whispered in a soft voice, *Hold still, precious one. It is almost over now. Feel my strength, Elizabeth. I am here, and I will never leave you.*

After the IV was in place, she quieted, exhausted and sniffling from the ordeal. Her lower lip quivered, and her tears were still wet on her cheeks. The doctor moved back from the table so that the nurses could bind an IV board to Elizabeth's arm and free her arms and legs from the straps. When they were finished, one nurse lifted the little girl while the other slid the board out from under her.

Now that the worst was over, David stepped to the door and called Lynne back into the room.

"I've started her on Acyclovir and an antibiotic. The Acyclovir may not be effective, as it's supposed to be administered within twenty-four hours of the initial breakout, but it's all we have. I've also given her something to help her sleep. I'll check back on her tomorrow. The nurses will call me if I'm needed," an unsmiling Dr. Childs told Lynne and David. "Right now, she needs to sleep so that her body's natural defenses can fight the infection."

The young pediatrician hurried back to a roomful of waiting patients at his practice while Elizabeth was wheeled to her room with her parents walking silently beside her.

A short time later, a lady from the admissions office brought the paperwork to the room for them to sign, and a nurse moved Elizabeth from the gurney to her bed. An orderly came in and left two trays of food, explaining that food for the patient and one parent was provided. The other parent would need to go to the cafeteria. It didn't matter. None of them were hungry.

"Mommy, I want you," Elizabeth said plaintively, holding out her free hand. Lynne looked at the IV in her other hand with the board bound to her arm to hold it straight. Elizabeth seemed so tiny with her dark, waist-length hair spread over the pillow and her glistening brown eyes, which seemed to take up half of her face, pleading for comfort.

Lynne wiped her tears covertly and plastered a smile on her face. She climbed into the bed with her child and held her, stroking her hair and carefully avoiding the IV and tubes. David collapsed in a recliner for the night. In a few minutes, they were all asleep. Every four hours, a nurse came in to check on Elizabeth, but they were all too tired to wake fully.

The family rested, but Xander, Niall, and Roark stood guard through the night, unmoving and unsmiling.

~~~~~~~~~~

Four days later

Xander wanted badly to take Elizabeth and go to a safe place. He had seen dark ones in the halls each time Elizabeth's door had opened. The place was crawling with filthy demons, though none had dared to enter her room. It would take a small army of them to withstand three protectors.

Lynne wouldn't leave the hospital without Elizabeth, and her child wouldn't have let her go in any case, so David handled everything at home – taking Janna to school, doing laundry, and bringing Elizabeth's favorite movies to play in the VHS player provided by the hospital. Every afternoon he picked Janna up from Peniel and together they came back to the hospital, giving Lynne enough time to take a quick shower in Elizabeth's bathroom and change into the fresh clothes Grace had sent her.

After one day of allowing adult church members to visit and being flooded with people, the hospital had proclaimed Elizabeth to be quarantined and prevented anyone except immediate family to enter her room. Elizabeth was bored and very cranky. She was ready to get the IV out and go home.

Finally, after eleven days of breaking out, there were no new lesions.

"Mommy, when will they take this thing out of my hand?" she asked Lynne, holding up her arm.

"Dr. Childs said that he would probably take it out today if everything looks good when he checks you, Sweetheart. We might even go home today!" Lynne said enthusiastically.

Lynne turned to the sound of the door being pushed open. "How is my favorite patient this morning?" he asked, after sitting on the foot of the bed.

"I think she's much better, Doctor. I don't see any new lesions."

"Take it out, please," Elizabeth said to him, holding out her bound arm.

"Let me check a few things first," he replied, turning to get her chart.

Elizabeth raised the arm with the board and was going to hit him when Lynne caught her arm and frowned at her.

"He said he would take it out; he promised," Elizabeth whispered indignantly to her mother, affronted that he was not moving fast enough to suit her.

"He will, El. Be patient just a little longer," her mother said quietly but firmly into Elizabeth ear.

Dr. Childs turned back with a quizzical expression, wondering what he'd missed. He pulled up Elizabeth's gown and looked at her stomach and legs, checked her arms, and looked in her mouth. As he scribbled on her chart, Elizabeth started trying to remove the bandages that held her IV board in place. In her opinion, she had been patient for a *long* time.

Stifling a chuckle, Xander agreed wholeheartedly with her assessment.

"Woah! Slow down, Elizabeth," the doctor said with a twinkle in his eye and an amused smile. "Let me help you with that." He caught her arm and began to undo the bindings himself. *It's good to see her back to her saucy little self.*

David came in just as the doctor was removing Elizabeth's IV and putting a band aid on the site.

"Are we ready to go?" David looked at Dr. Childs. *He's such a good man,* thought David. *Really kind.*

"I think so," replied the doctor, more cheerful than he'd been in many days.

David was beyond happy. He couldn't wait to have his family back home and together again.

David held out his hand to Dr. Childs. As they shook hands, he said, "Thank you so much for caring for my daughter. I want to invite you to come to our church, Tabernacle, out on Great Falls Road. We'd love to have you visit us."

"I'll think about it," replied the younger man with a smile.

Xander smiled knowingly at Niall and Roark. *Keegan is very skilled with his darts, but he is no match for the Great Physician. I doubt that we'll ever hear anything of that particular demon again. Vega will not be pleased.* He fixed them with a steely gaze as he spoke menacingly. *We must be even more vigilant, for they will never stop attacking until they have killed Elizabeth, and I will be slain before I allow that to happen!*

If Niall and Roark were surprised by the vehemence with which Xander spoke his last words, they kept their thoughts to themselves, only nodding in agreement.

~~~~~~~~

The group of dark ones assembled once more, grumbling and screeching in frustration. Vega was exceedingly displeased, and his expression ensured that someone would pay. As the pitch rose to a keening wail, Vega called for Keegan.

"Come before me to receive your payment, Keegan," Vega barked, glaring at him with undisguised hatred. "You know what my subordinates receive for failure? The same thing Kieran and Adrian got."

The others chortled, looking forward to the spectacle.

Vega motioned to Nyx who was perched in a corner of the ceiling, watching the proceedings with hawk-like eyes, awaiting his summons.

Shrieking in terror, Keegan turned to fly, but Nyx swooped down and grabbed him by the throat before he could make his escape, the long, sharp nails of his dark fingers sinking into the neck of his helpless victim. Vega's avenger held him in a vise-like grip with one hand, keeping him suspended in midair, wings extended and hovering, while he drew his sword and sent the smaller demon, howling, to his just reward.

Chapter 7

"Sing to Him a new song; play skillfully with a shout of joy."Psalm 33:3

Fall, 1995

Xander watched over Elizabeth and listened to her thoughts as she lay on her bed with her legs bent and her feet crossed behind her, happily coloring a picture of Jasmine, her favorite Disney princess. She had on her Jasmine dress-up outfit that Aunt Grace had given her for Christmas. *Aunt Grace gives the best presents*, flitted through her mind.

Observing his young charge had long since begun to give him an indefinable pleasure he had never before experienced. Of all the children he had protected since the creation of humanity, she had become more special to him than the rest. She was blessed with a beautiful mind and a lively spirit. *Elizabeth is a joy to me.* He had tried to stop the thought, but he was too late. The words had escaped him and seemed now to hang in the air. It unsettled him.

Niall and Alexis, in the music room with their charges, glanced at each other; then quickly looked in opposite directions.

They heard me, Xander thought uncomfortably. He groaned inwardly, and deliberately changed his focus back to Elizabeth, listening again to her thoughts as they leapt from her coloring to the melodies she was hearing. He smiled again.

Elizabeth's mind was humming contentedly as she listened to Janna's piano lesson. Lynne had begun teaching Janna to play six years earlier when she was eight, and Elizabeth had enjoyed listening to her mother's instructions and hearing the music from the time she was a baby. Five-year-old Elizabeth was captivated by all sorts of music. The wonderful sounds seemed to speak to her.

Janna was playing *Reverie* by Debussy, hoping to have it prepared in time for the spring recital, as Lynne listened and gave suggestions for tempo, dynamics, and fingering.

Elizabeth hopped off of her bed and began to dance around her room, moving slowly, pretending that she was a ballerina. Suddenly, she ran to the music room and threw open the door. Xander followed her, curious.

"I can do that!" she exclaimed to her surprised mother and sister.

"You're a little too young for lessons now, El, but I'll start teaching you, too, in a few years," her mother said, smiling at her indulgently.

"But I can do it now!" Elizabeth insisted stubbornly, her chin jutted out.

Xander could hear how perfectly reasonable it all seemed to her. She had no doubt at all that she could play the piece. He leaned his head to the side, a little puzzled. *What now?*

Niall looked at Xander skeptically. *She really thinks she can play the piano.*

Do you think it's possible? asked Alexis as she raised her eyebrows. *She's only five.*

I have no idea, Xander calmly replied. *I suppose it's possible. Our Master told me Himself that she was especially gifted.*

Even-tempered Janna rarely showed annoyance at anything her sister did, but she was annoyed with Elizabeth at that moment, both for interrupting her lesson and for thinking that she could play what it had taken years for her to master.

"No, you can't. I've been practicing for six years to get to this level. It takes a lot of work. Now, please go back to your room so that Mama and I can finish my lesson. I have homework to do," said Janna with a trace of irritation and a slight frown.

Elizabeth slammed the door and stomped back to her room, slamming that door as well, just to be sure that *everyone* knew she was *not* happy.

A small smile played around Xander's lips as he watched with amusement to see what she would do next. She never failed to interest him, nor did she disappoint him this time. He could hardly wait for someone from her family to peek in the door and see what she had done.

About fifteen minutes later, when her lesson was over, Janna hung her head, hiding her face in her long, dark hair.

"Mama, I'm sorry that I was mean to El. She's little, and she doesn't understand how hard it is to learn to play. I shouldn't have discouraged her."

Pushing Janna's hair back and lifting her daughter's chin with her hand so that she could look into her eyes, Lynne said tenderly, "Oh, Sweetheart, I think it would take much more than your gentle remonstrance to damage your sister's confidence. But, since you feel guilty about it, why don't you go talk to her? El loves you so much, and she wants to be just like you. Go tell her you love her, and apologize. You know she can't be angry for very long. She's probably already forgotten it. I love you, Janna." Lynne hugged her older child and kissed her cheek.

Xander heard Janna and Lynne talking. *Here comes Janna. This should be good.*

Alexis and Niall floated through the walls of Elizabeth's room, chuckling and looking forward to the reactions of their charges. If Xander's thoughts were any indication, it would be quite diverting.

Janna opened Elizabeth's door quietly and peered into the room. She put her hand over her mouth and silently backed away, shaking with suppressed laughter. Janna hurried to find her mother in the kitchen and put her finger over her lips, whispering, "Shhhh! Come with me, Mom. You just have to see this!"

Curious, Lynne followed Janna back to Elizabeth's room, and together they tiptoed over to her bed.

Elizabeth had pulled the covers over her head, and, right where her nose should be, she had taped a note. Mother and daughter leaned over together to read it, trying not to laugh.

To Janna

You hurt my feelings. You are mean, and you should say sorry! I am _very_ mad at you. You were being ugly to me. Jesus is NOT happy!

El

Lynne and Janna clapped their hands over their mouths as hard as they could, but they could not stop their giggles from erupting.

Xander, Niall, and Alexis had rarely seen anything so funny, and they all wore huge grins. Moments such as these were relatively few for protectors, and they enjoyed sharing the mirth with each other.

Elizabeth threw the covers down from her face and glared at her mother and sister, her eyes flashing and tears spilling down her cheeks. They were laughing at her! She jerked the covers back up over her head. *Humph!* Now she was angry *and* embarrassed.

Janna lay down beside her on the bed and wrapped her arms around the stiff little form as well as she could. "El?"

Silence.

Janna glanced back at her mother, who arched one eyebrow and shrugged her shoulders.

"Ellie? I'm sorry for being mean to you, and I'm sorry for laughing. Please forgive me. I love you so much." Janna's soft voice was contrite and pleading.

More silence, followed by sniffles and snubs. Suddenly, Elizabeth wriggled away from Janna and dramatically flung the covers away, marching off to the music room with her little nose in the air.

"I'll show you I can do it!" she announced, gathering her dignity about her like a robe. It might have made more of an impact had she not been wearing the Jasmine costume.

An odd parade of sorts followed behind the small, extremely determined child, marching down the hall to the music room. No one, angel or human, wanted to miss whatever would happen next.

Having arrived at her destination, Elizabeth climbed up onto the piano bench with great effort. Neither Lynne nor Janna dared to offer her help for fear of offending her further.

She sat quietly with her hands folded in her lap for a moment; then she reached up and began to play. No one was laughing anymore. There was total silence except for the mesmerizing sounds coming from the piano.

Lynne's jaw dropped. Elizabeth played *Reverie* nearly perfectly, from memory, making mistakes only when her small hands were unable to reach the octaves, causing her to play two notes instead of three. Even more astounding was the pathos with which she played. *A five-year-old should not have such depth of emotion. And her technique is amazing! She can't reach the pedals, yet she is playing the piece so smoothly that no one would ever miss the pedaling, and she's improvising to make up for the smallness of her hands.*

When she finished, Elizabeth looked up with an "I told you so" expression. She giggled when she saw Janna's mouth forming an "O" and her mother's hanging open. What she could not see was the trio of angels wearing similar expressions.

When they had at last found their tongues, Niall whispered, *Absolutely amazing.* Alexis answered, *Truly incredible.* Xander was too moved to speak. Her music had touched him deeply.

"Elizabeth . . . how did you know you could do that?" asked Lynne in a strangely quiet voice.

Elizabeth wrinkled her forehead in deep thought for a moment before replying, "I don't know. I just knew I could. I think God told me." She lifted her shoulders. "Didn't you like it? Didn't I do good?" Her eyes begged for approval.

"Darling, it was wonderful!" Lynne moved quickly to gather Elizabeth close and reassure her.

"Did you like it, Janna?" Elizabeth asked, peeping at Janna over her mother's shoulder.

"I loved it, El. Now I really *am* sorry. You were telling the truth, and I didn't listen. I promise to listen to you from now on. I love you. Are we okay?" Janna's eyes glistened with unshed tears.

"Yep!" Elizabeth chirped, wiggling out of her mother's hug, hopping down from the bench, and running to Janna to grab her around the waist. "I love you more. I win!" she proclaimed, looking up at her sister's face, eyes shining with happiness.

Lynne began Elizabeth's piano lessons that same afternoon. She skipped the primer books altogether, and had finished grades one and two by the end of the hour. Music theory was really what Elizabeth needed to learn, and she was soaking up all her mother could teach her like a sponge. Once she understood notation, she played anything in the intermediate levels at sight.

As soon as David, along with Roark, was home from the church, Lynne relayed the day's events to him. He had been a little cynical at first; Lynne did tend to exaggerate sometimes. Roark knew that it was the absolute truth, as he had shared the minds of the other three protectors as the event had taken place.

However, as David stood at the door of the music room and listened to her play, he realized that Elizabeth was truly gifted; she was a prodigy.

He knocked on the door, opened it slightly, and peeked in at his small wonder.

"Hello, El. That's really good. I like to listen to you play," he said casually. "How would you like to learn to sing, too?"

"Daddy! Do you really mean it? Would you give me lessons, too?" She beamed at him with pure joy.

"If you would like for me to, I would," her father replied, smiling at her.

"Yes, yes, yes! I love music! Let's start now," she said eagerly.

David spent the next hour with his younger daughter, learning humility. He had majored in theology, but had also minored in music, specifically vocal performance. His young daughter was far more talented than anyone else he had ever known. She had perfect pitch, and her voice had a wonderful, bell-like quality. The sound stirred his emotions, bringing tears to his eyes.

From that day forward, no one had to search very hard to find Elizabeth; she was usually in the music room, playing everything she could get her hands on, or singing while she accompanied herself.

~~~~~~~~~

About an hour's drive away in Charlotte, Gregory Wickham was also proving to be adept in his training, as well as far beyond his years in his accomplishments. Among the group of Satanists to which Cathy and George Wickham belonged were brilliant scientists, mathematicians, linguists, martial arts experts, sorcerers, musicians, witches, warlocks, physicians, and artists of all sorts. They were all more than willing to share their knowledge, gifts, and skills with the son of the Dark Lord.

Gregory had a mind that thirsted for everything they could offer him. His body moved gracefully and he enjoyed submitting himself to physical tests and training. It was as if the beautiful boy were a vacuum, sucking everything around him into the vortex of his darkness. He excelled at everything he attempted, and he attempted nearly everything.

He learned to be human, but he also learned to use his demonic side. Gregory could transform at will, charming people into doing nearly anything he wished with his hypnotic eyes and voice. The half-demon boy loved to fly through the walls to soar high into the atmosphere and look down at the world his father had promised him they would rule together.

Cathy and George were careful to file all the required paperwork with the state to support homeschooling Master Gregory. No one ever questioned them about it; all was in order.

Chapter 8

"But Jesus called for them, saying, 'Permit the children to come to Me, and stop hindering them, for the kingdom of God belongs to such as these. Truly I say to you, whoever does not receive the kingdom of God like a child shall not enter it at all.'"Luke 18: 16-17

Spring, 1996

Lucifer paced back and forth in the center of the warehouse, his guards hovering around his path, the black-cloaked principalities with their captains kneeling before him. His onyx satin robes flowed behind him, swishing against the floor as he turned again and again. The Dark Lord shook with uncontrolled anger, his eyes glowing crimson, making no attempt to disguise his rage. There was absolute silence, as no one wished to draw his attention.

Not only did the girl still live, but also it was Passover, the time of year he had hated with every fiber of his being for nearly two millennia. Every year, the words from Genesis rang in his ears, as if he were hearing them for the first time.

And the Lord God said to the serpent, because you have done this, cursed are you more than all cattle, and more than every beast of the field; on your belly shall you go, and dust shall you eat all the days of your life; and I will

put enmity between you and the woman, and between your seed and her
seed; He shall bruise you on the head, and you shall bruise Him on the heel.
Genesis 3:14-15

Lucifer remembered Jesus' final days on the earth as if it were yesterday instead of almost two thousand years ago. He thought that he had won, that he had confounded the prophecies, when Jesus had died on the cross, but he soon realized that he truly had been bruised on the head when the Christ had risen from the grave three days later. Jesus had conquered death, hell, and the grave, and Lucifer had tasted defeat. To his further chagrin, Christians had instituted a holy day during Passover as well, calling it Easter and celebrating the resurrection.

But it was far from over in his mind. Though he had lost that battle, Satan still had a plan to win the ultimate war, and that brought his thoughts back to the girl. She should be dead already! He threw back his head and howled in fury as he continued to pace, working himself into a frenzy fueled by anger and hatred.

Vega had been waiting for this summons with dread for the past year. He had tried desperately, over and over again during the past five years, to kill the human girl, but Xander had thwarted him at every turn. Her death consumed him, and Vega's terror at his failure to complete his assignment controlled his every thought. The huge demon waited hopelessly for the inevitable. In one way, it would be almost a relief to give up the struggle and be consigned to the oblivion that was outer darkness. He was utterly convinced that no one would be able to accomplish the Dark Lord's wishes concerning the girl. The only thing Vega would hope for was that Xander would someday share his fate. He despised Xander with all the passion of his evil being. He wanted to smite the guardian himself for frustrating all of his carefully laid plans.

Vega was not the only one who had been awaiting this meeting. The entire demonic realm knew of his impotence and eagerly looked forward to his punishment. Vega had no friends in the ranks. He was known to have sacrificed the lives of many demons in order to preserve his own. The other dark angels smirked, though their heads remained bowed, faces hidden beneath their hoods. The spectacle that would spell the demise of Vega would be most entertaining.

At last, Lucifer stopped abruptly in the center of the room, his blood-red eyes flashing a warning to any who would dare to speak. He lifted his chin, his demeanor haughty and arrogant, and fixed his icy gaze on Vega. The underprince shivered involuntarily from the coldness of his master's voice. His time had come.

"Vega, you can have no doubt as to the reason for this assembly."

There was total quiet. No one moved; not even the slightest sound was heard.

"Vega! Approach me." Satan's voice was steady and deadly.

Every head lifted to watch Vega slowly rise and move to kneel before their master. They salivated at the thought of what was to come.

"You pathetic creature. You have failed me for the last time," Lucifer spat out, suddenly extending his right hand and holding his index finger and his thumb together.

Vega began to choke and sputter, unable to speak.

Lucifer touched his fingers together with a little more pressure.

Vega crashed to the floor, clutching at his throat with both hands, his eyes bulging. His legs jerked in spasms.

Lucifer pinched the tips of his finger and thumb together tightly while gradually raising his arm. He stared at Vega with disgust, as if he were an insect to be squashed under his boot.

Vega levitated limply in the air, his head falling to one side and his tongue lolling out, as though he had been hung from a gallows. There was a puff of black smoke, and Vega was no more in this world.

The crowd of dark angels exhaled audibly. Their master was magnificent. No one could stand before him, and their admiration knew no bounds. Loud cheers and catcalls vibrated the rafters and echoed through the empty space.

The Dark Lord raised his hands; the silence was instantaneous.

"Nyx! Step forward," Lucifer commanded.

The tall ebony angel obeyed at once, a glint in his black eyes. He had tired long since of playing second place to the fool, Vega.

"Nyx, you are now underprince in Vega's stead. See that you do not follow his example of failure. Do not make me angry, Nyx. You would not like to see me angry," growled Lucifer.

"I will succeed, my master," said Nyx with a swagger.

"That would be wise," Lucifer replied succinctly, one eyebrow raised.

Lucifer turned on his heel and flew through the beams of the warehouse, faster than eyes could see, accompanied by his ever-present henchmen, their midnight cloaks quickly disappearing into the darkness.

~~~~~~~~

Pensively, Xander walked beside the Bennet ladies as they left home, musing over Elizabeth's thoughts that morning. The beauty of his countenance was marred by a slight frown. *Her dreams were disturbed last night. She does not seem happy now, either. Something is bothering her, but, oddly enough, all I sense is her fear. Why can I not hear her thoughts clearly? She is too young to have reached the age of accountability.*

Niall and Alexis followed the little procession. They heard Xander's worrying, but it seemed that he was always overly anxious about anything concerning Elizabeth.

It was Easter Sunday, and the daffodils and jonquils were in bloom. The dogwood trees again told the legend of the cross with their scarred petals. It was the time of rebirth.

Normally, Elizabeth would have been excited about her new Easter outfit, a beautiful white dress with lace scallops around the waist and hem, and tiny pink rosebuds on the bodice. Her mother had curled her hair and caught the sides with pearl clasps, letting it flow down her back in dark spirals. She wore new white patent leather shoes with her white tights. However, she was too distracted to enjoy her Easter finery, and her expression was glum.

She is even more beautiful today than she usually is. She loves to dress up. Why is she not happy? Xander asked himself.

As Lynne and her daughters walked to Tabernacle Church for Sunday morning services, Elizabeth tugged on her mother's sleeve and asked seriously, "Mommy, can I sit with you in big church today?"

Lynne looked at her daughter's upturned face. Puzzled, she asked "Don't you want to go to children's church and hear Miss Lolly tell the Bible stories? You always have fun in there, and you wouldn't have to sit quietly for so long."

"But, it's Easter, and I want to go with you and Sissy. I promise I'll be good. I want to hear Daddy sing today. He told me he's singing the special, and I want to hear you play the piano, too, Mommy. I can listen to Daddy preach. I promise I'll be good," she pleaded, her soulful brown eyes entreating her mother.

"You'll have to sit with Janna during the welcome time and congregational singing. Will you behave for Janna?"

"Yes, Mommy. I can be good, if I try very hard."

The trio of angels nodded at the truth of her words. *Out of the mouths of babes*, thought Xander.

~~~~~~~~~

Xander, Alexis, Niall, and Roark stood along the wall closest to the pew that held Elizabeth and Janna. As they had entered the sanctuary that morning, the angels of the various church members had saluted one another in greeting. The other light beings had seen Xander hundreds of times now, but they still showed the chief guardian the utmost respect and deference.

As they all took their places near their charges, the entire auditorium glowed gently with the light exuded from the hundreds of guardians. The presence of so many holy angels gathered in one place caused a spirit of warmth and love to settle over the congregation.

After Lynne had played for the congregational singing, she joined her daughters to hear David sing "Does He Still Feel the Nails?" Elizabeth listened intently to her father's beautiful baritone and thought about the words he sang. *Does He still feel the nails every time I fail? Does He hear the crowd cry, 'Crucify,' again? Am I causing Him pain? Then I know I have to change. I just can't bear the thought of hurting Him.* Her tender heart was moved as she visualized her sins nailing Jesus to the cross. *My sins are hurting Him*, she thought sadly.

Xander remembered standing by Mary as the soldiers had nailed Jesus to the cross. He could still hear the sounds of the hammers as they drove the nails through His flesh and into the wood. Niall, Roark, and Alexis relived those hours at the cross through Xander's memories. They bowed their heads in respect for what the Son had suffered willingly to save mankind. Any of the angels present that morning would have been honored to have ministered to Jesus during that time, but He had refused all attempts to alleviate His pain. As God the Father had turned from Jesus while he bore the sins of the world, the Son had been alone until His death. It was the only time in all of eternity that the Father and Spirit had been separated from the Son. The Trinity had experienced true agony during that time.

Xander thought solemnly of the words Paul had written in Hebrews 2:9, 14-15, *'But we do see Him who has been made for a little while lower than the angels, namely, Jesus, because of the suffering of death crowned with glory and honor, that by the grace of God He might taste death for everyone. Since then the children share in flesh and blood, He Himself likewise also partook of the same, that through death He might render powerless him who had the power of death, that is, the devil; and might deliver those who through fear of death were subject to slavery all their lives.'*

David had never been a "fire-and-brimstone" preacher, but this morning he had presented the plan of salvation and had referred to the Scriptures regarding hell, which God had originally created for the Devil and his angels, as a final destination for those who rejected Christ. After he finished his sermon and prayed, he stepped in front of the pulpit and asked if anyone would like to come forward for assurance of salvation, prayer, or counseling, and several members of the congregation came to rest on the kneeling benches to pray.

As he stood alone at the front of the church, a movement to the side caught his eye. He turned his head just in time to see a small blur hurling herself at his legs.

He knelt to hold his younger daughter, who was crying as if her heart would break. Xander moved quickly to her side, kneeling beside her with his hand on her back, and Roark took his place beside David.

"El, darling, what's wrong?" he whispered in her ear.

She wailed loudly, "Daddy, I don't want to go to hell!"

"Sweetheart, you're very young. I don't think you're on the way to hell quite yet."

"Yes, I am! I've told lies, and I've been bad! I've disobeyed you and Mommy! I'm going to hell!" she practically shouted, her voice breaking in her grief.

Elizabeth understands, though she is but five years old, Xander realized. *She knows that she is a sinner, and that she needs a Redeemer. She has reached the time of being held accountable at a younger age than most.*

David, looking up to a sea of amused faces, embraced his child and stood to his feet, holding her in his arms. Roark rose to his feet beside the pastor.

The other angels, as well as the humans, were smiling at the antics of Elizabeth, but as Xander stood to his feet, he could not force a smile he did not feel. It was as if a hand tightly gripped his heart, squeezing it to the point of pain. He could not bear her tears, and he fought fiercely to control his thoughts. Exposing his weakness to this entire body of guardians was unacceptable.

"Tom," David said to the chairman of the deacons, "would you mind coming up front and dismissing the service with prayer?" He looked out over the crowd of believers and added, "I think I have something I must discuss with my daughter immediately. I am her pastor, too."

Xander was glad to have an excuse to leave. He and Roark hurried to follow the pastor and his child.

David strode quickly down the aisle to his office, carrying his tearful child with him. When they were in privacy, he pulled Elizabeth onto his lap and kissed her cheek, holding her closely to him. Xander stood behind her, stroking her curls.

"My El, what is it that you want? You've told me what you don't want. Now tell me what you want."

"I want Jesus in my heart," she sobbed.

"El, Jesus loves you, but He doesn't want you to accept Him out of fear. He wants you to love Him."

"I do love Jesus," she said earnestly, the tears running down her cheeks, looking into her father's eyes. "You pray with me every night and read me stories from the Bible. You taught me that Jesus died for me, and I don't want to make him unhappy anymore because of my sins. I want to be like you, and Mommy, and Janna. I want Jesus to be my Savior, too."

"Then pray to Jesus and tell Him that, El. It will make Him very happy."

Father and daughter bowed their heads together, and Xander beamed as Elizabeth was born anew into the family of God. Roark smiled and put his hand on Xander's shoulder, sharing his happiness at his charge's decision. The salvation of one's charge was always a momentous occasion for a guardian, the most important moment in that person's lifetime, and the beginning of years of service.

Xander thought of the words penned by Luke, the physician, *'I tell you, there is joy in the presence of the angels of God over one sinner who repents,'* and he knew that there was a celebration in heaven, as well as in the sanctuary, over Elizabeth's decision.

"El, you are now my sister in Christ as well as my daughter. I have something I've been keeping for you just for this special day," said David tenderly. Her father set her on her feet, stood, and led her by the hand to his desk. He opened a drawer and took out a small box which he handed to his child.

She reached for the box, smiling in anticipation. As she removed the lid, she looked up at her father, her face radiant.

"I love it, Daddy," Elizabeth said, lifting the garnet cross and gold chain from the cotton. "It's just like Janna's. Can I wear it now?"

"Certainly, my angel. Let me help you with it." He fastened it around her neck, and they left his office hand-in-hand, Xander and Roark shadowing them. Elizabeth was ready to celebrate her first Easter in the family of God. She was happy once more.

~~~~~~~~

The holy angels were rejoicing, but there was no promise of joy that day for the fallen ones. Elizabeth Bennet was still very much alive, and she was now a servant of Jehovah God.

Nyx knew that he must redouble his efforts, and quickly, or he would suffer the same fate as his predecessor.

The new underprince convened a meeting in the strip mall with all of his underlords and powers.

"Hadrian!" called out Nyx in a voice of authority. "Come before me."

A mighty demon who was as large as Nyx dropped to one knee before him. Hadrian was the essence of all that was dark.

"Hadrian, you are now my captain. I have several plans for eliminating our problem, and I require your assistance."

"As always, I am completely at your disposal, Prince Nyx," Hadrian answered in a rough voice.

"I would expect nothing less. Astra, Blade, and Than, I have need of your skills. The rest of you will soon receive your assignments. For now you are dismissed."

The demons scattered throughout the dominion to cause destruction and strife while awaiting their orders.

Chapter 9

"'For I know the plans I have for you,' declares the Lord, 'plans for
welfare and not for calamity to give you a future and a hope.'"
Jeremiah 29:11

Spring, 1998
Greenville, South Carolina
Southern Association of Christian Schools Elementary Fine Arts Festival

Xander, Niall, Roark, and Alexis tracked their charges from room to room,
forming a hedge of protection around them. Elizabeth's pastel yellow dress
stood out in the crowd, making her instantly recognizable and easily
followed. The angels knew that if it was not difficult for them to see her, it
was also no problem for the dark ones. Xander well understood that Nyx
would be waiting for any opportunity to harm Elizabeth, especially after the
fate that had befallen Vega.

Xander took pleasure in listening to Elizabeth's performances at this annual
event. She had continued her piano and voice lessons with her parents, and
had progressed so well that she was now competing in several categories.
Lynne, David, and Janna were all at the Festival with Elizabeth, along with
many other students, teachers, and parents from Peniel Christian Academy
and sixty other schools. The annual event attracted more than fifteen
hundred people, more than one thousand of whom participated in art, music,

speech, spelling, Bible, and science fair competitions. Academic testing had been completed a month earlier at each participating school, and the results were to be announced at the end of the day, along with the winners of the day's competitions. The eight best performers in the music and speech categories would be showcased in the closing assembly.

Elizabeth was thoroughly enjoying herself; therefore, Xander was content as well. She had already sung with the choir and the ensemble, and they were now weaving through the crowd to the solo female vocal performance room for her age group. Lynne and Elizabeth waited just outside the door for her summons from the judges while the room filled with parents and students from Peniel and the other Christian schools. Janna and her father had gone in earlier to secure a seat on the front row as Roark and Alexis had joined the other guardians standing around the perimeter of the room.

"Mommy, I'm so nervous. There are so many people in there," Elizabeth whispered anxiously to Lynne after peeking into the room.

"El, you have nothing to be worried about. Everyone in there wants you to do well. I'll be with you, just as we've practiced so many times. You know every note perfectly. Just relax and enjoy sharing your music with everyone."

"Mommy, will you pray with me?"

"Sure, Sweetheart. Hold my hands."

Lynne knelt, holding Elizabeth's hands in hers as they bowed their heads. Xander and Niall placed their hands on the shoulders of the mother and daughter. "Dear Lord, thank You for Elizabeth and her gifts. Please help her not to be afraid, Father, as she sings, but help her to glorify You as she shares her song. In Jesus' name. Amen."

"Amen. Thanks, Mommy," said Elizabeth, her brown eyes shining with confidence.

As Lynne stood, the hostess came to the door and motioned for them to enter. Lynne handed her the judging sheets and music, and she walked to the piano at the front of the room and seated herself. The two guardians took their places beside their charges. Xander had, of course, drawn attention already that day, but those protectors who had not yet seen him raised their hands to salute him in greeting. He returned the gesture, and then stepped behind Elizabeth. The other guardians saw the little girl bathed in the light of the angel who towered behind her, and, to her human audience, she looked as bright as a sunbeam in her yellow dress. Her dark hair, which had never been cut, had been pulled back with a yellow bow and hung in loose curls to her waist.

Lynne placed Elizabeth's selection on the piano's music stand and smiled encouragingly at her daughter, who stood beside the piano. Elizabeth returned her mother's smile and faced the audience just as the judges looked up and nodded for her to begin.

"Hello. I'm Elizabeth Bennet from Peniel Christian School, and I will be singing *"Kyrie Eleison,"* one of my original compositions, arranged by my father, David Bennet." She glanced at her mother who began to play the introduction.

As Elizabeth started to sing, a silent stillness settled over the room. Her voice soared with perfect clarity, spanning three octaves, touching each note with just the right dynamic level, and enthralling everyone in the room. Those who had not heard Elizabeth sing before had never heard a child sing with such power and range, yet such tenderness. Her song was a plea for God's mercy, a prayer, and everyone in the room felt that they had been in His presence by the time she sang the final note. Her face was expressive, with her glistening eyes and double dimple. It was impossible not to be touched.

As the last note faded away, there was a pause, a moment in which no one moved.

Xander wanted to hug her, to tell her that she was wonderful, but there were too many eyes watching him. He instead satisfied himself with laying his hands on her small shoulders and looking down at her with a smile. *She is so special, so beautiful, inside and out.*

After a few seconds of stunned silence, the judges rose and began to applaud vigorously as the rest of the room joined them. Elizabeth bowed and ran to her father and Janna.

"Did you like it, Daddy? Did I sing it right?" she asked David as he hugged her tightly.

"El, it was just wonderful! I'm so proud of you," he answered with tears in his eyes.

"Can I have a hug, too, El? You did a great job!" Janna told her little sister, holding out her arms. Elizabeth beamed as Janna held her.

Lynne made her way over to her family, and they walked, together with their unseen escorts, down the crowded hall. Their next destination was the room for piano solo competition.

Again, David and Janna went in to find seats as Lynne waited outside the room with Elizabeth to help her stay focused.

"Mommy, I think I'm nervous again." Elizabeth's voice trembled slightly as she looked up at her mother. "What if I mess up?"

"El, you know this piece backwards and forwards. You have prepared well, and God will honor your work." Lynne again knelt to embrace her daughter. "Even if you don't play it perfectly, we'll all still love you, you know," she teased with a grin.

Yes, we will, Xander thought, and then quickly stole a glance at Niall to see if he had been listening. Niall showed no reaction. The wall was suddenly very interesting to him.

Elizabeth giggled at her mother's statement. "Mommy, you're being silly. I know you'll love me anyhow."

"Then there is no need to be afraid, is there?" asked her mother.

"No, I guess not. I'll just do my best, right?"

"That's all you can do, Sweetie."

When the hostess stepped to the door and called for them, Lynne gave her Elizabeth's music, led her daughter to the front of the room, and took the seat that David had saved for her.

Elizabeth stood by the piano, looking alone and very small. She lifted her chin with determination, smiled sweetly, and announced, "Hello, I'm Elizabeth Bennet, and I'll be playing 'Second Arabesque' by Debussy." She and her mother had chosen the piece because it was playful, the notes were within the reach of her small hand span, and it was written by Elizabeth's favorite Impressionistic composer. Oddly enough, Lynne had played the piece during her college years, twenty years before. *Now I'll hear how it should be played,* Lynn thought. *The teacher becomes the pupil.*

Xander, standing to her side away from the audience, placed a calming hand on her shoulder. He anticipated watching her hands move gracefully over the keyboard.

Elizabeth sat on the piano bench with her hands in her lap, focused herself with a silent prayer, and began to play. As soon as her hands touched the keys, she was lost in the music. It was as if there were no other people in the room. The music flowed and danced under her childish hands until the final *pianissimo* octaves faded away. She sat quietly for a few moments, still existing in the other world to which she traveled every time she played. Finally she rose and bowed to the audience.

The applause was thunderous, and Elizabeth's face seemed to glow with joy. She ran to her family, and as they were hugging her, the judges approached them. One of them reached out his hand to David and introduced himself as Dr. Edward Johnson, a faculty member of the music department at Converse College in Spartanburg.

"Mr. and Mrs. Bennet, we are all three in agreement. Your daughter is extraordinarily gifted. We have heard that she sings as well as she plays. Have you thought about engaging master teachers for her?" Dr. Johnson asked.

David and Lynne looked at each other, slightly embarrassed.

"Well, my husband has been giving her voice lessons, and I've been teaching her piano and music theory for the past two years, but, frankly, we're nearly at the end of our capabilities. However, we cannot afford to pay for master teachers," Lynne replied.

"We know of several people that we would like to contact on behalf of your daughter, if you would allow us to do so. I'm certain that something could be worked out as far as securing a sponsor to pay for voice and piano lessons for Elizabeth."

"I really don't know what to say. We are very grateful for your help," answered David.

"Could we have your contact information?"

David nodded at his wife.

"Certainly," said Lynne, scribbling on the back of a judging form she had in her bag.

"You'll be hearing from us shortly," Dr. Johnson said as he extended his hand to her and then her husband in farewell.

~~~~~~~

After the competitions for the day had ended, Lynne and Elizabeth went to check one of the showcase lists that had been posted throughout the facility while Janna and David went to the overflowing auditorium to find seats for all of them. Lynne was astounded to see that her daughter had been selected to perform both her vocal piece and her piano selection. Children as young as Elizabeth were not usually showcased, and in the ten years she had been bringing students, including Janna, to the Festival, she had never seen any student showcased twice in solo work.

Xander was so proud of Elizabeth that he thought he would burst with the joy of it.

Lynne controlled her astonishment and looked down with a broad smile at Elizabeth's upturned, questioning face.

"Elizabeth, you get to perform your piano and vocal pieces for everyone! That's wonderful. I know that you'll enjoy sharing your music with everybody." Lynne knew that she must be positive and show no trace of her own anxiety to her daughter.

"In front of all those people, Mommy? Both pieces?" Elizabeth's eyes were round and huge in her small face.

Niall leaned in to whisper in Lynne's ear, *Remember the Barbie that she wants.*

Lynne thought for a moment, and then cupped Elizabeth's chin with her hand and said, "El, I know that you've never performed in front of this many strangers before. I think you deserve a special prize. If you will agree to share your music with these people, you and I will go shopping together for that Barbie you've been asking for."

Elizabeth's expression immediately changed from fear to speculation. "Really, Mommy? The Ariel Barbie? You promise?"

"Absolutely. I promise. Pinky swear." Lynne's eyes twinkled as she extended her pinky finger to her daughter.

Elizabeth grinned and entwined her pinky with her mother's. "Pinky swear."

~~~~~~~~

At the beginning of the closing assembly the testing winners were announced, and Elizabeth placed first in each of the academic tests she had taken, which was no surprise to the group from Peniel Christian Academy. They all knew she had been so bored in kindergarten that, after a few weeks, Mrs. Mills had moved her to first grade. The summer after she finished first grade, Lynne had homeschooled her through second grade, and she had done the same the following two summers. Consequently, she was now in fifth grade, though she was only seven years old. Elizabeth had competed against fifth and sixth graders in the five tests she had taken.

Each time she went to the front to receive her awards, her massive guardian walked behind her, his hand on her back protectively.

Xander was stately as he shadowed Elizabeth to the stage for the final time that day. She had already performed brilliantly at the piano, receiving a standing ovation, and was now responding to the announcer's summons for her vocal solo. Niall went with Lynne to piano, across the platform from

Elizabeth. As her mother began the introduction, Elizabeth stepped to the microphone and looked out over the sea of humanity.

This place is huge! There are so many people! Her thoughts held a tinge of desperation.

Xander stepped up close behind her and leaned over, his sleeveless tunic showing his muscular arms as he bent them to place his hands gently on either side of her head while he whispered to her, *You can do this. God loves to hear you sing of His mercy. Sing to His honor and glory. You are not alone. You are never alone.*

I am not alone. I am never alone. The beautiful child began to sing, and her song transported her listeners to the very throne of heaven. Her performance was flawless, and as she finished, the hushed audience suddenly came to life. They leapt to their feet with shouts of glory to God, and the angels glowed more brightly than they had for almost two thousand years. Elohim was well pleased with her offering.

~~~~~~~~~~

The Prince of Darkness descended slowly into his son's bedroom and sat in a winged back chair. He leaned forward with his elbows on his knees, his fingers templed under his chin, and spoke softly, "Gregory, come before me. I wish to see you."

Lucifer's hooded guards grouped themselves into a semi-circle behind his chair, brawny arms folded across their chests.

Though it was midnight, the strapping seven-year-old eagerly left his warm bed to stand fearlessly before his sire.

"Yes, Father?" Gregory queried.

"How are your classes progressing, my son? Are you working hard at your lessons and learning the ways of men and of our kind?"

"According to my teachers, I am doing very well. I especially like the physical training and discipline – and flying, but I have no trouble with the maths, sciences, or languages. Sorcery comes naturally to me, and I am learning to appreciate the great works of art. Cathy and George have been taking me to playgrounds to meet human children and learn their customs. Father, humans are very easily led, aren't they?" Gregory questioned, his eyes wide.

Deception was second nature to Gregory. Even so, he was amazed at how little effort he had to use to deceive other children and adults. The boy was able to get them to do practically anything he wanted with trickery and lies.

Lucifer laughed. "Yes, Gregory. Learning to influence humans is an elementary skill, but one in which you must excel. You have not mentioned your music lessons. I am especially interested in hearing how you fare in that area."

Gregory drew his dark brows together thoughtfully. "Music is easy for me. The teachers say that I have a 'natural aptitude' for singing and playing instruments. Why do you ask, Father?"

The Dark Lord drew his son into an embrace, kissing the top of his head. He then pulled back from the boy so that he could see his face.

"Because you must be very skilled in music to accomplish our goals, my own. Elizabeth Bennet is supernaturally gifted in that area, and your musical talent can be something that you have in common with her. Gregory," said Lucifer, holding his son's eyes with his own, "the human girl, Elizabeth, can destroy all of our plans. Our enemy has gifted her in music for a reason. Though we don't know yet the purpose, we can use her gift against her. You must excel in music. Do you understand?" he questioned the boy gently, placing his hands on his son's shoulders.

Lucifer had never before loved anything or anyone except for himself, but in a twisted way, he now loved Gregory. *The boy is a part of me.*

"She must die, Gregory." Satan's voice was deep and hushed.

"Yes, Father. Your will be done." The boy had paraphrased Matthew 6:10, part of the Lord's Prayer, and he did not so much as blink as his eyes met his father's in an intense gaze.

Chapter 10

*"For our struggle is not against flesh and blood, but against the
rulers, against the powers, against the world forces of this darkness,
against the spiritual forces of wickedness in the heavenly places."*
Ephesians 6:12

A year later, 1999

Xander mused over the fairly quiet past four years. There had been no major
attempts against Elizabeth's life during that time, yet he knew without a
doubt that Lucifer had not abandoned his plans. There had been three
determined, orchestrated attacks, in addition to smaller, random tries.

He was strangely disquieted, for he could not remember any time in the past
when he had felt such an attachment to any of his other charges. Elizabeth's
music lessons at the college were going very well, and he took great joy in
hearing her play and sing. In fact, being around her made him happy; that,
in itself, was odd. Disguising his thoughts was taking more effort every day.

~~~~~~~

Xander, Niall, and Alexis flew in the frigid air just above the Mitsubishi
Galant early one morning as Janna drove Lynne and Elizabeth to school.
Lynne and David had bought the used car for her the previous year after she
had completed driver's education and a safety course, and had passed the

state testing for her permit and then her license. Lynne was strapped into the passenger's seat, and Elizabeth was behind her, studying a book and notes for a test.

Janna, a senior, was a careful driver; nevertheless, Xander was wary of teenagers behind the wheel. He scanned the area uneasily. Niall, hearing his anxiety, dropped back to guard the rear.

Valentine's Day had been the day before on Sunday, but Janna and her boyfriend, Chance Bingley, had gone out to dinner on Saturday night, and she hadn't given him one of his presents yet. It was in the trunk, and she was looking forward to seeing his face when she could give it to him at break time.

Chance is such a dream. He's really going to like his extra present. He's got a game tonight, too, so the timing is perfect. Her thoughts were blissful.

The road was unusually empty for a school morning. As they crested a hill before a long straightaway, Janna saw a stopped school bus and began to slow down. Remembering her driver's training, she came to a complete stop about two bus lengths behind the bus.

Why is she stopping way back here? thought Lynne. *Well, I won't fuss at her for being too careful.*

Janna glanced into the review mirror and saw a pickup truck coming at full speed, weaving back and forth. *Is that truck going to stop?*

Niall saw the pickup at the same time and recognized three hulking demons with the inebriated driver, draped over his shoulders and whispering into both of his ears.

Nyx has definitely stepped up his efforts. He has sent three of his best.

Astra, Blade, and Than had spent the past two years watching the Bennet family, and waiting for a moment such as this. They had cultivated a "relationship" of sorts with Tom Wilkins, and he was accustomed to hearing them in his mind. The voices in his head were the only friends he had.

The demons had stayed with the drunkard throughout the prior evening, encouraging him to drink until he could barely stand. He had spent the night carousing and playing video poker at a convenience store back up the road, finally stumbling out to his old F-150 pickup around seven in the morning. They even now continued the assault on Tom's mind, filling him with ideas of power and false confidence, convincing him to drive faster.

Blade left the speeding vehicle and flew in front of it for a couple of seconds at a critical moment, rapidly taking form to block the man's view of the stopped car and bus. Tom squinted at the dark object, his thoughts jumbled and incoherent. Blade dematerialized and flew back into the truck, allowing the morning sun shining in Tom's eyes to further blind and confuse him.

Niall heard his disorientation. The man wasn't even thinking of slowing down.

Xander! yelled Niall. *Blade blocked his view! He does not see the bus or the car! He will not stop!*

Niall, push the car! I'll take the bus! Alexis, talk to Janna! Xander's wing muscles strained to propel him at top speed as he flew directly into the bus, arms wide apart, and hands planted on either side of the rear door. The school bus had just begun to pull forward slowly when Xander pushed it ahead, accelerating the busload of children out of harm's way. He was careful to measure his power to avoid throwing the bus down the road.

Alexis, her honey hair streaming behind her, quickly dipped through the roof of the Galant, placed her hands on either side of Janna's head, and spoke forcefully into Janna's mind. *Take your foot off the brake. Janna, take your foot off the brake now!*

Niall flew at flash speed, silvery wings streamlined, to the back of the car, using his mighty arms to thrust it forward.

Janna's eyes were enormous with fear, but she instinctively obeyed the voice, still watching in the mirror as the pickup bore down on them. There was no time to tell Lynne and Elizabeth that they were about to be hit. Alexis rapidly flashed back, helping Niall push Janna's car to lessen the damage from the impending collision. A second before the small pickup going at least sixty miles per hour plowed into the Galant, Niall and Alexis shot up in the air, narrowly avoiding being crushed while in semi-solid form. The impact threw the Galant down the road, barely missing the moving school bus.

Behind the bus, Xander turned and planted his feet, catching the Galant as it flew forward, preventing it from becoming sandwiched between the bus and the truck.

The explosive sound of the crash brought several people hurrying out of their houses to see what had happened, and one of them returned home to call 911.

Tom Wilkins stumbled from the truck, a gash on his head dripping blood, and collapsed in a drunken stupor on the ground beside the road. Several bystanders went to see if they could help him as they waited for the police to arrive.

In the car, Lynne voiced concerned for her daughters. "Are you okay? Janna? Elizabeth?" Lynne tried to turn to look at Elizabeth, but felt pain shoot through her back and decided to remain still. "Girls?"

"My back and neck hurt, but I think I'm fine," Janna answered, her voice trembling.

"El?" Lynne called.

Janna looked at her sister in the rearview mirror. The back seat was bent at an odd angle, and Elizabeth appeared to be caught between the front and rear seats. All Janna could see was the top of her dark head, and she was terrified for her little sister.

"El!" Janna's voice rose with fear.

"Mom, Janna, I'm okay, but I'm stuck. I don't think I can get out by myself," Elizabeth replied in a small, frightened voice.

Xander had checked on Elizabeth during the accident, and he knew that she was not hurt. But he decided in that moment that she had worn the target long enough. She had been terrorized, threatened, and victimized, and he was tired of it. *These three dark ones will never hurt you again.*

As soon as the car stopped moving, he flew toward the truck with blinding speed, glorious in his fury. His eyes were blue steel, his jaws clenched, and his mouth set in a determined frown. He unsheathed his sword with stunning swiftness and dove directly through the windshield of the pickup, taking Than by the neck with his left hand in one fluid motion.

You will not have to wait for Nyx's sentence. I will carry it out this instant, right here! Xander shouted. Without pause, he cleared the roof of the vehicle holding the demon in a stranglehold, and, dropping him, sliced his head from his body. Not waiting to watch him disintegrate, Xander flew through him, keeping his eyes fixed on Blade.

Blade and Astra fled in opposite directions, shrieking.

Niall, you and Alexis take Astra. I want Blade!

Xander, determined that Blade would not escape him, spread his wings widely, took a few powerful strokes, and shot up into the air. Looking down, he located Blade and swooped down on the black-cloaked denizen of hell like an avenging hawk, his wings folded flat against his back. Blade was fast and strong, but he was no match for Xander. The protector picked up speed as he dove, knocking Blade from the air as he smashed into his back. Blade hit the ground with a resounding thud, and jumped, catlike, to his feet – but not fast enough. With a menacing smile, Xander raised his gleaming silver sword above his head with both hands and brought it down with the force of years of frustration through the dark angel's head and body, cleaving him neatly in half. Blade had no time to scream.

His work done, Xander glanced quickly around him and located Niall and Alexis. *Astra?*

Dispatched to the abyss.

Xander nodded his approval. The entire battle had taken no more than a few seconds.

Good work. Let the spies report that to Nyx, the chief guardian thought with satisfaction.

Within a few more seconds, the three protectors were by their charges, assessing the damage. The car, without question, was totaled. Elizabeth was still trapped in the backseat, afraid to move, and so panicked she was barely able to breathe. She had always had an extreme fear of feeling trapped in a small space. Her eyes were tightly closed against her claustrophobia.

Xander was able to get his head and arms into the back seat with her, though the rest of his body remained outside of the car. The seatbelt held her, caught in the small space left between the front and back seats. She kept trying unsuccessfully to get to the clasp and unbuckle the belt, but her hands were pinned in her lap where she had been holding the book. He could not leave her like that, caught and frightened, until the police and the EMT's had time to arrive. *This is a rural area. It might be twenty or thirty minutes before help comes.*

In a split second, Xander flew into the trees along the road and changed into human form, wearing a blue turtleneck sweater, jeans, and Nikes. Alexis and Niall followed his example, and emerged from the woods almost immediately after Xander, now.

The three angels ran from the shelter of the trees, which closely lined the highway, to the car to help their charges. Niall and Alexis easily opened Lynne and Janna's car doors, but Elizabeth's door had been crushed and was stuck fast.

Xander grasped the door handle and yanked it a few times to open the door, nearly tearing it off in his haste. Lynne caught a glimpse of him running toward them from the woods and had a vague feeling that she had seen him somewhere before. She was distracted from following the thought by Niall.

While Niall got contact information for David and the school from Lynne and went to a nearby house to call them, Alexis talked in quiet tones to Janna and held her hand. Niall could, of course, have read Lynne's mind, but he wanted her to have the comfort of knowing that all was being handled.

Xander leaned his head and arms in to the tight space to look into Elizabeth's eyes. "Are you all right?" He looked her over carefully, saw that there was no blood or other evidence of injury, and had confidence that he might be able to release her from her confinement if he could get the seatbelt off of her.

"Yes, sir. I think so. But I'm stuck. Can you help me?" she asked, turning her deep brown eyes imploringly to the man who had opened her door.

"I will try my best. What is your name?" he asked with a comforting smile.

"Elizabeth. What's yours?"

"How can I help you, Elizabeth?" he questioned, avoiding answering her.

"Can you unbuckle my seatbelt?"

"I think so. Do not be afraid. Nothing will hurt you while I am with you, Elizabeth," Xander said gently, looking into her eyes and asking for her trust with his own.

Xander tried to reach across her to get to the buckle, but the seats were too closely jammed together to admit his bulk. He then went around to the other side of the car. For some reason, that door was even more crumpled than the one on Elizabeth's side. He could open it of course, but not without making a spectacle of himself. People were certain to notice if he actually ripped the door off the car. Another idea occurred to him, and he went back around the car to Elizabeth's side.

"Ma'am, I'm going to cut the seatbelt, if you agree," he said to Lynne, who was still unmoving in her seat.

"That's very kind of you. Is she all right?"

"Yes, she appears to be unharmed," he replied, taking a switchblade from his pants pocket.

I've seen those eyes before. They're so blue. He could hear Elizabeth's thoughts.

She remembers me. He smiled, ridiculously pleased with the idea.

"Be very still. I will be careful, so just trust me."

'Trust me.' I remember that, too.

Showing her the knife, he said, "Elizabeth, I'm going to cut the seat belt very close to the seat. I promise that I won't hurt you. Are you ready?"

"Yes. Please do it quickly. I want to get out."

Before she had had time to finish her sentence, Xander had cut the belt and removed it from her.

"Can you move your legs now?" he asked. She nodded. "Good. Now try to slide them toward me. If you can lie down in the seat, I think I can slide you out."

Her jean-clad legs shifted in his direction, and she wiggled her upper body into the small space to her left. Xander slowly and carefully began to pull her through the tight triangle made by the bent seats.

"Do you hurt anywhere?" he paused to ask.

"No. I just want out. Don't stop, please," she nearly begged him.

He read her mind and knew that she was not experiencing any pain. The greatest source of her distress was her fear of enclosed spaces. Within a few minutes, Elizabeth was standing by her hero, looking up at him with adoration. Impulsively, she embraced the handsome young man, her arms tightly wound around his waist. He was her knight in shining armor.

Xander gasped, but then quickly recovered and leaned over to return her hug. Reading her thoughts, he felt the full force of her gratitude, and his heart leapt. *In all my millennia of existence, no one has ever done that while I held human form. I have given comfort, but I have never received a human touch like this one. Could this be what it feels like to have affection for another? She is such a precious child and unlike anyone else I have ever known.*

Her rescue was punctuated by the sounds of sirens, and Elizabeth released Xander to look toward the noises as a highway patrolman, an EMT, and a wrecker pulled up. Both the patrolman and the EMT came immediately to

Lynne and Janna to question them. As Lynne and Janna were talking to them, David arrived and pulled into a driveway. He immediately left his car to go to his family, a stern-faced Roark by his side. As soon as the Bennets were distracted by the patrolman and the EMT, the three angels unobtrusively walked into the nearby woods and quickly changed back into angelic form before anyone had realized they were gone.

After taking Lynne's statement and checking Janna's driver's license and registration, the patrolman went to talk to the driver of the pickup truck. The EMT checked the three Bennet ladies and said that although Elizabeth had no injuries, Janna and Lynne appeared to have whiplash. He told them that they would probably be very sore for a few days, but they would more than likely be fine. However, he recommended that they all go to the hospital ER to be examined.

The patrolman, who knew David, returned to tell them that Tom Wilkins's license had been suspended for the last ten years. He had a DUI on his record and had never bothered to have his license reinstated when his suspension had been completed. Once the EMT had bandaged the cut on his head, Wilkins was arrested, handcuffed, and put into the patrol car.

Janna and Lynne declined to have an ambulance called for them, but they agreed to let David take them to the hospital. He and the EMT helped them to get into David's car, but just before they left, Janna remembered Chance's gift in the smashed trunk.

"Sir!" she called from her open car door to the man who was hooking her car up to his wrecker. "I need something in the trunk. Can you open it?"

"I can pry it open if you want," he answered, taking a crowbar from his truck.

David went over to help the man, and together they forced the trunk open. Chance's present, a huge beanbag chair colored like a basketball, was popped open and firmly wedged in the right side of the trunk, directly behind where Elizabeth had been sitting. The Styrofoam packing had absorbed some of the impact of the crash, probably saving her from severe injury.

"I'm afraid Chance's present is not salvageable, Janna, but it appears to have served a higher purpose," David told her, chuckling grimly as he got back into the car.

Elizabeth went with them, their angelic escort gliding overhead.

Evil thwarted by a beanbag chair – my Master always has a plan, thought Xander, smiling.

Tilting his head to one side, another thought escaped his mind. *Perhaps the Almighty has a broader strategy which includes me. He told me, 'I will ask more of you when the time is full, and what I ask will not be easy for you.' He knows all. He knows of my struggles. Maybe it is all somehow part of His perfect will.*

Chapter 11

"Bless the Lord, you His angels, mighty in strength, who perform His word, obeying the voice of His word!" Psalm 103

Fall, 2004

Nyx and Hadrian met privately in the abandoned strip mall. None of Nyx's schemes to kill the girl had gone according to his plans, and he knew that his time was running out. Lucifer would soon take matters into his own hands, and that would spell the end for him.

"Hadrian, I have been watching the Bennet girl personally, and I think I have a way that we can finally finish this business once and for all. The underdemons are too stupid to follow instructions, so we need to do this ourselves," Nyx said angrily, his fists clenched, watching Hadrian for his reaction.

Hadrian rubbed the underside of his chin with his thumb as he carefully considered his words before making his reply, "Ummm . . .you want *me* to help *you* – just the two of us against Xander?"

Nyx nearly exploded with his rage. "Xander!" he sneered and pushed the long nail of his index finger into Hadrian's chest repeatedly, emphasizing his words. "*I* do not fear him, and *you* had better not either. Xander is not the one who holds your future in his hands. If you think that Lucifer will hold you blameless for our failure to carry out his orders you are mistaken. You are, after all, my captain. It would be in your best interests, as well as mine, for my plan to succeed. Even if you should escape the Dark Lord's wrath for my dearth of success during the last few years, consider this: should he eliminate *me*, he will make *you* underprince in my place. Then *you* will face Xander *alone*. Think on that."

Hadrian stiffened and drew himself up to his full height. "You are right, of course, Underprince. What is your idea?"

"I have several ideas that come from the same root." Nyx grinned impishly and both released wicked cackles which echoed off the walls of the empty building.

~~~~~~

Xander and Niall walked behind their charges as they entered Peniel Christian Academy on the first day of Elizabeth's senior year. She was fourteen, and had been gradually realizing over the past six and a half years that life could be difficult for those who were gifted.

Elizabeth gently shook her head and let out a ragged sigh. *Sometimes, I wish I were just like everyone else. They seem to have so much fun. I never feel that I belong. I'm too young to be accepted by my classmates, and I don't fit in with the kids my age because I'm a junior and they're in the ninth grade. At least I'll have a few classes with them this year. We'll all be in high school, and we'll be in P.E. and chorus together,* she thought wistfully as she walked the familiar halls.

Xander looked at her with a small frown, drawing his brows together. *Her thoughts are like this so often now. She wants to fit in so badly. I would rather she would be happy as she is.*

~~~~~~

Lynne had stopped homeschooling Elizabeth through the summers after she had completed fourth grade in the hopes that life would be more normal for her if she was not too far ahead of her age group. Nearly every day after school, Lynne drove Elizabeth to Converse College to take piano and voice lessons, as well as classes in music theory and composition. The college had agreed to use the class hours toward her college degree if she chose to attend Converse after her high school graduation. So far, patrons of the Petrie School of Music had paid for her lessons and classes. In return, Elizabeth had entered, and won, multitudes of vocal and piano competitions, and was developing a following in the music world. Her success had bolstered the reputation of the college's music department and had brought them many talented students. She was at her happiest when she was performing or composing, a fortunate circumstance, for most of her time was spent in honing her skills and using them.

Janna had attended Anderson University on a full scholarship as a S.C. Palmetto Fellow and had graduated with honors the previous spring. She and Chance Bingley, who had continued to date throughout their college years, had married in the summer. The young couple had chosen to live in Spartanburg, about a half hour's drive from their families. Janna was teaching elementary school and Chance had taken a position in a local bank while working on his MBA online.

While Elizabeth missed her sister, they were too far apart in age to be best friends. As it was, the Bennets and the Bingleys saw each other quite often on the weekends when the Bingleys drove back to Bethel to attend Tabernacle Church and have Sunday dinner with the Bennets.

Chance's sister Caroline was sixteen and a junior at Peniel. She and Elizabeth had been acquaintances in the elementary grades, but as Elizabeth had moved ahead and passed Caroline in school, their friendship had waned. Elizabeth hoped that she and Caroline could be closer again this year, and she was determined to work toward that end.

A few weeks into the school year, Elizabeth, with Xander ever present beside her, saw Caroline in the hall at school after they left Bible Doctrines and decided to make an effort at reviving the relationship. Because the school was small, juniors and seniors shared some courses; consequently, she and the older girl were in Bible Doctrines, physics, and chorus together for the first semester.

Caroline's guardian acknowledged Xander with a palm forward, and Xander returned the gesture.

"Hi, Caro," she said to the older girl, coming up to walk beside her. "How do you like physics?"

Caroline arched a finely tweezed eyebrow. *What could the perfect little twit want?* "It's okay, I guess," she answered without enthusiasm. "You don't seem to be having any problem with it. Of course, *you* never have a problem with any subject." Her voice was whiny and a little nasal. Xander flinched at the sound of it. He had been hearing her thoughts for many years, and had found nothing to admire in them.

Why would sweet, intelligent, gifted Elizabeth desire a friendship with this shallow girl? Xander sighed. *There is much I do not understand about teenagers in this age.*

The popular, older girl was tall, slender, and beautiful with caramel-colored, perfectly highlighted hair and eyes as brilliantly green as contact lenses could make them. Academics were not high on her list of priorities, but she saw an opportunity present itself with Elizabeth's overtures, and she was never one to waste a chance to better her position. She might not have the best grades in her class, but she was shrewd and manipulative. She managed to keep her scores just high enough to stay on the honor roll and be in the Beta Club.

Great. I hate being the 'smart one.' "Well, some are easier than others. Physics isn't my favorite class, but I manage to do okay, I guess." Elizabeth looked down at the floor. She would never admit to anyone that she had a one hundred or above average in all of her classes because she always answered extra credit questions correctly, and she turned in every extra project. In fact, Elizabeth had taken the PSAT with the other juniors in the previous year and had scored a perfect sixteen hundred. *I seem to be congenitally unable to do poorly in any academic subject or on any test. I wish I was as adept in my social skills.*

Caroline paused, as deep in thought as it was possible for her to be, and Elizabeth stopped beside her. "Maybe you could help me with my homework at lunch today, El. There are a few problems I didn't understand. Why don't you sit at my table?"

Elizabeth, see this girl for what she is – a self-absorbed, narcissistic individual who seeks only to use you. A friendship with her will bring you nothing but pain. Xander disliked for anyone to take advantage of Elizabeth and her gifts.

"I'd be happy to help you, Caro. I'll see you at lunch," Elizabeth said, smiling broadly. *Yes! I've always wanted to sit at that table with the rest of the cheerleaders and some of the jocks. Maybe now I won't be as lonely at school as I have been for the last couple of years.*

Exasperated, Xander threw his hands up in the air. *There are worse things than being lonely.*

The girls continued toward their next classes. Caroline had Algebra II while Elizabeth was one of four students in AP Calculus. *I wonder what else El would do to be my friend?* thought Caroline, looking smug.

Xander was not at all pleased as he read Caroline's thoughts, for he knew that she had no desire for a friendship with Elizabeth. The imposing protector fixed his eyes steadily on Ros, Caroline's guardian from the lower ranks.

Can you do nothing to restrain your charge? Xander asked, not unkindly. He knew that guarding Caroline would be a joyless assignment.

My chief, she has been this way from the time she was a toddling child. She has accepted the Master, but she does not live by His precepts for the present. Caroline does not listen to me. In fact, as her parents are non-believers and her brother is gone, I have no assistance with her from them or from other guardians, and she is influenced by dark ones. She does what is right in her own eyes.

Xander remembered the verse to which Ros referred. *Judges 21:25, 'In those days there was no king in Israel; everyone did what was right in his own eyes.'*

Ros inclined his head respectfully as Xander passed by with Elizabeth.

Caroline is not a good friend for Elizabeth, Xander said to Ros as he continued to walk. Ros nodded in agreement and hurried to catch up with Caroline.

Elizabeth was practically giddy and could hardly sit still through her classes until lunch.

Finally, the endless morning was over, and it was time to go to the cafeteria. Elizabeth stopped by the restroom to check her hair and the minimal makeup her mother allowed. She looked in the mirror and was glad she had on her best jeans and her favorite American Eagle hoodie. Looking at herself critically, she thought, *Well, I'm no Caroline Bingley – that's for sure – but I don't look too bad today. Now if I can just keep from sounding different from the others. Maybe I'll just smile a lot and keep my mouth shut unless someone asks me a question. Sounds like a plan.* She smiled and gave a "thumbs up" sign to her reflection in the mirror before turning to leave for the cafeteria.

Xander shook his head. She never saw herself clearly. He could hear what the boys were thinking when they looked at her, and more than once, he had forced himself to calm down before he hurt one of them. *She is maturing into a beautiful young woman. Her face is perfectly symmetrical with her pert nose, high cheekbones, and large brown eyes. Her smile is a photographer's dream – brilliant white, straight teeth and that double dimple! She is altogether adorable.*

Elizabeth had no idea of her power over human males, and Xander wanted it to stay that way indefinitely. While Xander's thoughts never strayed beyond admiring her beauty and goodness, the minds of the boys jumped easily from noticing her stunning appearance to having daydreams of a more intimate nature, featuring her engaging with them in various activities. Xander feared that he might one day seriously injure a hormonal teenaged male mentally undressing Elizabeth. So far, luckily, the boys had been afraid to approach her. She was young, the daughter of a minister and a faculty member, highly intelligent, and beautiful. Up until now, those things had been enough to make them think she would not welcome their advances, but he knew that someday soon, males would vie for her attention. He slowly let out his breath, rubbing his temples. *I wonder how her father would feel about being a pastor in Antarctica?*

~~~~~~~~~

Caroline and her crew were already seated when Elizabeth joined the lunch line. She loaded her tray and looked over at them. Caroline caught her eye, waved, and gestured to the seat between her and Grant Willoughby. Relieved that she had not been forgotten, Elizabeth carefully navigated the crowded cafeteria and shyly took the offered seat. Xander stood at her shoulder with his arms crossed over his chest and an inscrutable expression on his flawless face.

"Hi, El. Do you know all these losers?" Caroline asked teasingly, glancing around at the assembled group.

"I think so, Caroline. Thanks. Hi, guys," Elizabeth answered, smiling timidly and allowing her long, thick hair to partially hide her face.

"El!" A general chorus of welcome went up.

"El is going to help us with our physics homework. She's a hardcore nerd, you know." Caroline giggled, and gave Elizabeth a little punch on the arm. Elizabeth started. Xander frowned.

"Great. Break it out so we can copy it. I need to pass that class if I want to keep playing football," said Grant, the team captain, with a grin and a wink. *She's really hot. I've never noticed her much before. Hmm ... Maybe I should give this a try. I'll bet she'd look even better without that big hoodie on. I could probably help her out of it. She looks good coming or going, too. Very nice rear view.*

Xander's gasp was noticed by the angels near him, and none of them missed the look of fury on his face. They had all heard much worse thoughts from the boys around them, so they failed to understand why Grant's appreciation of a girl's body merited his scowl.

Niall, across the room with Lynne at the faculty table, knew the difference only too well. The lustful thoughts were directed toward Elizabeth. Niall caught Xander's attention with a slight motion of his head and raised his eyebrows at his chief, thinking so that only Xander would hear. *Xander, you are drawing the notice of every guardian in the room. Is that what you want?*

Xander resumed his dispassionate mien but retained his protective stance.

Elizabeth gulped. Grant was smiling, all those considerable charms and amazing good looks aimed right at her. *Did he just wink at me?!* But she couldn't just let them copy her work; that was dishonest. Besides, the teacher would notice if all their work was right for a change, and cheating was an expellable offense at Peniel.

"How about I answer your questions instead? Get out what you've done, and I'll help you with it," Elizabeth answered, forcing a smile she didn't feel. Caroline snorted. Ros looked away, embarrassed.

"That's going to be tough for some of us. We can't get it out if we haven't done it," replied Lydia Henderson, another of the cheerleaders, sarcastically. The other teens at the table laughed derisively.

"Then get out your book and some paper, and I'll help you get started."

"Why can't you just give us the answers?" Lydia challenged.

Though Grant and Lydia had no protectors, many of the other students in the group did. Xander raised his eyebrows and looked at each one of the guardians. They shrugged in response. Xander had never had a normal, modern teenager as his charge. Guarding Deborah, Esther, Ruth, Michelangelo, George Washington, Queen Victoria, and Jackie Robinson had not prepared him for this, and he was getting a fast education. *If some of these are Christians, what are the unbelievers like?*

Elizabeth wanted to be friends with these people, but enough was enough.

"Because if you show up with perfect homework after not doing any since school started, Mr. Blake will be suspicious, and if anyone sees you copying my work, we could all be expelled," Elizabeth said evenly, looking Lydia squarely in the eye.

"Burned!" said Grant, laughing loudly and pointing at Lydia.

She glared at him and held up three fingers. "Read between the lines, Grant."

Xander raised his eyebrows in question at Ros, who lowered his eyes. *The meaning of the gesture is a profanity*, he answered.

Though Elizabeth hadn't realized it, standing up to Lydia was the best thing she could have done. While Lydia would never like her, Elizabeth had gone up a notch in the boys' opinions.

"You can help *me*, gorgeous," Grant said, smiling at Elizabeth while everyone else was picking at Lydia. He moved closer to her and dropped his voice to a whisper, leaning in and speaking into her ear, "In fact, I think I'd like to become your special physics project. How about it? Want to be my private tutor? You can teach me, and maybe I can teach you some things, too."

Xander put his hands possessively on Elizabeth's shoulders and stepped closer to her. *You want to be taught, boy? I can do that. I think you need lessons in how to treat a young lady.*

Is Grant actually flirting with me? He can't be. He can have anyone he wants, and I'm nobody. Elizabeth smiled at him and reached for her physics book.

"I'll be happy to help you every day, Grant. If we want that state championship, you're going to have to bring up your grades."

"Whatever. Like the team can't do without you," sneered Lydia, looking at Grant.

The rest of the lunch period was spent working on physics homework. Elizabeth answered their questions and pointed out their mistakes, relaxing enough to smile and laugh with them. She made several new friends that day, and Mr. Blake got a pleasant surprise that afternoon in physics. His class was prepared for the first time that year.

~~~~~~~~~

Caroline caught up with Elizabeth as they were leaving school that afternoon. Ros nodded at Xander.

Caroline tapped Elizabeth's back to get her attention. "So, Chance says you go to Tabernacle Church?"

Elizabeth slowed to wait for her. "Yes, he and Janna come every Sunday, you know. Caro, you should join us this weekend. You could have lunch with us and spend some time with Chance." Elizabeth looked at her expectantly.

"I just may do that. I need to get back into church, and it would be good to spend more time with the fam. Chance says that you have a really big youth group." Caroline turned her eyes to look at Elizabeth speculatively. Xander watched the girl closely.

Something tells me that Caroline is not thinking of spending time with her family. I was not created yesterday.

"Yeah, we do. We have a great time together. Come check it out Sunday. We meet in the youth building at nine thirty, and service is at eleven."

Here it comes.

"I'll be there. I'll expect introductions to all those cute guys I've been hearing about."

Xander could not help himself. He actually rolled his eyes. Ros looked away, embarrassed again for his charge.

"Cute guys?" Elizabeth looked puzzled. *She wants to come to church to meet guys? Every boy in school wants to date her.*

"Lydia was telling me all about your group. She said there are some real hotties there."

"Oh. Lydia visited a few times over the summer." *Hotties?*

Xander echoed, *Hotties?*

"Doesn't Richard Williams go there? We were together in school through eighth grade."

"Richard? Yeah, he goes to Tabernacle." Elizabeth glanced at Caroline sharply, and a light bulb came on in her brain.

"Huh! That's interesting. Well, guess I gotta go now. Not everyone can just sit at a piano all day. Must be nice not to get sweaty at your practices. Cheerleading awaits. See ya'!" Caroline threw a plastic smile over her shoulder, her stylishly cut hair falling into place as she hurried off, Ros trudging after her.

~~~~~~~~~

Elizabeth really felt more at home among her church friends and was very active in her youth group at Tabernacle. Most of them attended public school and knew very little of her life at Peniel. The teenagers knew that she was extremely talented as they had heard her play and sing in church over the years, but they had only the vaguest concept of the scope of her gifts. She never talked about the competitions or her lessons and classes at Converse. Elizabeth herself felt like she was a freak, but she could not bear for the other teens to think of her in that way.

While they had been on a youth retreat during the previous summer, Elizabeth had become close to Richard Williams. He had just turned sixteen and was attracted by Elizabeth's long brown hair and smiling brown eyes which seemed to glitter when she was happy. Although Richard knew that she was intelligent and talented, he felt comfortable with his own abilities and gifts, so he did not feel threatened by her. He was a young man who had no problem with his self-esteem. Elizabeth never noticed boys looking at her, but Richard was very well aware of all the feminine glances he garnered everywhere he went. His light brown, wavy hair was tousled just the right way and gelled exactly the correct amount, and his light brown eyes sparkled with good humor. He seemed to be perpetually tanned and worked out to keep his six-pack and his muscles chiseled. Richard played football and baseball at Bethel High School; he was a shooting star. The girls sighed and called him "a hottie with a body," and he well knew that he could date any girl he wanted; he wanted Elizabeth.

For all his conceit, Richard was a good young man. He attended church, didn't drink (much), didn't curse (often), and had no use for a girlfriend who had slept around. Whereas other boys may have been put off by Elizabeth's innocence, it attracted him. He was a virgin (technically), and he fully intended to marry one (in the distant future). Richard and Elizabeth had gone through the True Love Waits series at the same time with the rest of the youth group, and he well knew what the promise ring from her father meant. David had given it to her at the completion of the study; she now wore it in place of a wedding band, vowing chastity until marriage. In fact, Richard had received a similar ring from his parents, but, ironically, he had lost it.

His family and the Bennets were well acquainted, not only because his family were members at Tabernacle, but also since his mother had taught Elizabeth in 4-K at Peniel. Richard had gone there himself until three years ago; he had been thirteen in the eighth grade, and she had been eleven years old in the ninth grade. Of course, she had been a little girl to him then. After that, he had transferred to the larger public high school to play sports so that he might have a better chance at an athletic scholarship for college. He had noticed her again this past summer at youth camp and was amazed at how she had changed. Elizabeth was now beautiful in every way, and he thought he deserved her. Though she was only fourteen, Elizabeth was mature beyond her years and was the smartest person he knew, all of which made her perfect for him.

Richard had made his decision; he would not wait around while some other guy snatched her up.

~~~~~~~~~

In the throne room of heaven, Michael and Gabriel knelt before the Throne of Grace, bathed in the pure holy light of His presence as they bowed on their knees in silence, their white robes puddling around them. The room was filled with the perfume of the prayers from the saints rising from the altar, poured out for their Father to hear their pleadings, praises, and supplications. It pleased Jehovah-Elohim, the Lord God, to answer the prayers of His children, for He cared for His creations.

Though the two archangels had been before their Master many times, the experience never failed to fill them with awe and wonder. They waited for

Him to speak, and finally, after several moments, the Almighty spoke in a low, gentle voice.

"Gabriel . . . Michael."

"Yes, my Master?" Gabriel responded. He never failed to thrill at the sound of his name coming from the One he served. "We hear Your voice and obey. What is Your command, O Lord?"

"I summoned you, my faithful servants, because I have heard your thoughts and your words. Speak to me of your concerns," Jehovah-Shalom said to His archangels.

Michael, the warrior, kept his head lowered submissively as he spoke. "You know all things, Almighty Creator. Just as You have heard our thoughts and words, You have heard the thoughts and seen the actions of our brother, Xander. Is all well with him, Lord?"

Gabriel added reverently, "He seems to be . . . overly involved with his charge, Master. Do you wish for him to be replaced? Michael and I, as You already know, are both willing to serve as guardians in Xander's stead if You so desire. Either of us would gladly don the tunic and wield the sword to please You and help our brother."

"I am well satisfied with both of you. You are exactly as you should be, as is Xander. He has done nothing which I did not foresee, and all that has happened has been according to My perfect will. Xander is serving Me in harmony with My plan for him. Do not be anxious for him. All is as I wish for it to be. It must happen this way."

The brilliant light vanished as suddenly as it had appeared. After a moment, Michael and Gabriel rose and looked at each other briefly before they turned to walk together down the long, golden hallway, quietly pondering the words of their Master.

Chapter 12

"For the Son of Man is going to come in the glory of His Father with His angels; and will then recompense every man according to his deeds."
Matthew 16:27

Hovering protectively behind Elizabeth, Xander frowned as he listened to the chatter of the teenagers in her church youth group one Sunday night. He did not enjoy being around Caroline Bingley at school, and now he had to suffer her presence at Tabernacle Church as well. Xander stood tall and rubbed his chin, glaring at the girl as he read her petty mind. *I can't stand that little twit or any of the rest of these losers. They're a bunch of rejects. Why do I have to put up with this? Only because Richard won't wake up and see her for what she is. It's just not fair.* Even her thoughts were whiny and irritating.

Xander made an effort to school his features into an expression of nonchalance. *There is a meanness about her, a littleness that Elizabeth does not see. Ros was right – she is definitely being influenced against Elizabeth. I wish that Elizabeth was not so desperate for her friendship. This one is dangerous. I will be watching her closely.*

Ros was beside Caroline, embarrassed at the direction of her thoughts, and Garnet, Richard's guardian, stood behind the couch alongside Xander, trying to look comfortable in the shadow of the gigantic angel. Xander stood nearly a head taller than the other assembled protectors. The two guardians were spending quite a bit of time together as Elizabeth and Richard's friendship deepened, but Garnet could sense that Xander did not approve of the relationship. He had no inkling concerning Xander's reasoning; it seemed to him a good match for both of them. Garnet's enigmatic chief kept his opinions to himself, and he would certainly follow Xander's example in that.

Caroline, who had begun attending shortly after Elizabeth had invited her a couple of months earlier, sat to Richard's left on a couch in the Shock Zone, as the youth building was called, while Elizabeth sat on his right. Caroline's striking good looks and eagerness to establish herself as a part of the group had made her initial acceptance a certain thing, though it had not taken long for most of the kids to realize for whom and for what reason she had come to Tabernacle. She was soon snubbing them and making sarcastic comments about Elizabeth behind her back as she zeroed in on Richard Williams like a lioness stalking her kill. Richard appreciated the attention of such a popular, attractive girl, but his focus on having Elizabeth for his girlfriend had not changed. Still, his vanity was flattered, and he enjoyed flirting with her.

"Richard, are you going to the homecoming dance next weekend? I wish we could have dances at Peniel, but all we are allowed is one a year – prom – and it's lame." Caroline tossed her head and pouted prettily, looking into his eyes.

Could she be any more transparent? Xander sniffed. He felt free with his thoughts here. None of the other guardians in the youth complex could hear them unless he spoke, and he was very careful not to do that. He was aware that Niall and Roark were somewhere on the campus, but they had long ceased thinking that his thoughts were unusual. *Odd. Strange is now my new normal.*

"Um . . . I haven't decided yet, Caro, but when I do, I'll be sure to let you know," he returned, then glanced at Elizabeth. Her parents had made it clear that she was too young to single date, but they had not ruled out a double-date or a group outing that was chaperoned by adults. He had been to her house several times to hang out, and she had gone to his house for dinner or to watch movies with his family. Richard's parents had recently bought him a black Mustang, and he was hoping that her parents would agree to let him pick her up for a date with another couple, friends of theirs from the church group.

Hearing his thoughts, Xander grudgingly admitted, *He is not completely without intelligence and judgment. She is too young, and he should turn his attentions elsewhere. He does show good taste, however.*

"El, do you dance?" Richard asked, tentatively, gazing at her. *Look at me, El. Look at me.*

She met his stare, and it startled her. *His eyes are so beautiful. I could get lost in them.* For a moment, Elizabeth forgot to breathe; then she laughed self-consciously. She lowered her eyes, her long lashes darkening her cheek. Peeking up at Richard through her eyelashes, she replied softly, "Only at home where no one can see me. I'm not very good at it."

While he did not care much for her unspoken thoughts or the increase in her heart rate, Xander liked her answer, though he knew it was not completely true. She danced beautifully, but she did not think so. Her self-esteem issues amazed him. *She is brilliant, beautiful, talented, selfless, kind, and humble. Why can she not see herself as I see her? However, Richard sees her much as I do, and, apparently, she admires him.* Xander groaned inwardly. He hoped that her reply to the boy would discourage him.

Caroline saw with disgust the look that passed between Richard and Elizabeth. She knew that she was losing control of the situation, and drastic times called for drastic measures. *What does he see in her? I'm prettier and more experienced. I could show him a really good time, and I would enjoy doing it.* She leaned over Richard, putting her arm on the couch behind him, and stared pointedly at Elizabeth's lap.

Ros gasped, reading her thoughts before she voiced them. He knew that she would say what she was thinking. While Xander heard Caroline's jealous mind, he did not yet realize how free she could be with her speech. Ros glanced at Xander, and then quickly lowered his saddened eyes. *I am sorry.*

"El, did you forget something back there in the restroom? Feeling a breeze? I think your fly is open."

In his surprise, Xander's composure slipped for an instant, and he spoke, *The hateful little baggage!* Every guardian in the room heard and looked toward him in shock. Xander exercised iron control, resuming his stony mask and unclenching his fists with a concerted effort.

Richard's face flushed, but he was not nearly as red as Elizabeth. She looked down and was mortified to see that her "friend" was right. Her jeans were gaping open. The top button had come off, and she had neglected to make sure that her zipper was locked at the top. It must have worked its way open as she had moved around. Because her top barely met the band of her jeans, her pink bikini panties were very noticeable. Elizabeth jumped up and ran blindly for the bathroom, tugging at her zipper.

Xander strode beside her, his fierce eyes belying his carefully blank expression.

Richard froze Caroline with an icy stare. "Why did you do that? You could have told her privately. Not cool, Caroline."

He got up to go after Elizabeth, but Caroline stood at the same time, putting her hand on his arm to hold him back. As he shook her hand off and jerked his arm away, she realized that she had made a serious tactical error. *He must like her more than I thought.*

I could have told you that, Ros replied in his thoughts.

"I didn't mean to embarrass her. I was trying to help her out. I'll go get her; you just wait here." Caroline injected just the right note of apology into her voice. He hesitated, and she hurried after Elizabeth. Richard followed her to the bathroom door.

Xander had continued into the bathroom after Elizabeth, leaning over her with his hands on her shoulders. She was too upset to feel the peace he was pouring into her. He had never seen her so out of control, and he was interrupted before he had a chance to speak into her ear.

Caroline, followed closely by Ros, opened the door to find Elizabeth sobbing over the sink. *Excellent!* Ros rolled his eyes. Caroline smirked, then quickly pasted on a smile and started to speak in a sugary voice, "El, I'm so . . ."

Before she could finish the sentence, Elizabeth whipped around and punched her in the nose. It was such a reflex action, that Elizabeth did not even realize what she had done until she saw the blood dripping down a stunned Caroline's shirt. She had not thought about it before she acted, so Xander was just as surprised as Ros. Xander clamped his jaws tightly together in anxiety as Ros's mouth hung open.

She deserved it! Xander said vehemently, defending Elizabeth.

"You HIT me, you little . . ." Caroline began screaming hysterically. Ros was frantically placing his hands on her arms and shoulders, but to no avail. *Be quiet, Caroline!*

"That's enough!" Mrs. Williams interrupted her sternly, barreling out of the last stall, holding up her palm toward Caroline. Elizabeth stared at the blood, horrified at what she had done. Tears still streamed down her cheeks. She was shaking, and Xander stepped to her side, rubbing her back with one large hand while stroking her arm with the other.

Elizabeth's mind was frenzied. *What have I done? How can I face everyone? I'm so embarrassed. I know better than to fight. It's against the rules! I've never hit anyone in my life! My parents will be so hurt by my behavior. Richard probably won't want to be my friend anymore. I want to crawl away and die. I always ruin everything!* While Xander comforted Elizabeth, he never moved his glare from Caroline. *Elizabeth, you are wrong. Your parents may be upset with you, but we will all still love you. Your friends will understand what happened.*

Mrs. Williams's guardian, Raymond, successfully kept his mouth from gaping open. The small space was becoming quite crowded, and Xander loomed large above them all. His expression was fierce, and if Xander's sharp glares had been daggers, Caroline Bingley would have been on her way to the morgue to have her pedicured toe tagged. The other guardians tried to back away from him, but there was insufficient room to do so.

"But she *hit* me! My nose is bleeding! It may be broken! I'm going to have a *black eye*!" shouted Caroline, grabbing paper towels as she bent over the sink.

"I think you'll survive," replied the older woman drily, handing her more towels.

Mrs. Williams had known both girls from the time they were babies, and she knew that if Elizabeth had struck the girl, she must have had a very good reason for doing so. She also was very well acquainted with Caroline Bingley, and was extremely tired of her constant phone calls to their house asking for Richard. Against her better judgment, she had finally told her son to give Caroline his cell number so that she would stop tying up their land line. It did not take much imagination to deduce that Caroline had probably pulled some stunt to humiliate Elizabeth in front of her son since Caroline was well-known at Peniel for her cattiness and manipulative ways.

Mrs. Williams pulled the sniffling Elizabeth to her shoulder and hugged her, stroking her hair. Xander continued his ministrations and whispered to her, *Peace, Elizabeth. Be calm, precious one.*

"I didn't mean to hit her. I really didn't. It just sort of . . . happened. I'm really sorry, Caro," Elizabeth choked out.

I am not, thought Xander privately, still holding Caroline with his stare.

"Let's get you some ice for those knuckles, Sweetie," murmured Mrs. Williams to Elizabeth, releasing her and taking her hand, looking at it with concern. "Can you open and close your fist without pain?" Elizabeth gave a slight nod. "Maybe you're just bruised," finished Mrs. Williams.

She socks me in the nose and you're worried about her? Caroline huffed. She thought several choice profanities and stalked out the door holding the bloody towels to her nose. The entire crowd of teens and adults was waiting outside the bathroom, listening to the brouhaha, and trying to figure out what in the world was going on. The sight of the regal, snobbish Caroline looking so ridiculous was a little too much for some of them, and a slight titter ran through the crowd. Incensed, she turned to leave, only to be met by Lynne Bennet coming through the door. *Can this night get any better? Now the mother? Could her father and Janna be coming, too? Do I have to put up with every Bennet in the country?*

"Caroline, dear, what happened? Did you run into something? Let me help you," Lynne said with genuine concern, reaching for the girl's shoulder. Niall was right behind her, looking at Caroline speculatively. He had "seen" the entire incident through Xander's thoughts.

"Maybe you should ask your freak daughter! The only thing I ran into was her fist," snapped Caroline angrily, jerking back from Lynne's hand as if it would burn her. Stomping through the door and out to her car, she slammed her door and spun out of the parking lot. Lynne stood rooted to the spot, stunned by her vitriol.

I need patience, and I need it now, Xander mused, listening to Caroline's hateful comments through Niall.

After a moment, Lynne turned and looked questioningly at Richard who shrugged and bit his lip. He could not believe El had punched Caro in the nose, but he would not deny that she had brought it on herself.

Ha! Even he agrees with me. Richard had just gone up a notch or two in Xander's estimation, and he disliked the young man a little less.

I'll get even with her. She'll be sorry she ever touched me. Nobody makes me look stupid, Caroline promised herself venomously as she sped home.

Ros, flying overhead, frowned as he listened to her thoughts. He knew that Xander was listening as well, and he hoped that Caroline would not do anything foolish.

~~~~~~~~~

Monday at school, Caroline acted toward Elizabeth as if nothing had happened, though the slight bruise under her eye proved that it had. As the days passed, they continued to work on homework at lunch, and Caroline smiled and spoke when they met in classes or in the hallways. She also kept attending Tabernacle, holding her head high and ignoring the knowing smirks. Slowly, she built back Richard's trust in her. He really believed that Caroline had forgiven Elizabeth, and he wanted them to be friends again.

Elizabeth was wary, but she intensely disliked conflict and was ashamed of the way she had acted. Her guilt gnawed at her and eroded her distrust of

Caroline. She convinced herself that Caroline had not mistreated her purposely and concluded that it had all been a big misunderstanding.

~~~~~~~~

Lucifer and his entourage took form in the Wickham residence, black robes settling around their feet. Cathy and George immediately knelt before him. They had been expecting the Dark Lord and were ready with their reports.

"You may stand. Where is my son?" Lucifer intoned, looking toward the couple.

"He is with his music instructors, my lord. His progress is nothing short of phenomenal, and his performance is brilliant," answered George, getting to his feet with his wife. Standing or kneeling was of no significance. Lucifer still towered at least a full head over them and dominated any space he occupied.

"Ah, yes. I can hear him singing now. Who accompanies him?"

"He usually accompanies himself, my prince, as he has surpassed the skills of his teachers. He plays to perfection every instrument that he handles, and his vocal technique is beyond compare."

"Certainly. I would expect no less of Gregory. Bring him to me." His voice was deep and commanding, exuding confidence that any request would be instantly obeyed.

Cathy quickly climbed the stairs and went to the music room, motioning for Gregory to follow her. At his questioning look, she inclined her head. "Your father is here to see you."

"You may go now. Use the back entrance," Gregory addressed his music masters in a clipped voice. He and his guards then quickly preceded Cathy down the stairs to the room in which his father waited.

Satan smiled when he saw his son. Gregory, at fourteen, was nearly as tall as he was, strapping and muscular, with the perfect body of an Adonis. He could have been the model for the multitudes of statues and paintings of the Greek god, the archetype of youthful male beauty. The Dark Lord clasped

Gregory by his shoulders in greeting while dismissing Cathy and George with a nod of his head. Lucifer then released Gregory and stood back to look at his face.

"Are you doing well, Gregory?"

"Yes, Father. I think I have made rather exceptional progress." Gregory lifted his chin with pride as he answered.

"Excellent, my son. I hear good reports of you from all of your instructors. Music has always held a certain fascination for me, and I am very interested in your musical tastes. What is your favorite kind of music, Gregory?"

"I can play anything I attempt, Father, but I think the modern forms will be the most useful. I have observed from watching television and spending time on the internet that young human females are very impressed with those who play and sing in bands. I am proficient on the drums, all types of guitars, and all keyboards. Singing in that style is not a challenge. My guards and I have flown over the arenas when popular artists are playing concerts, and it seems that humans lose their inhibitions under the influence of that style of music more than any other. It has a raw power, an anger, a sensuality. I can use it."

"I am certain that you can; however, do not neglect the classical forms. Elizabeth Bennet is an *aficionado* of Debussy in particular, though she is well-versed in all types of music. She is also a composer and arranger. Have you been working on any original compositions?"

Gregory's amber eyes darkened. "I have, but she would not care for my work in that area, I am sure. My guards and I daily fly over her home, her school, and that college she attends. I have spent many hours observing the girl, being careful to remain undetected. My style is too *avant garde* for her. I can compose music she would like, but there would be little pleasure in it for me."

Lucifer spoke softly but convincingly. "Composing her kind of music may not give you pleasure, Gregory, but destroying her with what she loves will bring you, and me, great satisfaction." He looked into his son's eyes with a calculating expression and put a hand on his shoulder. "You are very young, but I think it is time that I took some of your training into my own hands.

126

There are many routes to pleasure, and you are old enough now to appreciate them."

Gregory smiled broadly, and his eyes held a wicked sparkle. "Indeed, Father. I am very eager to start that part of my education."

"I have human servants who specialize in all the sensual arts, Gregory, and they can teach you how to pleasure a human woman. They can also teach you other ways that you will not share with Elizabeth. These servants will be willing to do anything you want, my son, and you are free to learn it all. Only remember that some pleasures are best kept secret. There is nothing wrong for you, Gregory. Whatever the world can provide is yours for the taking, for it is mine to give. You have only to express your desire. We were meant to be worshipped, and others were meant to serve us in all things. The earth is your footstool; if you can imagine what you want, you can have it. We can share these experiences. I have long looked forward to this time. Are you ready, this very night?" At that moment, Lucifer was the essence of perversion, the very Devil, and he smiled lasciviously at his beautiful son. He clapped the younger version of himself on the back in camaraderie.

"I have been ready for several years, Father." Gregory laughed, but it was a chilling sound.

Lucifer with the combined guard forces joined Gregory in his laughter as they abandoned human form and become one with the night, flying toward their assignation with evil like a dark cloud.

Chapter 13

"For He will give His angels charge concerning you, to guard you in all your ways. They will bear you up in their hands, lest you strike your foot against a stone." Psalm 91: 11-12

Spring, 2005

Xander stood rigidly with his back toward Elizabeth. She was singing as she showered, and he was unaccountably discomfited. He closed his eyes tightly so that he could not see her reflection in the mirror that was before him. Never in all the years he had been a guardian had he ever felt uncomfortable watching over his charge in private. He tracked her thoughts carefully, listening to make certain that she was safe, but he studiously avoided "seeing" what she saw in her mind. Every few seconds he opened his eyes to scan the ceiling for dark ones. *Am I losing my mind? What is wrong with me?*

He needed to be in the room with her to keep her from harm, but he was feeling more embarrassed with each passing second. In the past few weeks, he had considered standing in the hallway by the door, but he realized that it was imperative to prevent Niall and Roark from seeing him there. They would wonder why he had left her unguarded. It simply was not done. Even though his fellow guardians were gone with their charges at the moment, he felt the weight of his responsibilities toward Elizabeth and could not leave her. Besides, either of the guardians could return home at any time. *Why do*

I feel like a voyeur when in ten millennia it has never bothered me before? What is happening to me?

He was relieved to hear the water stop followed by the sounds of Elizabeth toweling herself dry and dressing. His daily torture session was drawing to a close at last. Xander moved behind her as she stopped before the mirror to comb her hair. *I'll put on my makeup after I get back from getting my hair done,* she thought to herself.

She really does not need that paint. I am glad that she wears very little of it, was Xander's reaction.

She would be going to the Peniel prom with Richard in a few hours, and her mother would soon return from her errands to take Elizabeth to have her hair done professionally. Lynne had accompanied her to get a manicure and a pedicure the previous evening.

Xander had never before been to a prom. Janna, of course, had gone the four years she had been in high school, but Elizabeth, and, therefore Xander, had always stayed with Aunt Grace on those nights. Queen Victoria had not attended proms; nor had any of his other charges done so. He had observed balls and state occasions, but "prom" seemed to be a modern concept.

Elizabeth's thoughts were happy. *I can't wait for tonight! It's going to be the best night ever. I absolutely love the dress we found! Doubling with Char and Billy will be so much fun, and my date is going to be the hottest guy there. I hope Richard is going to like the dancing, even though it's kind of corny. I really don't want to make a fool of myself dancing in front of everyone, so it's a good thing I've been practicing in front of the mirror. I think it's paid off, though, if I do say so myself. And Laser Tag afterwards is going to be awesome!* She hummed a cheerful tune.

Because the school had only about fifty juniors and seniors, freshmen and sophomores were also allowed to go to their annual prom. It was innocent enough. It was very well chaperoned, as there were always nearly as many adults in attendance as there were students. Lynne and David had agreed to allow Elizabeth to invite Richard only because they would be there themselves as chaperones. Elizabeth was ecstatic that her parents had agreed to let Richard pick her up for the prom; they would be double-dating with Charlotte Lucas and Billy Collins.

Charlotte was a senior at Peniel, and she and Elizabeth had become fast friends in the past few months. Both Charlotte and Billy were in the Tabernacle youth group, and Elizabeth's parents fully approved of them. Billy was the son of Mary Collins, Lynne's close friend in the ministry, and he attended Sunday morning services at the smaller church which his father pastored.

Charlotte's brother, Joshua, was Elizabeth's age and was a freshman at Peniel. He was also one of Elizabeth's closest friends, and she was glad that he would also be at the dance.

Dance. Elizabeth chuckled at the misnomer. *I wonder what Richard will think of it. Our music is vetted by the faculty, and our dancing is nothing like what the kids do at public school proms. Well, he can't say he wasn't warned.*

Lynne and Niall arrived. "El! Are you ready to go? I picked up Richard's boutonniere. It's in the 'fridge."

A fresh-faced Elizabeth practically bounced into the kitchen to meet her mother. "Yep! Let's go. I'm ready to be stunningly, breathtakingly beautiful," she proclaimed, striking a model's pose.

You already are, Xander thought tenderly from behind her.

"Well, I'm sure Rhonda will do all she can, but she can work only with the raw material provided for her. You poor little thing. We have to tie a pork chop around your neck to get the dog to play with you," Lynne replied, deadpanning, and ruffling her daughter's hair.

They left the house laughing together at Lynne's remark. Xander and Niall exchanged a smile at the horseplay.

~~~~~~~~~

Richard, Charlotte, and Billy arrived promptly at six o'clock to pick up Elizabeth. Garnet and the other two guardians stood along the wall, watching the proceedings.

The prom was actually a catered dinner at the local country club, followed by a DJ, karaoke, and dancing. Their pictures were scheduled with the photographer at six thirty, and they did not want to be late.

Lynne greeted the teens and led them into the living room while she called for her daughter. Xander had waited in her bedroom, staring at the walls, while she finished dressing. When he heard Elizabeth mutter, "This is as good as it's going to get," he turned, and his stomach tightened. He was overwhelmed by her loveliness. She was fastening rhinestone earrings into her pierced ears, leaning close to her vanity mirror. His breath caught in his chest as he gazed at her.

She wore a chiffon overlaid gown that was midnight blue at her bodice lightening to a turquoise just below her tiny waist. Rhinestones were set in a spray pattern across the front of the gown, continuing down one side, drawing the eye to a short train. The dress fit her slender five foot six form perfectly, accenting the curve of her hips and narrowing at her knees only to flare out from there to the floor. Elizabeth's glossy brown hair had been gathered up in the back to fall in a cloud of loose curls to her shoulders. Tendrils escaped at her ears and on her neck. She was a picture of innocence flowering into young womanhood.

Neither Queen Esther nor King David's Bathsheba could rival your beauty, Elizabeth. How will I bear to hear the thoughts of those teenage boys tonight?

Elizabeth did one final turn in front of the full length mirror on the back of her door before she opened it and walked gracefully toward her date. Richard's eyes widened as he saw her, and Xander had no cause to disapprove of his thoughts, for he was speechless, both audibly and mentally.

There was silence, and then everyone seemed to speak at once.

"Wow! . . . Just . . . wow! You look wonderful, El," Richard finally stammered.

Elizabeth's face lit up with a breathtaking smile. "You are quite dashing yourself, sir. Definitely GQ material," she joked, taking his boutonniere from her mother and pinning it to his lapel. In turn, he handed her a florist's box with a wrist corsage that matched her dress. Obviously, their mothers had coordinated the effort. Richard's vest complemented Elizabeth's gown perfectly.

"Oh, my. You two look like you just stepped out of a magazine," said Lynne, admiring the handsome couple. "Char, you and Billy look great, too. Now you'd better get going so that you don't miss your appointments with the photographer." She kissed her daughter's cheek. "We'll be there right behind you. David should be home any minute. Drive carefully."

"I will, Mrs. Bennet. Don't worry," Richard assured her.

Lynne handed Elizabeth a duffle bag containing her clothes for Laser Tag. Elizabeth had packed it earlier and left it by the door.

Xander, where is your formal toga? asked Niall, speaking aloud. Xander was looking altogether formidable, but his expression changed from a scowl to a smile at Niall's remark.

I forgot to pick it up from the cleaner's. This old rag will have to do. However, I did polish my sword for the occasion, he responded as he followed Elizabeth to the car.

The protectors, other than Niall, listened to the banter with astonishment. When did Xander grow a sense of humor?

Richard and Billy opened the car doors for their dates; Elizabeth waved to her mother from the front seat. Lynne waved back, and Niall stood with her on the porch until the teens drove down the driveway and out of sight, their four guardians gliding above the car, gently glowing and watching – always watching.

~~~~~~~~

After dinner and so many pictures that Richard and Elizabeth thought they would be permanently blinded by the flashes, the dancing began. The teens danced in lines and groups to music that was upbeat – and usually old. Since the same dances were done each year, the older teens had taught the younger. Richard attempted the unfamiliar patterns good naturedly, joined Elizabeth for the Macarena, the Cha Cha Slide, and the Electric Slide, among others, but he took a seat during the Cotton-Eyed Joe. Lynne saw him sitting alone and went to sit with him for a moment.

"Richard, why aren't you dancing? You've been doing so well."

"Mrs. B., I could catch on to the others; they were simple, but this is like a level ten. Can't do it. Josh Lucas is picking up my slack."

Lynne searched the dance floor and spotted Elizabeth dancing with Josh. They appeared to be having a wonderful time together. The two of them were like brother and sister.

Lynne smiled at Richard. "You've been a good sport. I think you've earned a little rest. Don't be out too late. Two o'clock, okay?" After much deliberation, she and David had decided to let Elizabeth stay out later and go with a large school group for their post-prom activity.

"Yes, ma'am. I'll bring her home when Laser Tag closes," he replied. "I have a curfew, too."

As the music changed to "One Sweet Day" by Mariah Carey and Boyz II Men, Richard stood, excused himself to Lynne, and went to claim Elizabeth. She looked up at him and smiled shyly as he took her hand, pulling her away from the group, drawing her into his arms for their first slow dance. He listened to the lyrics, "Sorry I never told you all I wanted to say. And now it's too late to hold you, 'cause you've flown away, so far away." *It won't be that way with us – not after tonight. I am going to tell her how important she is to me. I love everything about her – her eyes, her sweetness, her scent, her mind.*

Xander fumed as Richard's hands slid to her waist and Elizabeth rested her head on his shoulder. *I do not think proms are suitable. There is too much intimacy. Two hundred years ago, he would have had to marry her had he held her in that way.*

Niall and Roark exchanged a knowing look. *Do you object to the dance, or to Richard's thoughts?* asked Niall.

Both! answered Xander emphatically, glowering.

~~~~~~~~~

Following the prom, the teens had changed clothes at the country club before going to play the games, and Elizabeth had given her formal outfit to her parents. Apart from hearing lascivious thoughts constantly from the teen male population concerning other activities in which they would like to engage with Elizabeth, and that final time she had danced with Richard, Xander had been comfortable at the prom. There were so many guardians there that the light permeating the building was a warning beacon to the dark forces, and Richard's mind was not the sewer that characterized the minds of so many of the other young men. He truly respected Elizabeth. *She could do much worse,* mused Xander.

The Laser Tag arena was a different story entirely. It was dark; there were not as many guardians, and there were quite a few non-believers there giving entry to demons. Xander practically glued himself to Elizabeth. He stayed close enough to touch her at all times.

Caroline Bingley, Grant Willoughby, and Lydia Henderson came in with the rest of their crowd after the others had already put on their vests. Nyx and Hadrian arrived with them.

The underprince and his captain are now hounding Elizabeth themselves? Garnet, you and Ros will need to be on high alert in here. Elizabeth is the target, not Richard or Caroline. Keep her in your line of sight at all times. He wished that Niall and Roark were with him, but Garnet, Ros, and the other guardians would have to be sufficient cover.

Feeling a tap on her shoulder, Elizabeth turned, surprised to see Caroline.

Wonderful, thought Xander. *Linda Blair is here with her contingent. I fully expect to see her head start spinning at any moment along with the projectile vomiting of pea soup.*

"Hi, Caro. You looked fabulous at the prom. I didn't know you guys were coming to play, but I'm glad you did."

Like I would miss seeing Richard. Right. Caroline's thoughts were loud and dripping with sarcasm.

"You looked very pretty, too, El. It's crowded here. Looks like fun," Caroline answered, sounding bored, and scanning the group for Richard. *You looked very pure, just like a Bible beater. One day Richard will want more, and I'll be there waiting. Hmmm. It's really dark in there. Maybe I'll just bump into him tonight. Full body contact.*

Richard came up from behind Caroline to join Elizabeth, putting his arm around her possessively. "Hello, Caro. El, come on. We're all ready to play. Catch you later." He nodded to Caroline, took Elizabeth's hand, and led her toward the game room.

Xander and Garnet shadowed their charges into the darkened playing area. *We need to keep track of Nyx and Hadrian,* said Xander. Garnet nodded his agreement.

Caroline was steaming. *Richard barely acknowledged me, but he had loads of attention for the vestal virgin.* Grant and Lydia came up, and Lydia handed Caroline her equipment.

"What's up, Caro? Mad, again? The luscious Richard blow you off?" Lydia teased.

"Whatever, Lydia. He was just ready to play, and so am I. Let's go," she snapped.

"Chill, Caro. It's no big deal. You have the best looking dude in the place with you," Grant said, throwing his arm around her shoulders.

They went to find the others. Ros followed glumly. *She just will not let it rest.* Nyx and Hadrian sneered at him.

Caroline spent her time tracking Elizabeth, tripping her several times in the dark. Elizabeth never saw her because she was good at hiding. *Wow, I never knew I was so clumsy. I need to be more careful before I break something – like my leg,* Elizabeth thought.

I may break something myself before this is over – like Caroline's neck, thought Xander. He had caught Elizabeth each time she had fallen, preventing her from suffering any real harm.

Ros knew that he could do nothing to stop Caroline as long as she allowed the evil ones free reign in her life. Angels never interfered in the free choices that humans made. They made suggestions, but a human was never forced to follow the ideas that were planted. She consistently chose to listen to Nyx and Hadrian rather than him. There was no help for it unless she repented of her backslidden condition and asked the Master for forgiveness. He had seen it happen many times with other humans, but Caroline was far from being in that place in her life at this time. *Maybe when she's older . . .* Ros thought with hope.

Gregory, in dark form, floated through the ceiling and perched up in a corner of the room, observing the two girls and enjoying the spectacle immensely. As he did not intend to engage the enemy that night, he had only two guards with him to attract as little attention as possible. He knew that as long as he confined himself to watching, Xander and the other guardians would leave him alone. Gregory was not stupid; he knew that he was not ready to fight Xander . . . not yet. But he could learn many things about Xander and Elizabeth by being quiet and unobtrusive. He could still take advantage of his anonymity. Xander had glimpsed him and assumed he was just another demon, but he did not yet know who he was. The chief guardian was familiar with the powerful demons who had existed for millennia; however, Gregory was a few months shy of fifteen years. Nobody in the holy angelic realm knew him. Gregory was careful to keep his face hidden under his hooded cloak to preserve his secret identity for the time being. *They will all recognize me very soon, and bow to me.* Gregory allowed himself a small, self-satisfied smile.

He noticed that Caroline Bingley particularly hated Elizabeth, as he had heard her words against the girl on several occasions, and he saw Nyx and

Hadrian using their influence with her, planting thoughts in her mind. *They must have some sort of a plan using that girl. Tripping Elizabeth may be a fun game, but it will not achieve our goal. I will tell Father to give them a little more time; however, unless I see something better than this very soon, I will have to take action myself.*

~~~~~~~~

Richard had dropped Billy and Charlotte off at Billy's house to get Billy's car, and he and Elizabeth continued alone to her house. Richard had always been very careful not to press Elizabeth for more physical contact than she was prepared to give. He had kissed her many times, short chaste kisses, but as his attraction for her had grown, he wanted more. As he drove her home, Jessica Simpson singing "Take My Breath Away" came on the radio. *El really does take my breath away. Tonight was wonderful. She was happy and playful. I think she may be ready to take it a little further.* He reached for her hand, and she responded. They held hands the rest of the way to her house.

Maybe he's not so different from the others after all, growled Xander. *He should think about his driving and keep his hands to himself – preferably on the steering wheel.*

Xander, he is thinking of a more serious kiss. That is all. Richard is a good boy, Garnet replied, defending his charge. *Surely you cannot object to a kiss? He truly cares for her. He is not trying to use her. Be reasonable.*

Xander mulled over the question and Garnet's sound logic. He should not object to a kiss, yet he did.

They pulled up fifteen minutes before her curfew. *Good timing,* thought Richard. He turned off the car and looked at Elizabeth. She was ethereal in the moonlight. The pins had fallen from her hair as they had played Laser Tag, and it lay in loose curls around her shoulders and down her back. She smiled shyly at him.

I cannot blame him. Who could resist her when she smiles like that? He is not made of stone, Xander admitted grudgingly.

137

Richard cleared his throat, suddenly nervous. "El, you are so beautiful and special. I know you're young, but we've been together for more than seven months now. You are so important to me, and I'd like to make it official. Will you be my girlfriend?" His beautiful eyes pleaded with her. She had no feelings for anyone except Richard, and she could not refuse him.

"Yes, Richard. I don't want anyone else but you." Her deep brown eyes were serious.

"Do you trust me?" he asked, leaning closer to her, and whispering his question in her ear.

"Yes. I trust you." She was puzzled by his question.

Wrong answer, thought Xander privately.

 Richard took her into his arms and kissed her gently. She kissed him back, and then he ran his tongue tenderly against her closed mouth. It shocked her, and he felt her little gasp parting her lips. He slowly deepened their kiss and she responded tentatively, pulling him closer.

As she grew bolder and started to put her fingers in his hair, Xander felt his heart rate accelerate with hers, but for a different reason.

Niall! called Xander gruffly. *Rouse Lynne. I think it is time to turn on the porch light.*

Garnet glanced at him, and then looked away.

The porch light came on and the spell was broken. Pulling back a little to look into her dreamy, slightly unfocused eyes, Richard said softly, "I guess I'd better let you go in now. We don't want to make the 'rents mad. I wouldn't want them to decide we shouldn't see each other." She nodded slowly.

Richard got out of the car and came around to open her door; then he walked Elizabeth to the porch. When, Elizabeth retrieved her house keys from her purse and unlocked the door, he noticed that her hands were trembling. Richard took both of her hands in his, pecked her on the cheek, and breathed, "Good night, my sweet El. I'll call you tomorrow."

She answered, "Good night," smiled at him, and went blissfully into the house to her waiting mother.

Richard went back to his car with a spring in his step and a huge grin on his face. *Yes! She said yes!*

Niall watched with concern as Xander trudged behind Elizabeth with his head down. He dutifully followed to her room, ready for another session of staring at the ceiling and the walls while she prepared for bed. *At least she is alone with me for now, though she does not know it.* His sadness threatened to overwhelm him. He wished that he could close his eyes and sleep.

Chapter 14

"Therefore, since we have so great a cloud of witnesses surrounding us, let us also lay aside every encumbrance, and the sin which so easily entangles us, and let us run with endurance the race that is set before us."Hebrews 12: 1

Xander stood to the side as fifteen-year-old Elizabeth crossed the stage to receive her high school diploma. Though he strove to maintain a neutral expression, his pride in her accomplishments was evident by the gleam in his eyes. *She is truly amazing. I am privileged to guard her.*

In the awards ceremony that morning, Elizabeth had won academic, citizenship, and outstanding conduct awards. In addition, she had been recognized, of course, as valedictorian, as well as a National Merit Scholar. Scholarship offers had poured in from around the country, but Elizabeth had declared her intentions to finish her bachelor's degree in music at Converse while working toward a BS in theology from Liberty University online. Because she had begun working on her BA at Converse several years prior, and she had numerous AP credits, her class load there would be fairly light. She planned to finish her undergraduate work at both institutions in two years, and afterward continue her master's studies in music performance at Converse and Worship-Ethnomusicology at Liberty in the same manner. If all went according to what she hoped, she would be working on her doctorate by the time she turned nineteen. Until then, her mother had decided to leave her teaching job at Peniel and had accepted a position tutoring English at Converse. That way, Elizabeth could live at home with her parents, and Lynne would drive her back and forth to Converse until she was ready to move out on her own for her doctoral work.

During the graduation exercises, Elizabeth gave her valedictory speech and sang a solo, "*Con Te Partiro* (Time to Say Goodbye)," and then joined the choir for "*Hine Mah Tov*," a song based on Psalm 133:1, "How good and pleasant it is when brothers live together in harmony." Senior choir members had joined together for "Friends Are Friends Forever," by Michael W. Smith, and the program ended with the senior ensemble singing, "A Claire Benediction," by John Rutter. Charlotte Lucas was in the choir and ensemble, and Elizabeth truly felt that she and the older girl would remain close; Charlotte had decided to attend Converse with her in the fall, commuting with Lynne and Elizabeth for at least the first year.

Xander and the other guardians stirred in astonishment as they listened to Elizabeth sing in Italian and Hebrew and realized that the English speaking audience heard every word *in English*, though she sang in languages that were foreign to them. Because the songs were translated on the video screens, and the choir members knew the English words for the songs, most of the humans failed to notice anything amiss. The few in the choir, faculty, and audience who did detect a deviation from the norm simply wondered why Elizabeth had chosen to sing in English; Elizabeth herself did not know there was anything different from any of her other performances. In the confusion following the program, no one thought to mention it to her.

Xander drew his brows together and mused, speaking for the entire host to hear, *How can this be? It reminds me of the Day of Pentecost. 'And they were amazed and marveled, saying, Why, are not all these who are speaking Galileans? And how is it that we each hear them in our own language to which we were born? . . . we hear them in our own tongues speaking of the mighty deeds of God.' Acts 2:7, 8, 11. Has the Almighty made her special in more ways than we have already seen? I have not noticed this before. If this is a gift, it has been dormant until now. What He has wrought is wonderful! He is mighty in this place.*

Niall, Roark, Alexis and the others looked to him for an explanation. He shrugged, but his face glowed brightly with the glory of God. *I do not know, but I am certain that El Shaddai will reveal His purpose in His time. Let us praise the great I Am, Who was, and is, and is to come!*

The angels hummed as they raised their faces heavenward and lifted their hands in holy worship to the Alpha and Omega, the King of Kings, and the Lord of Lords, and the glory of the Lord filled the place. The light grew until it permeated the building, and shone from every window and crack like beams of sunlight through the clouds. All of heaven heard the offering, joining in the exaltation, and the omnipotent, omnipresent, omniscient, immutable God received their praises and was well pleased.

~~~~~~~~

Richard came to her graduation, driving separately from his parents so that he and Elizabeth could attend a graduation pool party given by her Aunt Grace, who had graciously invited all the Peniel juniors and seniors. Grace lived about ten miles out of town in a heavily wooded area. Lynne, David, Janna, Chance, and Richard's parents had agreed to help chaperone.

Xander was pleased that Niall, Roark, Alexis, and Hector, Chance's protector, would be at the gathering. He was increasingly edgy about Elizabeth's safety since Nyx and Hadrian were now seen regularly hovering around Caroline Bingley.

Charlotte, her brother Joshua, and Billy rode with Richard and Elizabeth to the party. Xander and Garnet, along with Edward, Alistair, and Skylar, guardians to the other couple and Joshua, provided an intimidating escort. Xander had communicated with Ros at graduation, and he had confirmed that Caroline would be there; consequently he would be on guard for her mischief.

"Oh, Richard. It's beautiful!" Elizabeth exclaimed as they drove through the trees strung with white lights circling the driveway. The fairy lights extended to the back of the house, strung through the magnolias and crepe myrtles, making the backyard pool area seem magical as the lights twinkled in the moonlight.

"Just like you," Richard replied, leaning toward her for a quick kiss before they all got out of the car. The couples walked hand-in-hand toward the pool where teens and adults were already gathering.

Xander and the other protectors followed their charges closely enough to touch them, sometimes walking with the young people and at other times hovering above them.

After greeting everyone, Elizabeth and her friends used the upstairs bedrooms to change into their swimsuits. Within a few minutes, the happily chattering group came down the stairs, headed for the tables full of refreshments.

Caroline, Grant, and Lydia had arrived in the meantime. They had dropped by Caroline's house and changed before they came. The underprince and his captain walked boldly with them, ignoring Ros and glaring at Xander and the other guardians with contempt. The denizens of hell had observed the happenings at graduation and knew that something extraordinary had taken place. The air between the holy and the fallen seemed to pop and crackle with electricity. Each side waited for the other to make a move. Xander's hand rested on the hilt of his sword, ever ready to wield his weapon.

Caroline hurried to intercept Richard at the buffet area. He turned as she touched his arm.

"Hello, Caro," Richard said, subtly moving his arm away from her hand. He was growing tired of her constant pursuit, and of her insults to Elizabeth, but he had no wish to offend her.

"Richard! It's always good to see you." Caroline knew that she looked good in her bikini. Her suit was the smallest one at the party, certainly, and it left hardly anything to the imagination. Most of the other girls kept on their cover-ups or T shirts until they were ready to swim, but Caroline saw no need to hide her assets. If her sparkling personality would not attract Richard, she would use any other advantages she had.

Elizabeth turned, holding a plate of snacks, and smiled at her. "I'm glad you came, Caro," Elizabeth said. She knew that Caroline was after Richard, and that she really was not her friend, but she tried to be courteous to everyone.

"Catch you later," Richard said over his shoulder to Caroline as he steered Elizabeth by a nod of his head toward some chairs by the pool.

Miffed, Caroline followed them and stood close enough to hear their conversation, though she acted with indifference. Ros trailed her, watching Nyx and Hadrian who stood on either side of her, whispering in her ears. When she heard Richard and Elizabeth making plans to go four-wheeling the next day in the woods behind his house, she broke into their conversation.

"That sounds like fun. Can I come along? I've always wanted to ride a four-wheeler."

Richard looked at her in amazement, and then he glanced at Elizabeth. She was struggling to hold back a laugh.

"Uh . . . sure, I guess. If it's okay with El." He gave Elizabeth a small grin, letting her know that the ball was in her court.

Wow. Thanks, Richard, for leaving it up to me, she thought with a little moue, though she recovered quickly. "We had no clue you'd like four-wheeling, Caro. You'll get dirty, you know."

"No problem. I like getting dirty occasionally," Caroline purred with a leer at Richard.

Richard looked decidedly uncomfortable. Elizabeth took her measure. *I'll just bet you do. Good luck with that move on Richard.*

"Is two o'clock good for you, Richard?" Elizabeth queried.

"Sure. Fine," he said with little enthusiasm. His highly anticipated plans for one-on-one time with Elizabeth were shot.

"I'll be there. I know where you live," Caroline said and turned to go back to Grant and Lydia.

Mission accomplished. Nyx and Hadrian grinned evilly and followed her, while Ros trailed behind, his dejection evident in his countenance.

Stalker much? thought Elizabeth.

Elizabeth reached down for her drink which she had set on the concrete to her left, her head turned right toward Richard, laughing at his dour expression. Unknown to her, lurking in the shrubbery behind her, a huge rattlesnake was coiled, awaiting his chance to strike. Just as she lowered her hand for her cup, the serpent shot out of the bushes, its mouth wide open and deadly fangs extended. Though it made no sound, the movement of the snake caught Xander's attention, as did the darkness surrounding the serpent. The skin of the viper should have reflected the light, but it didn't. It rather seemed to absorb it. As the snake went for Elizabeth's hand, Xander caught it with lightning-quick reflexes and slung it into the woods behind the house. His vise-like grip ordinarily would have killed a serpent; this one merely looked at him with cold, dead eyes and slithered away.

Garnet's eyes were wide with shock. Xander had caught and thrown the beast so quickly that none of the humans had noticed, but all of the guardians had seen the incident, as had Nyx and Hadrian. It was obvious from their surprised faces that they had not planned the attack.

The party continued as if nothing had happened. Elizabeth picked up her drink and resumed her conversation with Richard, totally unaware of her brush with death. She felt chilled from a sudden breeze and wrapped herself in her beach towel.

Xander, deep in thought, remembered how the serpent had felt when he had touched it. He had sensed a vile presence within the snake. It was unusual for demons to inhabit animals; he knew of only two with that ability. He thought back to the serpent in the Garden of Eden, beguiling Eve.

The snake was possessed by either Lucifer or Dark Spirit. Xander spoke aloud so that all the angels could hear him. The protectors were astonished that one of the two highest ranking demons had made an appearance and orchestrated an assassination attempt. It had happened only a few times in human history. Another oddity was that the serpent had left without more of a fight. *It was a test. He has not given up, only upped the ante.* The holy assembly nodded in agreement.

No one there was more amazed than were Nyx and Hadrian. Beyond that, they were terrified. They knew that if their plans for the next day did not succeed, there would be no more opportunities for them. Their master had decided either to enter the fray himself, or to send the most heinous of all his servants to carry out his will.

There was nothing more to be done this night. The underprince and his captain flew away in a swirl of their black, hooded robes to plot for the morrow and make needed adjustments to the path in the woods.

Undetected, Gregory perched on a tree limb, high above the lights of the party, with his father who held the snake coiled about his arm, gently stroking the reptile. *Watch and learn, my son.*

The unholy trinity observed while their guards hid within the limbs of the tall trees, blocking the light of the moon and stars.

~~~~~~~~~

That night, while Xander was watching Elizabeth sleep, Gabriel, clad in the garb of a guardian, appeared in her room. *Xander, you have been summoned. I will guard Elizabeth until your return.*

Xander hesitated, a look of uncertainty on his face.

Do not be anxious, Xander. Nothing will happen to Elizabeth during my watch. My sword is as sharp as yours.

I am not worried about that, Gabriel. I know that you can protect her.

What then?

Xander looked away for a moment, and then gazed into the dark blue eyes of the archangel.

Xander's voice was low as he spoke. *We have never been parted since her conception. The thought of leaving her is . . . uncomfortable for me.*

Gabriel's look was penetrating as he held Xander's eyes with his. *And yet, you must answer the summons.*

Yes, I must. Sighing, Xander took one last glimpse of Elizabeth sleeping peacefully; her dark hair was spread across the pillows and a single beam of moonlight peeked through the curtains and illuminated her face. His expression changed from one of misery to resignation as he opened his wings and flashed through the ceiling, into the night, and out of the atmosphere. The curtains stirred in the breeze, and Elizabeth shivered and unconsciously drew the covers closer to fend off the chill.

~~~~~~~

Upon his arrival in the golden city, Xander went immediately to the throne room. He was surprised to see Michael there waiting for him, wearing a tunic and full battle armor, standing beside several large articles made of a golden metal.

The dazzling, pure light of Elohim suddenly filled the place. The two angels dropped to their knees and bowed their heads.

"Xander, I have called you away from your duties because there are things that you need in order to successfully protect your charge."

The protector's dark head remained bowed, but there was a question in his mind.

"Speak, Xander."

"What more do I need, my Lord? I have my sword."

"You are now facing an underprince and his captain, and I know that Lucifer has called Dark Spirit and another to his side. Guardians have never been armed with defensive weapons, but you will need them now. Michael, the mighty warrior and the captain of the host, has had the artisans craft a shield and breastplate, as well as arm and leg guards, which I have blessed, specifically for you. After you have prepared yourself, he will show you how to best use your new weapons. Michael, proceed."

Michael and Xander rose to their feet and the warrior strapped the arm plates to the guardian's brawny forearms, the shin guards to his muscular legs, and the breastplate over his broad chest and shoulders. He gave Xander the round shield and showed him how to slip his arm through the straps and hold it with his hand. Michael illustrated how to move the shield to its greatest advantage. It was not large, but it was enough to deflect the blow of an opponent.

Satisfied, Michael unsheathed his own sword, put his shield on his arm, and walked a few paces away. Turning to face Xander, he instructed, "Attack me, and then defend yourself."

The massive angels were evenly matched. Michael's advantage in height by a few inches found a counterpart in Xander's muscular bulk. They were both highly skilled in battle and faster than the blink of an eye. The competition was a fair one.

Xander had always favored a direct frontal attack, but Michael spun and whirled, holding his sword tightly across his chest, flipping himself over Xander to catch his most vulnerable area – his back. The guardian learned the new strategies quickly, and found that the shield and plates, which had at first seemed cumbersome, could be used to his advantage both offensively and defensively. The coverings and shield were surprisingly lightweight and strong. No sword could pierce them, and while he could hang the shield from his breastplate on the hip opposite his sword when it was not in use, there was no need to remove the armor; the flexible guards molded to his body perfectly.

They practiced through Elizabeth's earth night, and the clashing of their swords resounded throughout the halls of heaven and echoed around the holy places. As the hours passed and news of the event spread, hundreds of angels gathered at the doors and in the hallways, watching the training session in fascination.

Knowing their curiosity, Jehovah-Magen spoke graciously. "You may enter."

The throng streamed into the cavernous room, lining the walls and hovering high above the training session. Michael's moves and attacks became more complicated as Xander learned. He feinted from side to side, leaping and suspending himself in the air, kicking and spinning until he was a blur. When he was not flying, Michael pulled his translucent, flexible wings so close to his body that they seemed like a second skin. The guardian quickly absorbed the warrior's instructions, mirroring his moves and creating new strategies.

Watching Xander and Michael battle over and over, with first one and then the other claiming a victory, was an unheard of spectacle.

When the earth night was nearly done, Xander turned what seemed to be a sure win for Michael into a loss with a stunningly innovative maneuver. Before Michael could react, Xander, using his wings to catapult himself, twisted and spun in the air, suddenly attaching himself to the giant angel's back, over his tucked wings. Xander caught Michael in a bear hug, his arms pinning Michael's arms and his sword across Michael's chest. The guardian effectively immobilized the warrior, his right hand grasping the hilt of his sword and his left hand holding to his right wrist. Had Xander chosen to do so, he could have released his wrist and flown backwards, slashing with his sword and beheading Michael before he had a chance to turn around. The murmurs in the room erupted into cheers.

"You can release me now," Michael said with a smile and a twinkle in his green eyes. As Xander leapt off the captain's back, thrusting his sword back into its sheath, Michael knelt before the Ancient of Days, saying, "I think Xander is ready, Jehovah-Chereb."

Xander and the other angels made obeisance, bowing low in silence.

"You are now my guardian warrior. You have appropriated the full armor; therefore, stand firm, having put on the breastplate of righteousness and taken up the shield of faith with the sword of the Spirit. Are you prepared for the battle, Xander?"

"I am ready, my Lord. Thank you for your care in providing the weapons. I will use them to Your honor and glory as I face the evil ones."

"Your work has pleased me. You have done well. Return and defend your charge."

The brilliant light folded in upon itself and disappeared.

Michael and Xander stood and clasped hands. "Thank you, Michael."

"It will be thanks enough for me to see you defeat Nyx and Hadrian. Remember that we will be watching your victory."

The room shook with the combined voices of the multitudes of angels, cheering and encouraging their brother with fists raised.

Xander nodded, flew from the room at dizzying speed, and arrived back in Elizabeth's room just as the sun was rising on Saturday. She was still sleeping as quietly as she had been when he had left her, dreaming of a handsome young man with light brown hair and sparkling eyes.

Gabriel put his hand on Xander's shoulder. *Adonai will be with you today. Go in His power.*

Then stretching out his shimmering wings, he soared through the walls and back up to heaven.

Chapter 15

"For I am convinced that neither death, nor life, nor angels, nor principalities, nor things present, nor things to come, nor powers, nor height, nor depth, nor any other created thing, shall be able to separate us from the love of God, which is in Christ Jesusour Lord."
Romans 8: 38-39

The sun rose over the horizon on Saturday, throwing brilliant shades of blue, pink, and violet across the eastern sky; however, the magnificent dawn with the promise of a beautiful day was wasted on Xander, who was intensely focused on shielding Elizabeth during her upcoming afternoon outing with Richard and Caroline. Because neither he nor Garnet could go themselves, the protector had summoned a scout and sent him ahead to look at the trail. Carson had reported back to Xander, first by telepathing as he walked the area, and later by meeting with him at the Bennet home. It was as the chief guardian had suspected; Carson had seen Nyx and Hadrian altering the course to make it more dangerous. Richard would be confident that he knew the trail, but in reality, there would be hidden hazards at every turn.

Niall and Roark had been amazed at the change in Xander's appearance that morning. Of course, they had known that Gabriel had taken the guardian's place while he answered a summons, and they had read his mind as soon as he had returned, reliving the night's training through his thoughts, but to actually see him was another thing altogether. He was the only one of his kind now – a guardian warrior, personally tutored in the arts of warfare by Michael himself.

The day seemed endless to Xander as the hands of the clock inched ever closer to the appointed time. While waiting, he went through all he had learned the night before, reviewing every detail in his incomparable mind. He fidgeted unchacteristically as he counted down the hours. Finally, just before two o'clock, Lynne and Elizabeth left the Bennet home, accompanied by Xander and Niall. Lynne and Delores Williams had arranged that she would drive Elizabeth to their home and Delores would bring her back home after dinner.

As they drove up to the Williamses' home, Elizabeth saw Caroline's red Lexus convertible. Xander heard Elizabeth's thought, *Of course she would be here early – trying to get Richard alone.*

The guardian settled from flight, standing atop Lynne's car, his golden armor gleaming in the sunlight as he probed the area with his eyes and his mind. *I will need every skill I learned from Michael,* he thought, his face an inscrutable mask to Garnet and Ros. They were both staring at him openly, mouths agape at the formidable sight of Xander in the battle armor of a holy warrior. *Good,* thought Xander. *Perhaps Nyx and Hadrian will be intimidated as well. I wonder where they are. They must be waiting for us in the woods; I smell the putrid odor of evil in the breeze.*

Richard had been on the porch swing for a while, watching for Elizabeth, and Caroline was nestled as close to him as she could possibly get without actually sitting in his lap. He squinted from the glare of the light off the car, but he did not wait for Lynne's Honda to come to a complete stop before he bounded off the porch and opened Elizabeth's car door. Caroline sauntered lazily after him, her skin-tight tank top and short-shorts showing her figure to its best advantage.

"Be careful driving that four-wheeler, Richard," Lynne said to him, looking through Elizabeth's open door without turning off her car. "You will be carrying precious cargo."

Richard returned her smile, saying, "I'm always careful with El, Mrs. B. Don't worry. You can trust me to watch after her." Caroline rolled her eyes behind his back as he helped Elizabeth from the car and closed the door. The guardian could have known her stabbing thoughts from the look on her face, but he listened anyway. *I may just throw up,* he heard.

Xander glared at her. *Maybe we can arrange that, Caroline, if you desire it.*

The guardian had seen many women like Caroline before. There was absolutely no mystery in their approach to men. He took in her appearance, thinking, *Strange attire for riding a four-wheeler. Elizabeth is dressed more sensibly for an afternoon in the woods – jeans and a T shirt. She will not be scratched by every twig.* He approved of her modesty and practicality.

Lynne backed out and drove away, waving at Delores and her husband Jim, who had come to the front door shadowed by their protectors. As Delores and Jim returned her farewell, Niall copied his charge's wave to Xander, smiling. *Have fun!* Then more seriously, *I wish that I could be at your side today.*

Xander growled in response. He would have preferred to have Niall with him during the coming ordeal. He had grown accustomed to Niall and Roark, and he knew that he could depend on them. They worked well together. Garnet and Ros would have to be enough, however. He shook his head. He could not allow himself to dwell on negative thoughts.

He followed as Richard led the two girls into the garage. The young man grabbed a towel from a shelf by the door leading into the house and tied it to the handlebars of the ATV. More than once, he had been glad that he had taken a towel for small cuts and scratches. The girls went back outside while he backed the four-wheeler out into the driveway.

"Who wants to go with me first?" Richard asked, imploring Elizabeth with his eyes. He had no desire to be alone with Caroline in the woods. Caroline was eyeing him speculatively, sizing him up like she was imagining his performance potential. Richard saw her look and felt like a side of beef at an open market.

Neither angel nor human could mistake the look on her face. Xander could well understand Richard's desperate thought, *Somebody shoot me now, please!*

Xander shuddered and agreed. *Death would be preferable to being caught by oneself with that shrew.*

"El?" Richard queried, the hope in his voice grating on Caroline's nerves.

Before Elizabeth could reply, Caroline quickly took control of the conversation. "I don't see why we can't all ride together. The seat is big enough; El and I don't take up very much room," she said. She had no intention of waiting around with Richard's parents while her quarry took off with El for hours.

If the three of us ride together, I can get out of being alone with Caro. I'll still be with El the whole afternoon. Win-win! Richard agreed to her idea immediately. "Sounds like a plan. El?"

"I guess so. Don't you have just two helmets, though? Who wants to ride without a helmet?" Elizabeth asked.

"The law doesn't say that we have to wear helmets, El. Lighten up," Caroline said derisively.

"I know the trails like the back of my hand, El. We'll be okay," Richard added, reaching for Elizabeth's hand. *I'd go naked if it would get me out of being alone with Caro.*

Elizabeth hated to be a spoilsport, so she reluctantly gave in to her friends. *After all, it won't kill me to ride without a helmet just this once.*

Xander fumed. *No helmet? You need this armor more than I do. For heaven's sake, do not make this anymore difficult.*

Caroline moved to take the place behind Richard, but he smoothly pre-empted her by saying, "El, you're in the middle. Put your arms around me and hold on." Elizabeth did as instructed, and Caroline squeezed on behind her, grasping Elizabeth's waist with distaste.

Richard started down the trail to the woods, and Xander spoke with Garnet and Ros as they flew over the four-wheeler. *Nyx and Hadrian have altered the path to make it very dangerous. Even now, they await us in the woods. Garnet, you will, of course, protect Richard. Ros, I may need you to help guard Elizabeth. Caroline will be doing whatever Nyx and Hadrian suggest to her. You will have no influence on her, and she is unlikely to be hurt. Both of you be ready to do battle.*

The teens rode deeper into the woods, chatting and laughing. They were several miles in when Richard noticed a few areas that seemed steeper than he had remembered, but he reasoned that the recent rains had eroded the gullies. As the track became rougher, he began to regret that he had allowed Elizabeth to ride without a helmet. He had promised her mother that he would protect her, and he knew that the Bennets, as well as his parents, would not have approved of the choice they had made.

Garnet spoke sharply to Richard. *Slow down! You are going too fast.*

Richard was too flooded with adrenaline to listen. Though he saw the trail was in poor shape, he still thought that he knew it well enough and could handle it without any problem.

Ros had taken the right of the vehicle, Garnet was on the left, and Xander flew above, his dark waves ruffled by the wind, close enough to touch Elizabeth.

As the undergrowth became thicker, Richard had more difficulty seeing clearly. He came over a hill with too much speed and did not notice the fallen trees piled just on the other side of the crest. The four-wheeler climbed the trees that had been placed to act as a ramp and was airborne for a few long seconds, coming down on the front tires because of the weight of the three teens pushed forward on the seat. The back tires came up, and Richard jumped off the vehicle to the left side, instinctively rolling as he had been taught to do.

Caroline, acting on an idea planted earlier in her mind by Nyx and Hadrian, pushed Elizabeth forward with all her strength, and Elizabeth's head hit the handlebars as she flipped over the four-wheeler. Caroline leapt to the right just before the four-wheeler turned over and came to rest upside down on Elizabeth, who lay with her face up under the handlebars. Her guardian was anguished. He had not been able to cushion her back and protect her front simultaneously. All that he could do was to hold up the four-wheeler in flight, keeping it from crushing her completely.

Xander, still in angelic form but solid enough to move objects, picked up the ATV, lifting it off of Elizabeth, and threw it against a tree. The three teens were all unconscious and Richard and Caroline had minor injuries; however, Elizabeth was bleeding profusely from a gash on her forehead at her hairline where she had hit the handlebars.

Xander had never sworn before in his existence, but he was sorely tempted to do so at this moment. Before he had time to think that thought to its completion, Nyx and Hadrian took solid form before him, smirking maliciously, swords at the ready.

"Garnet, Ros!" Xander called, taking form himself, unsheathing his sword with his right hand, and taking up his shield with his left. The two protectors, who had been kneeling over their charges, immediately sprang to their feet, solidified, and pulled their swords from their sheaths. Good and evil faced each other.

Nyx and Xander were nearly the same size, both huge and rippling with strength. Hadrian was slightly smaller than either of them, but significantly larger than Garnet or Ros. Xander telepathed to his two companions, *Engage Hadrian. I will fight Nyx.*

The two smaller guardians attacked Hadrian from different sides, effectively separating him from the underprince. Hadrian stepped backwards as they charged, seeking an advantage with a tree to protect his back. Garnet struck the first blow, neatly slicing off Hadrian's left arm which evaporated in a foul-smelling puff of black smoke. Hadrian let flow a string of profanities, and kept slashing with his sword in his right hand. He nicked Ros's leg, but then turned away to defend himself against Garnet's charge.

Nyx dropped his robe and advanced slowly toward Xander, who awaited his attack crouched in a defensive posture, knees bent and feet set at shoulder width, arms forward, with sword and shield ready. Moving so quickly that human eyes could not have seen him, Nyx bared his teeth and flew straight at Xander, raising his sword high over his shoulder as he swooped down toward the guardian. Xander launched himself over the dark one, who then crashed into a tree instead, losing his balance. The demon righted himself, putting his back against the tree to steady himself, and then ran forward for another attack. Xander turned quickly to face him and was ready for him, shield up. Nyx lunged at the stalwart protector, bringing his arm around to slash his sword at the area beneath Xander's breastplate. The holy angel deflected the sword with his shield and used his wings to flip himself, twisting midair and landing lightly a few feet from Nyx's back. Dropping his shield and springing upward with his muscular legs, Xander used both hands to swing his sword. The arc of his sword had already begun as Nyx spun to face him, and he slashed his sword to the left, neatly beheading the vile giant. Nyx disintegrated without a sound and disappeared into oblivion.

Xander landed and pivoted to see how Garnet and Ros fared. He was just in time to watch Ros sever Hadrian's right leg as Garnet sliced him through the waist. With a fresh onslaught of shouted curses, Hadrian followed Nyx into hell.

Xander narrowed his eyes and saw Ros's leg leaking light from his wound. "You are injured?"

Ros responded rather proudly, "It is but a scratch, my chief."

The entire battle had taken but a few earth seconds.

The three angels turned their attention to their charges. Richard and Caroline were regaining consciousness, but Elizabeth remained still, the blood flowing from the wound in her forehead. She did not appear to have any broken bones. Xander's thoughts sped through the possibilities. They were at least two miles into the woods, and no help would be coming for several hours unless he took action. The woods were too dense for any rescue vehicle to drive through, the four-wheeler was wrecked and could not take the teens out, and, even if Richard became lucid enough to use his cell phone to call for help, too much time would elapse between the moment his parents received the call and the time it would take them to actually find the teenagers. Richard and Caroline could probably walk out, but Elizabeth would certainly not be able to do so. She needed help immediately.

He swiftly made his decision and telepathed his plan to Garnet and Ros. So that he could fly, Xander remained in solid, angelic form, while the two other protectors morphed into their human counterparts. They needed to take action before their charges awakened. Garnet quickly retrieved the towel

Richard had tied to the handlebars of the four-wheeler and took it to his chief. Xander tied it around Elizabeth's head to stanch the flow of blood; he then scooped Elizabeth carefully into his muscular arms, hugged her tenderly to his broad chest, and soared with her above the woods.

Richard awoke first and surveyed the wreck with confusion. Garnet, dressed for a hike in the woods as was Ros, squatted on his haunches beside the boy.

"You were in an accident. You should call your parents and tell them that my friend and I will walk you back to your house."

"Where is El, my girlfriend?" Richard's voice began to rise in agitation as he looked around frantically.

"Is that the dark-haired girl's name? She's going to be fine. She has a head injury, so another friend of ours who was riding alongside us as we hiked has used his transportation to take her to the hospital. Your parents should call her parents to meet them there."

Richard struggled to his feet. "Let's go. Caro, are you okay?"

Ros was helping Caroline to stand. "This sucks. I'm filthy and scratched up, we're stuck in the woods, and you expect me to walk for miles back to your house while El gets to ride out." Her beautiful face was marred by her jealous expression.

Richard was disgusted. Any concern he had harbored for her evaporated in an instant. "Caro, you can stay here if you want. El would have had on a helmet if you hadn't come, and you wouldn't have so many scratches if you had worn jeans and a T shirt. Who asked you to come, anyway?"

Richard's guardian interjected, "Both of you are very unsteady on your feet. My friend and I will carry you out. You should make that phone call first." He nodded at Richard.

Garnet and Ros, while not large by angelic standards, were, at more than six feet tall, bigger than either of the humans.

Richard called his parents, and he and Caroline climbed on the backs of their angels to be carried out of the woods.

~~~~~~~~

Xander kept to the wooded areas, flying just above the treetops, talking gently to Elizabeth the entire time. "Elizabeth, we are almost there. Do not give up. Please, Elizabeth, hold on. I am with you, and I will never let you go."

As they streaked through the air, the branches and leaves of the forest waved from the wind created by Xander's powerful wings.

The guardian looked for a protected place to land and spotted a small copse of trees just behind the hospital. Seeing that Elizabeth was still limp and unconscious in his arms, he dropped lightly to his feet in the cover of the trees and assumed human form, dressed casually in appropriate clothing for an afternoon of riding in the woods. Xander lowered his cheek to her face and whispered, "We are at the hospital, Elizabeth. You are safe. Your parents will be here soon, and I will not leave you. All will be well."

They had been in the air only a few minutes.

He fleetly ran with her to the Emergency Room and swiftly approached the admissions desk.

In a commanding voice, he said, "This young lady has been in an accident and her head is injured. She has been unconscious for more than five minutes. Her name is Elizabeth Bennet, and her parents are on the way."

The astonished clerk looked up at the largest, most beautiful man she had ever seen. Recovering her voice, she called for a gurney, and a nurse answered immediately. Hating to release her from his arms, Xander nevertheless laid Elizabeth carefully on the bed. She was beginning to stir, so he allowed the nurse to wheel her away while he slipped through a door marked "Employees Only." He eyed the scrubs with interest. It took but a second to change his form, this time to one wearing scrubs, a hospital ID, and a face mask.

Within seconds, he was trailing behind Elizabeth's gurney as they went into an examination area.

"What's up with the face mask?" asked the nurse, looking at the tall stranger curiously. Surely she would have remembered seeing *him* before. He was huge, and what she could see of him was gorgeous, especially those blue eyes. Her guardian recognized his chief and raised his arm in salute. Xander made no response except a slight nod of his head.

"I could be coming down with a cold, and I did not want to infect anyone else. This is my first day here."

He answered the question on her face and in her mind.

"Oh, okay," she answered, forcibly turning her attention back to her patient.

Elizabeth moved her head and groaned in pain. With great effort, he restrained himself and allowed the nurse to do her job.

"Well, hello. Glad to see you back with us. Does anything else hurt besides your head?" the nurse asked as she cleaned her head wound and put gauze over it.

"My chest," Elizabeth replied, frowning with the pain of breathing.

Xander stood beside the gurney, across from the nurse, and spoke calmly to his charge. "You're going to be fine. I saw your friends, and they are well." Elizabeth was relieved to hear that Richard and Caroline were not seriously injured.

The nurse glanced at him curiously, but continued to do her job, taking Elizabeth's temperature and blood pressure.

Dr. Moore was just coming in, a protector following him, and David and Lynne were right behind them with Niall and Roark. Xander stepped back so that the doctor could stand in his place. Dr. Moore assessed her with the swiftness of a doctor used to trauma patients.

The nurse spoke quietly. "She says that her chest hurts."

"She's going to need stitches for that cut, and she appears to have a concussion. We'll need to do a neurological exam, chest X-rays, and a CT scan. She'll probably need to stay overnight for observation."

"Does anyone know what happened?" asked David.

"Can you answer that?" the doctor asked Elizabeth.

"The last thing I remember is riding the four-wheeler with my friends in the woods. I don't know what happened. I was there, and, suddenly, I was here." She looked weary and fearful. Xander spoke peace to her mind, *Everything is going to be fine, Elizabeth. Be anxious for nothing. Do not worry nor fear. You are not alone.*

She became calmer.

Dr. Moore left to order the CT scan and X-rays, and orderlies came shortly to wheel Elizabeth to yet another room. Xander stepped behind the curtain to the adjoining exam area, and finding it empty, took angelic form. He was back in the room with Elizabeth before anyone noticed that he had disappeared.

In the meantime, Delores and Jim had brought Richard and Caroline to the ER to be checked out. The Bingleys had met them there, and Richard, surrounded by their guardians, had told them what had happened. Fortunately, he and Caroline were treated only for minor abrasions, but his parents were very unhappy with him for taking the girls riding without helmets. He was forbidden to ride three together anymore. Richard knew he had been wrong, and he took the correction with good grace. He felt terrible for being the cause of any injury to Elizabeth.

The scan revealed a serious concussion, so after Dr. Moore closed the wound on her forehead with tiny stitches, he had her admitted for the night.

After she was comfortably ensconced in her hospital bed, Dr. Moore stopped by before he left for the evening. His guardian saluted Xander who returned the greeting.

"How are you feeling, El? Any pain?" Dr. Moore had kind eyes that crinkled in the corners when he smiled.

"My chest hurts, and my head aches. Will I have a scar?" Xander chuckled at her small tribute to vanity.

By then, Dr. Moore had heard the full story of her accident. "I'm not surprised that it aches. That's a big lump you have. Fortunately, your ribs aren't broken, though four of them are cracked. I've ordered pain meds for you; that should help. The cut was right at your hairline, so the scar should not be visible. It will serve as a reminder to be thankful that you're still alive. You could have broken your neck. Next time, no riding without a helmet, and no more than two at a time."

She, along with her parents and the assembled guardians, nodded in agreement.

Xander was relieved that the day was drawing to a close, and that Elizabeth was safe. He leaned over Elizabeth, putting his head by hers on the pillow, and felt as if he were drawing breath for the first time in two days.

~~~~~~~~~

Lucifer and Gregory had watched the entire debacle from high in the trees.

Watching Xander fly away with Elizabeth, Beelzebub turned to his son, saying bitterly, "I am surrounded by incompetence, my son."

"Do not be concerned, Father. It will not be long before I can take care of the girl for you."

The Prince of Darkness smiled malevolently at the thought of his Gregory, his only son, avenging all the injustices he had suffered. It would be glorious indeed.

Chapter 16

"Now it came about, when men began to multiply on the face of the land, and daughters were born to them, that the sons of God saw that the daughters of men were beautiful; and they took wives for themselves, whomever they chose. The Nephilim were on the earth in those days, and also afterward, when the sons of God came in to the daughters of men, and they bore children to them. Those were the mighty men who were of old, men of renown." Genesis 6:1, 2, 4

September, 2005

Xander knew as soon as he followed Elizabeth into the Bennet home that the enemy had been there. The demon's scent, the smell of evil, hung in the air – yet something was not right about the odor. He had not encountered anything remotely like it for many thousands of years. There was a faint human aroma mixed with the unmistakable stench of a dark one. He wanted to track the fiend through the house to find out exactly where he had been, but he could not leave Elizabeth unprotected for even a moment.

Niall had noticed the evidence of an intruder as well. His nose was still stinging. *Have you ever smelled anything like that before?*

It reminds me of many humans before the flood, and of the giant Goliath and his brothers, as well as the Canaanites, though it is even more potent. Keep very close to Lynne.

Niall shuddered at the mention of the Nephilim. The ancient sexual sins of the fallen angels was a forbidden subject. They were so wicked that the Almighty had wiped all trace of them from the earth during the Great Flood, thus protecting Noah's, and therefore Jesus', bloodline from the genetic contamination of their iniquities. Demons again produced offspring with the human Canaanite women after the flood, and Jehovah had mandated the elimination of the idolatrous inhabitants of Canaan when Joshua led His people into the Promised Land. The mating of the dark ones with human women was a taboo which had stained and scarred the collective psyche of the light beings.

Surely you do not think there is another Nephilim. I will be no more than an arm's length from Lynne at any time. Niall felt as edgy as did Xander. He remembered the description of the Canaanites as told by the men who had been sent ahead to spy out the land for Joshua in Numbers 13:33. *'There also we saw the Nephilim (the sons of Anak are part of the Nephilim); and we became like grasshoppers in our own sight, and so we were in their sight.'*

Xander and Niall tracked their charges throughout the house, all of their senses heightened to the extreme.

Lynne and her daughter had just dropped Charlotte off after she and Elizabeth had completed their first day of college classes. A weary Elizabeth climbed the stairs and went directly to her room to put her bookbag by her bed. Xander noticed that the scent grew stronger as they neared her room. Once she opened the door and they stepped inside, the vile smell was overpowering. *The thing has been here – in her room.*

She normally practiced her music before she began her homework, but this day she was bothered by something about her bedroom. Xander heard her mental distress. *What is wrong in here? What is different?* She began to look carefully around her room, sensing that things were out of place somehow.

Elizabeth and Xander noticed several things at the same time. The framed pictures of Richard and her on the dresser had been turned face down. She shivered and felt the tiny hairs on her neck stand on end. Looking behind her, she saw that her clock had been moved from her bed table to the floor. Her bed looked as if someone had been lying on it. She tried to think rationally through her terror. *The door was locked. Mom had to unlock the deadbolt for us to come in. Maybe I knocked the clock off and didn't make the bed well. Did I lie down before we left for school this morning? I must have. Get a grip on yourself, El.*

Xander was beside himself with anger. *He actually took form and lay on her bed. What audacity! Is this a challenge to me?*

The guardian knew that Lucifer himself had stopped the fallen angels from procreating with human women to avoid the judgment of the Almighty from decimating his ranks. Though a few demons still had sexual relations with human women, any woman who conceived from the union was murdered or forced to have an abortion. *Lucifer knows the price for creating a halfling; surely he would not allow it.* He reconsidered. *Just how far would he go to harm Elizabeth?*

Elizabeth had nearly convinced herself that it was all just a figment of her imagination when she observed her windows. They were both wide open, though she was certain they had been closed and locked when she had last been in her room. She never opened those windows because of the air conditioning. They were actually painted shut. Nothing was missing, so theft was not a motive. It was almost as if the sole reason for the "tricks" was that someone wanted her to know that he had been there, undetected. Her sense of safety had been destroyed.

Xander pondered carefully each item which had been selected – both the manner in which those items had been disturbed and why those items were chosen. His anxiety grew as he began to see the symbolism. *The picture of her with Richard was turned down – their relationship is threatened; the clock was moved – this is a perilous time for her; the bed was used – a sexual relationship is contemplated; the sealed windows were opened – the dark ones have access to her.*

"Mom!" she called, stepping from her room to the head of the stairs. "Please come up here. I want to show you something."

She hesitated at the door, not wanting to re-enter the room without her mother. Xander stood behind her, a gentle hand on each of her shoulders.

Elizabeth, do not be afraid. I am with you always. Nothing shall harm you, as God is my witness.

Lynne frowned slightly at the unusual request. Hearing the note of fear in Elizabeth's voice, she decided that it must be important and hurried up the stairs with Niall close on her heels.

"What's wrong, El?" Lynne asked, looking at her daughter's frightened face.

"Come look. Someone's been in my room."

Lynne went into the room and looked around as Elizabeth pointed out the things that were out of place. She picked up the phone by her daughter's bed and called David.

"David, can you come home right away? It looks like we've had an intruder, though it seems that only El's room has been touched."

David and Roark immediately came home from the church. After looking through the house, he determined that nothing was missing, but David decided that he would still report the incident to the police. A policeman came to take the report and dust for prints, but there were none in the room except for those of the Bennet family and Charlotte Lucas.

Roark read the minds of Xander and Niall, a horror-stricken look on his face. *It cannot be.*

And yet it is. Xander smiled humorlessly at the policeman's report. *Of course there are no fingerprints. A dark one, or whatever this abomination is, does not leave such evidence behind.*

~~~~~~~~~

Xander was even more alert than usual, if that was possible, as Elizabeth, Lynne, and Charlotte traveled to Converse the next morning. Elizabeth and Lynne had not slept well, knowing that the sanctity of their home had been violated, and their fatigue only added to their stress. As soon as Lynne had stopped to collect Charlotte from her house, Elizabeth had filled her in on what had occurred the previous evening. Xander also spoke to Edward of the intrusion, warning him of the possible presence of a Nephilim.

Niall, Edward, and Xander were edgy, and they barely nodded to each other upon parting ways at the college as they put their entire concentration on keeping their charges safe.

Lynne and Niall headed to the tutoring lab as Elizabeth and Charlotte paused to speak to a group of students. After exchanging greetings with their friends, the two girls, followed by their guardians walked to the next building. Charlotte and Edward continued to her class, calling over her shoulder to Elizabeth, "I'll see you at lunch, El. Try not to worry yourself to death, okay? I'll text you between classes."

Elizabeth managed a small, nervous smile for her friend and walked slowly to her first class. She had always been able to discipline her mind, and she determined not to think of someone in her room, touching her things and lounging on her bed. It was Friday, and she had every reason to be excited and happy. She would focus on the good things instead.

Xander listened to her mental struggle and was pleased that she had decided to think about the work she had to do and the good things that would be happening in the next few days. She blocked her anxious thoughts and cheered herself considerably by focusing on her weekend plans and instead chose to actively practice the precepts of Philippians 4:8-9, *'Whatever is true, whatever is honorable, whatever is right, whatever is pure, whatever is lovely, whatever is of good repute, if there is any excellence and if anything is worthy of praise, let your mind dwell on these things. The things you have learned and received and heard and seen in Me, practice these things; and the God of peace shall be with you.' I'll see Richard tonight at his football game, and we're going to hang out at his house with Char and Billy afterwards. Tomorrow morning I can sleep in, and tomorrow night we're going with the youth group to hear Louie Giglio speak in Charlotte; Chris Tomlin will be singing. Josh will be there, too. It's going to be awesome! Sunday morning, we'll be at church together, and we're all going out for ice cream Sunday night after youth group.*

Xander rolled his eyes a little at her constant stream of inner chatter about Richard, but if it made her happy, he would bear it with good grace. *She will not suffer if I can do anything to prevent it. I would gladly die to save her.*

Elizabeth was distracted by her mental monologue and failed to notice a young man followed by two extremely large men hurrying from the alley between two classroom buildings and quickly walking straight towards her on the sidewalk. The youngest of the three was on his cell phone and had turned his head as a group of girls called his name and waved at him. He was waving back and smiling at the coeds when he and Elizabeth collided. She dropped her books, and they bumped foreheads as they both bent down to collect them.

That was no accident, thought Xander. *He saw her and turned his head on purpose so that he could run into her.* He looked closely at the two men behind the boy. He knew them; they were personal guards to Lucifer. *Why are they taking human form to guard him? Does he know who they are? Who is this young man?* Xander fixed his impenetrable gaze on the guards and stepped more closely to Elizabeth. They showed no fear of the guardian. Their faces were carefully expressionless. *They obviously do not want a fight. They are not threatening Elizabeth in any way. Why are they here? To guard this boy?*

"Oh, I'm sorry! I wasn't paying attention." Elizabeth began, raising her eyes to the most beautiful being she had ever seen. She immediately stopped talking and stared at him, mute. His jet black hair was just a little shaggy above his amber eyes, his full lips were sensual, his nose was straight and perfect, and his lightly stubbled jawline was strong and firm. He had the longest, blackest eyelashes she had ever seen. He was tanned, muscular, and superbly healthy; there was no physical flaw in him at all. Her eyes roamed over his face for she could not absorb so much male perfection in just one look. As they both straightened up, he seemed to keep getting taller. He looked like a bodybuilder and moved with catlike grace. She wanted to touch him to make certain that he was real.

Xander was surprised to find that he could not hear the boy's thoughts. In all of time, there had been only a few humans whose minds were closed to him. There was something strangely familiar about this young man. Then, a breeze stirred and he caught his pungent smell combined with those of the two demons. *This human was in Elizabeth's room yesterday. He must have had his guards with him. That would account for the mixture of scents.* The guardian's eyes became steely as he clamped his hands on Elizabeth's upper arms.

Gregory could not read Elizabeth's mind, but he did not need that ability to know what she was thinking; her thoughts were written clearly across her stunned face. He smiled with the full wattage of his personal charm turned solely on the innocent girl, and she caught her breath. He was even more glorious when he smiled. Just when she thought he could not possibly get any better, he spoke, and his voice caressed each word, as if he said them only for her. There was no one in the world except for the two of them.

He handed her the books he had retrieved for her. "No, it was entirely my fault. You must allow me to make this right. Let me buy you lunch today?"

She wavered; she couldn't seem to manage a coherent reply.

"Umm . . . I promised to meet my friend, Char, for lunch."

"Then we'll be a threesome. I'll take you ladies wherever you'd like to go. Do you think she would mind if I joined the two of you?"

Elizabeth, think of Richard, said Xander into her ear, a little desperately. The fact that he was willing to remind her of Richard underscored in his mind that the situation was precarious.

"Ah . . . I don't know you, do I?" Elizabeth's instincts finally kicked in. *What am I doing, ogling a total stranger? I have a boyfriend, named – what is his name?*

His name is Richard, Elizabeth. Richard.

"We haven't been properly introduced, but that's easily taken care of. I'm Gregory Wickham. We can get to know each other better over lunch – with your friend, of course."

"Uh . . . I'm El Bennet." *And I'm usually more articulate than this.* She blushed. *Richard! His name is Richard!*

"So, El, are we on for lunch?" Gregory was beyond smooth, and he had no doubt of being accepted. No human had ever turned down any request he had made. This girl would be no exception. Using his considerable magnetism, he held her stare.

Say 'no,' Elizabeth. Please walk away.

She did not seem to be able to look away; his eyes were locked on hers. She suddenly remembered to breathe.

"I guess – if it's okay with Char. I'll text her after this class. I'm going to be late if I don't hurry."

"Don't let me hold you up. I wouldn't want to make you late and get you into trouble. Just give me your cell number and I'll text you in a couple of hours to get your answer. I hope you won't disappoint me. I hate eating alone." He pouted just a little.

Oh, please! thought Xander.

"Do you have anything to write on?"

"Just put your number in the palm of my hand. You already have me in the palm of yours." He held out his hand to her, palm up, and one of the men behind Gregory handed him a pen which he gave to Elizabeth. He could have written the number as she said it, or remembered it with his perfect recall, but he wanted her to touch him.

He is very good at this. Xander groaned internally at his come-on line, but Elizabeth missed his meaning entirely.

"Who are your friends?" she asked, hesitating, looking at the unfriendly men.

"Those are my bodyguards. Dad is very protective." Gregory chuckled lightly.

"Bodyguards? Are you a prince or something?"

"Or something. You're going to be late if you don't go ahead and write your number." He extended his hand closer to her.

No, Elizabeth. Do not do it. He is leading you into a trap.

She paused for a second, ignoring that voice in her head for the first time in her life, and then wrote her cell number on his palm.

"We'll have to stay here on campus," Elizabeth said. She was not about to get into a car with those two creepy goons, and as gorgeous as Gregory might be, or maybe *because* of how gorgeous he was, she did not quite trust him either.

"That's fine. Whatever you want, El," Gregory said without missing a beat, though he would rather have taken her somewhere with more ambience and privacy.

~~~~~~~~~

Of course Charlotte agreed to meet Elizabeth and Gregory for lunch, given Elizabeth's description of the young man. There were a few male day students at Converse; however, the student body was overwhelmingly female. Having lunch with a guy at the school was a rarity, but this meal could prove to be a high point of Charlotte's year.

The girls met Gregory in the dining hall, and Charlotte was glad that Elizabeth had told her in advance about his amazing good looks; otherwise, she would have stuttered like an imbecile and embarrassed herself to no end. As it was, she barely managed to say hello and give him her name. Edward heard her mental confusion and looked at Xander with a frown. *Who is this guy? And look at his escort.*

He must be important to Lucifer. Those two belong to his guard.

Elizabeth was as stricken with his movie star looks as she had been the first time she had seen him.

I have never known Elizabeth to be so taken with how a young man looks. She is usually very sensible.

For the first time in his long existence, Xander wished to appear in human form to be seen. Elizabeth would have a reaction to him similar to the one she was having for this human boy, and he well knew it. Gregory might be more handsome than any other human male, but human women had always found his appearance to be pleasing as well.

171

Gregory already had a table set for them and pulled out their chairs in turn, insisting that they wait to be properly seated. He was charm personified. His bodyguards sat at a nearby table, watching with interest and admiring the work of their master's son. Xander and Edward stood beside their charges, arms crossed.

"I hope you don't mind, but I had some lunch brought in for us. I don't eat cafeteria food. Do you like Sonny's Brick Oven Pizza?"

"Yes!" the girls said together," laughing.

"Are you kidding? You've saved us from the dining hall for a day. Awesome!" Charlotte exclaimed. "My digestive system is very impressed!"

Before they ate, both girls bowed their heads for quick, silent prayers of thanksgiving for the food. Gregory looked at them, smiling sardonically, thinking they were thanking the wrong deity, but he remained silent. While the chief guardian could not read Gregory's mind, Xander fully understood his expression.

As they chatted through the hour, Elizabeth and Gregory found that they had much in common. Gregory was also majoring in music, they were the same age, and they were both juniors. Elizabeth had done the course work for the first two years while she was in high school, and Gregory had taken CLEP tests for all courses except for those he needed in music. As they compared schedules, they found that they would have many music classes together. In fact, they were to have a piano performance class that very afternoon, and with that newly discovered coincidence, they compared notes on the pieces they would play if their professors called on them.

"My, my. You certainly don't look fifteen," said Charlotte, suddenly feeling very old and dull at eighteen, sitting with two brilliant child prodigies.

"I had a growth spurt this past year," Gregory explained with a heart-stopping smile. "My mom complained that she could never keep enough food in the house, and I had to have new clothes every couple of months."

"Interesting," was the only reply she managed. *Whoever picked out his clothing today certainly did an outstanding job,* she thought. *That sweater hugs him like it was tailor-made for him, and I had no idea anyone could look that good in khakis. His outfit definitely did not come from Target.*

"Well, this has been a treat, but I have to go to class now or I'll be late," Elizabeth announced, standing from her seat. "Thanks, Gregory. I really enjoyed it. I'll see you at two thirty."

"Ladies, we'll have to do this again. Next time I won't run you down, El. I promise to watch where I'm going from now on."

As the three teens left the table to go their different ways, Xander was almost certain that Gregory had looked directly at him and winked, as if he could see him.

It stirred a memory of someone else with amber eyes and black hair.

Chapter 17

"Be of sober spirit, be on the alert. Your adversary, the devil, prowls about like a roaring lion, seeking someone to devour." I Peter 5:8

May, 2006

Lucifer, the Son of Perdition, sat imperiously on an immense regal throne in his counterfeit glory; Gregory was seated a little lower at his right hand. Father and son were resplendent in their black satin robes lined with crimson and detailed in gold thread. The royal guards stood in a semi-circle behind the dais in their hooded robes lending an air reminiscent of the ancient kings to the proceedings.

The Adversary had summoned the underprinces of all the dominions and their captains from across the globe to appear before him in the abandoned warehouse and had included Ryu and Tala, two high ranking demons from the southeastern portion of the United States, in the command. Speculation as to the purpose of the rare, worldwide meeting was rampant, and the evil beings buzzed like a hive of angry hornets. When the cacophony had reached a fever pitch, their sovereign lifted a hand. The gesture produced an uneasy quiet immediately.

He spoke deliberately, with great malice, biting each word. "The Bennet girl continues to waste perfectly good air, though six major attempts and countless smaller ones have been made on her life. My son has made more headway toward our goals in a few months than have the combined forces of all my servants in sixteen earth years. The last attempt, nearly eleven earth months ago, was a dismal failure resulting in the banishment of two of my most highly placed dark servants by Xander and his cohorts. They did not even survive the battle to appear before me. I was cheated of the satisfaction of dealing with them myself. It is unacceptable."

A thunderous roar of disapproval erupted from the assembly. Apollyon, the destroyer, allowed the sound to wash over him, basking in the hatred of Xander pouring from his followers. After several minutes in which the vibrations of the shouting threatened to collapse the building, he again raised his hand for silence.

"I have decided that a subtler approach is required and have summoned my entire council today to announce that my son will now be in charge of disposing of the girl. This will be his first official act as my second in command. You will obey him as if I myself were speaking. We are one from this moment forward. When you see him, you are seeing me. You will bow to him as you bow to me. Any attack on him will be viewed as an attack on me. If he requires your assistance, you will give it. Do you understand?" He paused after each short sentence. The menace in his voice brooked no opposition.

As one, the dark ranks dropped to their knees and bowed their heads before father and son, their masters.

Beelzebub, the ruler and lord of the demons, the Dark Lord, stood with hauteur.

"Ryu and Tala, approach us."

The dragon and the wolf, aptly named, rose, stepped forward, and bowed together before their monarchs.

Gregory rose to his feet slowly and lifted his chin a little higher as he addressed the two. He pronounced each word distinctly and with great deliberation. His authority rested on him like a prophetic mantle.

"I have chosen you. The positions of underprince and captain of the southeastern dominion of the United States have been vacant for too long. There is confusion among the ranks. Ryu, you are now underprince and Tala is your captain. You will assume the regular duties of your stations and control your subordinates as I handle the Bennet girl. In order to persuade her to accept me as more than just a friend, we must first end her little romance with the human boy, Richard. Nyx and Hadrian had the ear of a girl, an oppressed believer named Caroline Bingley. Because Xander and his cabal have ended their evil influence over this human female, you must give her new guides. She thirsts for revenge and is filled with envy and jealousy. Her carnal desires for the boy have made her an easy target and weakened the influence of her guardian. Your top priority is to make certain that your underlings use her backslidden condition to our advantage. I have been watching your dominion, and I suggest that you use Donovan and Akuji. Their skills could prove to be useful. They must begin immediately to establish a relationship with the girl. Understood?"

"Yes, my liege," answered Ryu.

"It shall be done," added Tala.

The Dark Lord looked proudly at his son. Gregory's plan was sound. Success was within his greedy grasp.

~~~~~~~~~

Xander smiled brightly as he followed Elizabeth and Richard throughout the house. Her adventure had begun when she found a letter in their mailbox from the church secretary addressed to her.

"What could Mrs. Goodwin be sending me?" she had asked Richard. It was Friday, and he had come over to the Bennet house after school to watch a movie and join Elizabeth and Lynne for pizza. David was in Romania leading a team from the church on a mission trip.

As Elizabeth had opened the letter, she had laughed aloud with delight, dark eyes sparkling with pleasure. It was a treasure map with a letter from the Dreaded Pirate David, handwritten on thick yellow paper that had been crumpled and torn around the edges to make it appear old. The letter told her of a treasure hidden somewhere in the house and provided a riddle leading to the hiding place of the next clue. Her father had prepared the surprise for her before he left the country and had given the missive to his secretary to mail. He had hidden clues, written on the distressed paper, all over their home, with each clue leading to the next and her promised surprise in the place indicated by the final clue. It was obvious that he had put much thought and work into the unexpected gift for his daughter to bring her happiness while he was away.

"This is awesome! My dad is the best!" she exclaimed as they unraveled the first riddle.

Richard joined her as they ran from room to room, her infectious giggles resounding throughout the house as they deciphered the rhyming clues until they found the treasure – her favorite Trolli sour gummy worms and a bag of Ghirardelli caramel-filled chocolates – under her bed.

Xander and Garnet had enjoyed the pleasant break from the near-constant demonic attacks. *It is good to see them laughing like children,* said Xander. Garnet nodded in agreement. He had been concerned about his charge's mood for quite some time.

Richard had not shown much joy in the past few weeks. He was nearing the end of his senior year of high school, and no colleges had offered him athletic scholarships. His grades had never been stellar, but his low spirits had caused him to study even less, and he would be doing well to pass all of his subjects in his final semester. Because Elizabeth's scores had always been perfect, Richard had not shared his problems with her. She had repeatedly asked him what was wrong, but he had avoided telling her. He hated the thought that she would feel sorry for him, or, worse, that she would think he was stupid. He would graduate high school, but he would lack any scholarship money, and he well knew that his parents could not afford to send him to college. Richard knew that he could work his way through school, or that he could take out student loans, but neither option was very attractive to him. Realistically, he had never decided upon a major or any job that he wanted to do; therefore, going to college seemed rather pointless. He was drifting in no particular direction.

~~~~~~~~~

Late in the next afternoon, Richard's cell phone buzzed to alert him to a text message. He flipped it open and saw a message from Caroline Bingley.

"Party at Grant's house tonite. Wanna come?"

He had no plans because Elizabeth was being featured in a piano exhibition and seminar at Converse. She had invited him to join her, but he had told her that he had a school assignment to finish. Consequently, Elizabeth and her mother had left without him early that morning. *I'm nearly finished with my project. Why not go to the party? I might actually have a good time.*

Garnet frowned from behind him and leaned forward to speak into Richard's ear. *This is a bad idea. Do not go. Caroline and her crowd will be drinking. El would not like this.*

Richard looked at himself in the mirror. "El will never know," he said to his reflection.

Quickly, he answered Caroline's text. "When?"

Her answer was immediate. *She must have been waiting with her fingers on the buttons.* Garnet did not like this new development at all. Anything associated with Caroline Bingley was sure to bring trouble to Richard.

"8. B there or b square. ;)"

"k"

Richard bit his lip for a few moments, considering what he was about to do. His handsome face stared back at him. Then he shrugged his shoulders and headed down the hall for a shower. *I can handle this.*

Garnet looked up to the heavens in exasperation before he followed Richard to the bathroom.

Richard's parents had gone to another couple's house for dinner and would be gone for a couple of hours. He wrote them a note telling them where he would be and left it on the kitchen counter.

~~~~~~~~~

Caroline was looking out of the window of Grant's living room when Richard pulled up in his black Mustang. *He is SO hot! Finally I'll get him alone without that little twit. He's been with her for about a year and a half now, and it's for sure she hasn't given him any. This will be almost too easy.*

He could hear the ear-splitting music when he turned off the car's engine.

Before Richard had time to put his hand on the front door knob, Caroline was opening the door. She took his hand and pulled him inside, smiling up at him seductively. After spending an hour deciding what to wear, she was quite satisfied with the effect of her choice. "Sexy and ready" was her aim, and she fairly screamed it. Caroline wore a black pushup bra under a cream see-through, short-waisted blouse, leaving enough buttons unbuttoned to display her ample cleavage. Jean short-shorts showed her long, tanned legs to advantage while her espadrilles lifted her heels to tighten her calf muscles. She was beautiful and trashy, and she knew how to work it.

Richard's eyes flew wide open in shock. Her message was for him, and it was unmistakable. *I came to have a good time, but not THAT good of a time. She's probably slept with a hundred guys. I could catch something really nasty from her,* he thought. *Besides, I love El,* he added belatedly, feeling a little guilty at his deception. Elizabeth thought he was spending the evening with his parents.

Garnet followed Richard into the house, and what he saw there did nothing to cheer him. Ros was the only other guardian in attendance. The room was packed with demons of all sizes and shapes, and the house reeked with the smell of evil.

"Hello, handsome! I'm so glad you came. Grant's parents are gone for the weekend, so the house is ours." Caroline entwined his fingers with those of her right hand, slowly licking her lips as she raked her eyes up and down his body in a clear invitation.

Donovan, the dark warrior, stood behind Caroline with Akuji, whose name meant "dead and awake," denoting his gift for manipulating drunken humans. The powerful demons stroked her arms and reminded her constantly of all the things she wanted to do *with* Richard and *to* him. She relished the lurid thoughts and dwelt on them. Caroline had visualized having Richard for nearly two years; she had dreamed of it almost every night. She had spent hours undressing him in her mind. It did not matter to her what she would have to do to get him into bed because tomorrow was nothing to her. After all, she did not want a relationship with him, so the consequences of a one-night stand were unimportant. Her goal, her obsession, was to possess him for one night. This was not about romance or love – it was all about having what she wanted and settling a score with Elizabeth. She had not forgotten the humiliation of being hit in the nose and walking around with a black eye for a week.

Elizabeth will pay for what she did. The little twit will hurt like she hurt me. She will be embarrassed in front of all of her friends, and she will lose Richard. Nobody treats me like that and gets away with it. I wish that she could see me with Richard. Actually, that's a great idea! I think it can be arranged.

Garnet and Ros heard her vindictive thoughts and looked at each other with disgust. Caroline's debauchery was reaching a new low.

Caroline took Richard's arm and steered him over to Grant, Lydia, and her other friends. "Grant, take care of Rich for a moment while Lydia and I go to the girls' room."

Lydia looked at her with a question in her eyes. "Come on, Lydia. We'll be right back, guys. Don't go anywhere," Caroline said to Richard in a sultry voice, kissing his cheek lightly as she released his arm. She and Lydia disappeared into the half-bath on the first floor of Grant's house.

Grant handed Richard a beer, saying, "It's about time you had some fun, Richard. I remember when we used to hang out together, before you hooked up with Saint El."

Richard accepted the beer with a small frown. "El's great. She has nothing to do with this. We're still together."

You won't be after tonight, stupid, passed through Grant's mind. *Maybe I'll give her a call in a couple of days. Being her rebound could be fun.*

Richard was on his second beer by the time Caroline and Lydia returned. He was feeling a pleasant buzz. More kids kept streaming in, and the music pounded in his head. The "Promiscuous" video was playing on MTV, and the sensual images stirred memories and longings in him. He was technically a virgin, because he had never had full intercourse, but he had done everything except that. Since he had started talking to Elizabeth, he had been chaste – they had never done more than kiss and hug – but the images of the things that he had experienced before she was his girlfriend were as fresh in his mind as if they had happened yesterday. They were burned into his brain.

Garnet heard the directions his thoughts were taking and tried to talk to him, but he realized that it was pointless. Donovan and Akuji leered at Garnet, knowing that he was powerless to stop what was happening. They had no intention of attacking Richard physically; therefore, Garnet's sword would remain sheathed.

Every time Richard finished drinking one beer, another seemed to appear miraculously in his hand, and he kept drinking until he no longer felt guilty, or stupid, or like a loser. The drunker he got, the better Caroline looked to him. In his mind, he was brilliant and witty. Everyone laughed at his jokes, he thought he was important, and in his alcohol-induced euphoria, he forgot all that he had been taught at Tabernacle and Peniel. The youth pastor had warned them that an inebriated person gives up control of himself, and that putting oneself in that situation leaves a believer open to satanic attack. He felt all-powerful, impervious to demonic influences.

At eleven, Grant went to his room and called Richard's parents to let them know their son was spending the night at his house. Mrs. Williams was not happy that Richard was with Grant, but she was glad to know that he was safe. He was, after all, old enough to make some decisions himself. She chose not to interfere, fearful that she would embarrass him in front of his friends, deciding instead that she and Jim would talk to Richard about it the next day. "Okay, Grant. Just remind him that we will expect to see him at church tomorrow morning."

"Sure thing, Mrs. Williams. I'll tell him that for you. 'Bye." Grant guffawed as he hung up the phone. *This is epic.*

By twelve, Richard staggered and his speech was slurred. He had not noticed Caroline slipping a little blue pill, which she had stolen from her dad's medicine cabinet, into one of his bottles. His need for relief increased to the point that he offered no resistance at all when she led him to a spare bedroom and lived out her fantasies.

Garnet was grieved. He and Ros turned their faces away as the demons encouraged Caroline to go farther and farther in her wickedness. Ros knew that Caroline really did not need anyone to spur her on. Certainly, he could do nothing to stop her. She had given herself over to a reprobate mind.

The two holy angels were unable to prevent what was happening; their charges were willing participants. The dark ones reveled in their victory while the two guardians were subjected to the sounds of coupling. While the demons exulted, the light beings wept as another saint fell farther away from God. Garnet and Ros threw back their heads and cried aloud in anguish at Richard's betrayal of all that was good and lovely. Garnet knew that his charge truly loved Elizabeth, and that the choices he had made this night would have dire consequences. Sin was fun for a season, but there was always a reckoning.

A few miles away at the Bennets' home, Xander's eyes flew open from his meditation as he heard their cries. Lifting his head, he saw what was telepathed by their minds. He watched over Elizabeth in the dim light, innocently sleeping and dreaming of the young man she loved so dearly, and two tears escaped from his sorrowful eyes, rolling slowly down his cheeks. He bowed his head and covered his face with his wings, aching for the pain she would feel when Richard's actions were revealed. *How could he do this to Elizabeth? Her heart will be broken. How will she bear it?*

Then he began to think more deeply about what was actually happening. He knew that Donovan and Akuji controlled Caroline, and that Gregory was always accompanied by Lucifer's guard. Xander began to put the pieces together. *Could this have been orchestrated to clear a path for Gregory with Elizabeth?* Gregory was pure evil. Xander could feel it every time he was around the teenager. He clenched his jaw tightly as he thought of the lives that had been affected by this night's work, the irreparable harm that had been done. *This is a different kind of attack altogether; the approach has changed. A more insidious intelligence has planned this.*

In his mind, Xander heard the Holy Spirit speak, *The hour grows darker. Be evermore watchful, my guardian warrior. 'Finally, be strong in the Lord, and in the strength of His might. Put on the full armor of God, that you may be able to stand firm against the schemes of the devil.' Ephesians 6:10-11.* Xander nodded his understanding to his Master . . . *and so the onslaught begins anew, my Adonai Jehovah. I will be ever diligent . . . ever watchful.*

Richard was totally oblivious to the coming storm. He did not know he had been drugged. He had actively taken part, thinking he was dreaming, and he never noticed the flashing light as Caroline posed with him, smiling lasciviously, for Lydia's camera. He was past caring about anything, and he was certainly no longer a virgin in any sense of the word.

Chapter 18

*"He who conceals his transgressions will not prosper, but he who
confesses and forsakes them will find compassion. How blessed is the man
who fears always, but he who hardens his heart will fall into calamity."*
Proverbs 28:13-14

Garnet and Ros remained by Richard's side, silent and motionless, as they
had been throughout the long night. Across the room, Donovan and Akuji
faced them boldly, excited and eager for the teenagers to wake up, ready for
the flood of emotion that would surely follow, waiting to feed off the anger,
hatred, and panic that would fill the room. They had done their jobs well,
and many lives would be mangled and ruined this day. Lucifer's son would
be pleased with them.

Across town, the Bennets, the Williamses, and Chance and Janna Bingley
were in the Sunday morning worship service at Tabernacle; everything
seemed to be normal. Xander, Niall, Roark, Raymond, Sacha, Alexis, and
Hector stood close to their charges, knowing the inevitable heartbreak that
awaited them and ready to offer as much comfort and peace as they could.
The guardians knew that the events of the previous night would cause a
tsunami of pain, and that the ripples of hurt from those actions would
continue in the lives of their charges for many years. They knew that the
effects of sin were never limited to the people who committed the

transgressions. Innocent people were always caught in the web, and the suffering was spread wider than anyone could imagine when they were first entertaining thoughts of the temptation at hand.

~~~~~~~~

Richard squinted at the sunlight streaming in through the windows of the strange bedroom. *Where am I?* He vaguely remembered a party at Grant Willoughby's house and stared at the ceiling trying to recall what had happened. The clock by the bed read 11:30, and somewhere in the fog that enveloped his brain he realized that it was Sunday morning; he had missed church. *My parents will not be happy with me. El must be wondering where I am.*

His mouth felt like cotton and tasted like old socks. He was surprised to find that he was completely naked under the sheet. His head pounded. *Now I remember why I stopped drinking.*

"Hello, Hotness," said a sultry voice from beside him.

He closed his eyes tightly. *Oh, God, please tell me that that isn't who I think it is.* A hand began to stroke his chest and make its way southward. He jumped as if he had found a rattlesnake in bed with him.

"Are you up to another round?" the voice asked.

Richard grabbed her hand and raked it from his body. He turned his head and looked into the eyes that had tracked him for nearly two years. She leered at him possessively, and he wanted to vomit.

"*Another* round?"

Caroline was beginning to get irritated. This was not the response she had expected from Richard after he had enjoyed a night of being treated to her superlative skills.

"Yes, Einstein. *Another* round! I lost track after a couple of hours."

"I don't remember the first round, and I would rather drink Drano than touch you," he told her, looking her straight in the eye.

"Oh, really? Sucks for you. You had no problem with *touching* me last night. Many times, in fact." She rolled away from him, left the bed, and began to gather her clothes.

"So, you really scored, huh? You got me drunk and did me. What did that do for you, Caroline? Before this, I put up with you and your stalking. Now I'll avoid you like the plague that you are."

She whirled to face him, conveniently ignoring the fact that she had drugged him. "You think you can treat me like this? I'm not a slut that you can use and then throw away, Richard. You will regret the things you just said," she spat at him in spite, her eyes blazing.

"That's *exactly* what you are, Caroline, and I won't regret one word of it! That's a promise."

Richard got out of the bed, turned his back to her, and began to dress as quickly as he could. All he could think of was getting home and taking a bath. He shivered with disgust at himself.

"That's what you think! You will be very sorry for the way you've talked to me! And, just to be crystal, you weren't that great. Actually you were a big disappointment."

Donovan and Akuji exulted in the destruction and followed Caroline out the door with Ros trailing dejectedly behind them.

Richard heard the door slam, and he suddenly knew that making Caroline angry probably was not the smartest thing he had ever done. Garnet thought, *Making her angry really did not change the outcome. She had already planned what she would do. However, now she will receive greater satisfaction in soiling the lives of those around her.*

~~~~~~~~~

Richard made it home just before his parents got back from church. He went straight to the bathroom, undressed, and got into the shower, not even taking the time to go to his room for clean clothes. Wrapped in a towel, he brushed his teeth and had just made it to his room when he heard a car pull up into the driveway. Richard grabbed jeans and a T-shirt from a drawer and started dressing, his mind buzzing. He knew he was in big trouble.

Garnet stayed by him, knowing that the coming catastrophe could not be stopped and that there was little he could do to help Richard. He would have to face the consequences of his actions. He would have to reap what he had sown.

As soon as Richard's dad was through the kitchen door, he headed for his son's room. Not pausing to knock, he opened the door, stepped into the room, and looked at his son. Sacha was close behind him. "We missed you at church, Richard. It must have been something very important that kept you from calling us to let us know you were okay. Your mom and I have been worried." Jim Williams spoke quietly, but firmly.

"Sorry, Dad. I overslept at Grant's house. It won't happen again."

"That's all? You overslept? If you have a problem, Richard, you know that you can talk to me."

"No, there's no problem, Dad. Everything's fine."

Jim looked unconvinced, but he turned to leave the room. He paused and looked back with his hand on the doorknob. "You should call El. She wanted to know where you were. We didn't tell her anything, but I advise you to be honest with her." He left the room, closing the door behind him.

Richard sat heavily on his bed, holding his cell phone. He pulled up El's number and hit "call."

"Hello, Richard?"

It was wonderful to hear her voice. "Hi, El. I'm sorry I missed seeing you at church this morning."

"I missed you, too. Where were you?"

"I spent the night at a friend's house and overslept." *It's the truth.*

Do not lie to her, Richard.

187

"Whose house?"

Tell the truth, Richard, Garnet said into his ear.

"A guy from school. You probably don't know him." *She doesn't know him very well.*

Richard, she is far from being an idiot. She will see through your dishonesty.

"I thought you had a project to do, and then you were going to spend time with your parents."

Garnet was exasperated. Richard was so focused on extricating himself from trouble that he was digging his hole deeper with every word.

"Those were my plans. He called when I was just finishing my project, so I went over to hang out. We were watching movies and it got late, so I stayed at his house." *This is getting worse, but if she knew the truth, she'd dump me.*

"Oh. Okay." She sounded hurt.

Xander stroked her hair gently. She sensed Richard's deception, but she wanted to believe him.

"I'll see you tonight at youth. Mom has lunch ready, and I know Janna and Chance are probably at your house. I gotta go. Maybe we can hang out and talk after church." His voice held a note of finality.

"Fine. I'll see you tonight. 'Bye." Her lower lip quivered. Something was not right, and she knew it.

"'Bye. Love you, El." *At least that is the truth.*

"You, too." Elizabeth could not say the words he really wanted to hear. She lay face down on her bed, trying to figure out what was wrong with Richard. Xander stroked her back and whispered, *It will be all right, my little one. Everything will be well. God will give you the strength to bear what you must.*

Richard pushed the button to end the call. He hated lying to her, but he knew that she would never understand what he had done. He could not wrap his mind around it himself. *What if she finds out? El is the only good thing in my life right now. I can't lose her.*

Garnet looked at him sadly. *You already have.*

Richard's mother called to him that lunch was ready; he wearily walked to the dining room and took his seat, avoiding the eyes of his parents. It was obvious to them that something was very wrong with their son, and his mother was certain that Grant and Caroline had a great deal to do with whatever was bothering him. After a few minutes of silence, Mrs. Williams excused herself from the table and went to his bathroom. She found the clothes he had worn to Grant's house and put them to her nose, sniffing. Holding his jeans and shirt between her index finger and her thumb, she went back to the dining room.

Garnet, Raymond, and Sacha stood along the walls of the small room, watching with trepidation as the drama unfolded.

"Richard, would you like to explain to your father and me why your clothes smell like a brewery?"

Richard hung his head; the food was like ashes in his mouth. *Maybe confessing to drinking will keep them from asking about anything else,* he thought.

Now you are using a portion of the truth to hide the rest of your sin. Garnet tried to reason with him.

"Grant had a party at his place last night while his parents were gone. I didn't know they wouldn't be there when I went. Everyone else was drinking, and I did it, too."

His father wore a pained expression. "I thought you had stopped drinking, Richard." Raymond stepped behind him and placed a hand on his shoulder.

"I had stopped, but I slipped up last night. It won't happen again."

"No, it won't – at least for the next month. You're grounded from everything except school and church. What did El say when you told her?"

Richard's eyes were round. "I couldn't tell her that, Dad. She wouldn't understand at all."

"You should have been honest with her. If she finds out from someone else, it will just be worse, you know," his father replied.

"I'll tell her at youth tonight. Okay?"

"That's a good decision, Richard. A relationship that isn't based on trust is worthless. Besides, she will find out from the other kids who were there."

I just hope that's all she finds out about, Richard thought morosely. *Anyhow, that would be my word against Caroline's. El will believe me.*

His mother took his clothes to the laundry room and returned to the table.

"I need to finish my project. It's due tomorrow."

His parents watched him as he trudged from the room, head down and shoulders slumped. They knew their son well, and both of them felt that there was more to the story than what he was telling them.

~~~~~~~

Xander and Garnet were ready for what was to come at Tabernacle that night.

As soon as he arrived at youth, Richard immediately went to Elizabeth, sat down beside her on the couch, and took her hand in his. They were listening to the youth pastor speak when his cell phone buzzed.

"Richard, I think you just got a text," Elizabeth said into his ear.

"No, I didn't," he answered quietly, averting his eyes. Garnet blew his breath through his nose, his lips drawn firmly together in a line. *Tell the truth!*

Richard's phone buzzed again, insistently.

"It might be your parents. You'd better look at it," Elizabeth whispered.

Reluctantly, he took the phone from his pocket. The window indicated two messages from Caroline Bingley. *Oh, no! This can't be happening!*

Elizabeth looked over at his phone. "What could Caroline want?"

Xander had a very good idea what Caroline wanted. She knew that Elizabeth and Richard would be in their youth group at this time, and she had chosen to text him when he would be with Elizabeth. From his place behind her, Xander placed his hand on Elizabeth's shoulder.

"I have no idea." His voice was monotone, emotionless.

"Aren't you going to open the messages?" Elizabeth looked at him, puzzled.

"I have no interest in anything she has to say."

That's odd. "Well, I do."

Elizabeth put her hand out for the phone. Richard did not give it to her, so she took it from his hand. They had always looked at each other's messages. She didn't understand why this time should be any different. Xander began to rub her shoulders. *Be calm, little one.*

She tapped in his password and the messages appeared.

"El, I need to talk to you first," he began to plead. But it was too late. She had read Caroline's texts.

You should have told her what really happened. You should have gone to her house after lunch, said Garnet aloud. The other guardians looked at him. He controlled his thoughts and held his peace.

"I had a great time last nite. Let's do it again soon. Caro"

That message was followed by a more explicit one.

"I luv knowing I was your 1st time. U were the best I've ever had. Don't worry. I won't tell El. This will be our little secret. Caro"

Xander heard the scream in Elizabeth's thoughts and wanted so badly to take her pain to himself. He would gladly have borne the hurt in her place.

Hot tears stung Elizabeth's eyes as she threw the phone into his lap and ran from the building. Richard went after her, barely clearing the room before he started calling her name and begging her to wait for him. Xander and Garnet hurried after them.

She stopped in the parking lot, and Richard tried to put his arms around her. She twisted away and stood with her back to him, crying.

Xander moved in front of her and embraced her. He looked at Richard, and Garnet saw the anger in his steely eyes.

"El, let me explain." *Do not touch her, Richard,* Garnet spoke loudly into Richard's mind.

"Is it true?" she choked out between sobs.

Xander wanted to wipe her tears away. Her pain was his pain; her sorrow was his sorrow. He bent and put his lips to the top of her head. *Give your heartache to me. I will bear it for you.*

"Let me tell you what really happened."

"I'm all ears, Richard. Did you sleep with Caroline?" She turned to look at him.

Garnet raised his voice, nearly shouting. *The truth, Richard! Be sure your sins will find you out. You cannot continue to hide the truth.*

Richard hesitated a moment and drew in a deep breath. "No, I didn't. She's lying. I did go to a party at Grant's house last night, and I got drunk, but I never slept with Caroline."

Xander lifted his head and vehemently questioned Garnet. *Can he not tell the difference between truth and falsehoods? He does not deserve her.*

"Why did you make up the lies about spending the night at some guy's house and oversleeping? I eat lunch with Grant nearly every day. I know him very

well, and I've talked enough about it that you should realize I know him."
She was no longer crying, but was staring at him, her eyes boring into his.

"I was afraid of losing you, El. I know how you feel about people getting drunk, and I thought you wouldn't be able to forgive me."

"Richard, it's harder to forgive being lied to than it is to understand when you make a bad decision. I'm not perfect either. I mess up all the time, and I know how easy it is to get in over your head. Just don't lie to me. We have to be able to trust each other."

Garnet tried one more time. *Richard, tell her what really happened. This could be your last chance.*

Richard gazed at her and thought about making a clean breast of the whole, ugly situation, but he just could not bring himself to say the words. *How can I tell her that I had sex with Caroline? She already believes me. Even if Caroline tells her what we did, she has no proof. El will never take her word over mine.* He decided to keep his secret. *God, I promise that I will never do anything like that again.* Relief washed over him. El knew that he had gotten drunk, and she had forgiven him.

Just then, Joshua Lucas strode up, his guardian, Skylar, in his wake. Joshua, who was like a brother to Elizabeth, could tell that she had been crying, and he glanced at Richard with eyes that were hard and cold. Xander stepped to Elizabeth's side as Joshua hugged her, turning her away from Richard. Hating what he had to do, Joshua spoke into her ear. "El, you need to come with me."

Elizabeth looked up at Joshua and smiled. "It's okay, Josh. I know what Richard did last night."

Joshua leveled a glare at Richard over Elizabeth's shoulder, pushing her hair from her tear-stained face. "You *know*? Exactly what did he tell you?"

Xander reached out to touch her arm.

"He said he went to a party at Grant's house last night and got drunk. That's why he missed church this morning." Joshua pushed her away a little to look into her face. Her eyes were so trusting that Joshua felt physically ill. Skylar felt the force of Joshua's emotions and put his hands on the boy's shoulders.

"That's all?" Joshua hissed, his eyes locking with Richard's as he looked over Elizabeth's back.

"What else is there? Richard?" Elizabeth turned to look him full in the face.

She has given you another chance. Think, Richard. You must tell her, pleaded Garnet.

He will not, the coward. He thinks that he can cover his sin. He will wait for the proof, said Xander tersely.

Richard lifted his chin in challenge to Joshua and returned his stare. "Nothing. There's nothing else." *Nothing you can prove, Josh.*

"Come with me, El." Joshua took Elizabeth's hand and pulled her with him, their guardians right behind them. They went to the main church building and into her father's office. Joshua already had the computer booted up and had logged into his Myspace.

Joshua took a deep breath and put his hands on either side of Elizabeth's face. He looked into her eyes with kindness and compassion. She began to breathe quickly, and Xander moved to her side. Skylar and Garnet stood in front of the desk, watching the tragedy unfold.

"This will be hard for you, El. I'm so sorry to have to hurt you this way, but I don't know what else to do. Sit down, and pull up your page," Joshua said gently. After she sat in her father's chair, Joshua leaned over her and placed his head beside hers. Her page came up, and Joshua spoke again. "Now pull up Caroline's page." Richard stood behind them so that he could see the monitor. He felt an impending sense of disaster. *What has that witch done now?*

As Caroline's page came up, Elizabeth could not make a sound. Then she began to gag and retch. Joshua grabbed the trashcan and shoved it under her face just in time. She leaned over it and vomited until her stomach was empty. He handed her some tissues, and she wiped her mouth. Xander's reaction was visceral. His insides twisted; he had never known such pain.

He nearly doubled over from the weight of it himself. *How can she stand it, Lord?*

Using the mouse, she clicked through the pictures. Caroline had made an album of her night's activities with Richard, entitled "There's a first time for everything!" and she had commented on every picture. There must have been sixty shots at least, and they were up close and sharp. Richard looked sleepy and drunk, but he was obviously nude and actively participating in a wide variety of sexual acts with a naked, leering Caroline. She was all over him, greatly enjoying herself, smiling and unashamed. Nothing at all was left to the imagination. It was pornographic and depraved.

Richard hung his head in shame. *I wish that I could die.*

Garnet stepped beside him and put his arms around him. *Richard, you will survive this. You will learn from this. You will be stronger. Do not despair.*

Elizabeth, unnaturally calm, went back through the pictures, reading the comments. She knew that all of their friends and many adults could see the pictures. She went to Richard's page. It was full of comments from Caroline, Grant, and Lydia extolling Richard's sexual prowess and the great time they all had getting drunk together, telling him to look on their pages for "a surprise." Lydia was proud of her role as the official photographer, and she bragged about her skill. Elizabeth then looked at Lydia's and Grant's pages; both of them had posted the entire album, too. She took a deep breath and returned to Caroline's page, sitting quietly and staring at the screen for a moment. The only signs of her agitation were the way she twisted her hands in her lap and the tightness of her jaw.

Xander felt completely useless. He had never known what it was to be incapacitated by agony. He wanted to make everything better for Elizabeth, but he realized that she would have to find her way through the pain. *She is a faithful servant, and she is strong. Dear Lord, please help me to comfort Elizabeth. Please give me the words. Help me to help her, Lord.* He had never prayed before, but it was as natural to him as breathing. He did not even realize that he was praying.

Elizabeth turned and looked up at her childhood buddy. "Thank you, Josh. You've always been a true friend to me. You need to go now. I'll be all right." Her voice was quiet, but controlled. Joshua patted her shoulder and left the room with Skylar, pulling the door closed behind him.

She turned the swivel chair to face Richard. He stood like a statue, shocked and mute. "Did you think I would never find out, Richard? Did you think it was all right to do those things as long as I didn't know?"

Xander knelt beside her. *Peace, my little one. You are the handmaiden of the Lord. Feel His comfort.*

Richard went to his knees in front of her, putting his hands on her legs. Garnet bent over him, his hand on Richard's back. "El, I'm sorry. I know I should have told you the truth. I thought I had dreamed all of it until I woke up in bed with her this morning, and I didn't know anyone was taking pictures."

"So, that's why you lied to me – first at your house over the phone, then in the youth building when you got the texts, and again outside in the parking lot? You lied to me because you thought you wouldn't get caught? You lied because you knew I wouldn't believe Caroline? You lied because you didn't know Lydia was taking pictures?" Her voice rose a little with each question. *Be calm, my little one.* She took a deep breath to settle herself. The tears began to roll unchecked down her cheeks.

"El, I lied because I didn't want to lose you. I couldn't tell you what I'd done. It made me sick." Richard began to sob with his face in her lap and his hands on either side of her thighs. His shoulders heaved, and he shook with pain. "I never meant to hurt you. I love you so much. You have to believe me. Please forgive me." He thought his heart would burst from his chest. "You can't possibly hate me as much as I hate myself."

Garnet bowed to his knees by Richard and spoke into his mind. *It will be well, Richard. God still has a plan for you.*

She gently stroked his wavy brown hair. "I could never hate you, Richard, because I love you. I believe you, and I forgive you, but I can't trust you anymore." She spoke very softly, and her heart broke a little more with every word she uttered. "I can't be with someone I can't trust to tell me the truth,

196

even when it's hard." Her voice broke on the last word, and Xander rubbed her back, willing his strength to help her.

Richard looked up at her, his beautiful tear-tracked face twisted with his despair. "You're breaking up with me? Please don't do this, El. Please don't leave me. Everything is caving in around me; you're my rock." Garnet put his arm across Richard's shoulders.

Elizabeth loved him. She loved his eyes, his face, his humor, his confidence, his childlike delight in surprises – she loved all of him, and she could not imagine her life without him. She would be alone again. Richard had filled her hours with phone calls, long talks, texts, sweet kisses, and laughter. She wanted to tell him that everything was all right. She wanted to comfort him – to hug him and tell him she would stay with him. But she could not. *I am with you, my Elizabeth. You are not alone. You will never be alone.*

She breathed deeply, held it a moment, and sighed, slowly releasing her pent-up breath, and Richard heard her answer in that sigh. "Richard, I should not be your rock. God loves you more than I ever could. He is your rock, and you should ask Him for forgiveness. Don't make this harder than it has to be. You haven't lost me – I'll always be your friend. You can call me if you need to talk, and I'll always be there for you as a friend." *Stay strong, my little one.*

"But that's all, isn't it? Just a friend – no more than that." His voice was dead, flat, hopeless. *Accept it, Richard. Be strong in the Lord and in the power of His might.*

"That's right, Richard. We won't ever be more than friends again. Don't wait for that to change, because it never will," she replied kindly, but firmly.

Somehow he stood, pulled her into his arms, and hugged her, kissing her cheek before he turned to go. Xander stood with her, his hand on her arm.

As Richard left, he saw her father coming down the hall. Richard fled in the opposite direction, ran to his car, and drove home, Garnet flying above his car. His parents were his friends on Myspace, and he wanted to tell them the truth himself, before they saw the comments splayed across his page. He also was in a hurry to block Caroline, Grant, and Lydia from ever accessing his Myspace again. He should never have trusted them in the first place. Richard laughed bitterly at the irony. *Who am I to be talking about trust?*

Chapter 19

"Now Joshua was clothed with filthy garments and standing before the angel. And he spoke and said to those who were standing before him saying, 'Remove the filthy garments from him.' Again he said to him, 'See I have taken your iniquity away from you and will clothe you with festal robes.'" Zechariah 3: 3-4

Xander stood behind Elizabeth in her father's office, holding her tenderly, his strong arms around her shoulders. She was a porcelain sculpture, pale and motionless.

As David approached his office door, he saw Richard running down the hall away from him, and he knew that something terrible had happened. He and Roark hurried into his office where his younger daughter, a large piece of his heart, stood facing the door with an empty, forlorn expression on her beloved face. Seeing her father's concern displayed in his eyes broke her calm, and raising her hands to her face, she began to weep, pouring out all the pent-up emotions she had felt in the past hour. Her father quickly crossed the room and hugged her fiercely to him as she buried her face in his chest. Xander stepped to Elizabeth's side, still stroking her arm and whispering words of peace. *You are beloved. You do not have to go through this alone, Elizabeth. Accept the peace of your Heavenly Father. He loves you more than any human ever could. I am with you. I will always be with you.*

David Bennet was well known to be a long-suffering, even-tempered man; he had rarely been truly angry in his lifetime. However, upon seeing his baby girl suffering and heartbroken, his rage flashed red hot. *I should have protected her; I should have been able to do something to prevent this. What has Richard done to her?*

Roark spoke into his mind. *Pray for strength, David. Pray for peace. You must be the father she needs now. You must let go of your anger and trust in God's promises. He will never give you more than you can bear. When you are weak, He is strong. All things work together for the good of them who love Him.*

Lynne, entering David's office to meet them for the ride home, was shocked at the scene before her. Elizabeth was sobbing hysterically as David crushed her to his chest. Lynne, followed by Niall, approached her husband and daughter, and she was stunned at his expression – he was livid. She had never seen her husband so angered, and it unnerved her; she was speechless.

Tentatively, Lynne moved beside the couple and put her arms around both of them. Niall touched her back, saying, *Pray for them.*

Lynne wondered, *What in the world could have happened to upset El this much and to make David so angry? Dear Father, please help my husband to calm down. Please help El get through whatever has made her cry like this. Please give me the words to say and the strength to do the right thing. Father, my loved ones are hurting, and I don't know what to do. I don't know what to pray for right now. Give me the words. Interpret my heart.* The tears ran down her face as her mother's heart ached for her daughter and her husband.

After a few minutes during which Lynne continued to pray, Elizabeth's cries began to quiet, and David relaxed his grip on her, though he still held her in his arms.

"Sweetheart, what's wrong? Let us help you," Lynne whispered to Elizabeth.

Elizabeth turned her face toward her mother. In a broken voice, she choked out the words, "I wish I had a heart that had never loved him."

What has Richard done? Lynne noticed that the computer on her husband's desk was running. She stepped to it and ran the mouse over the pad to re-activate the monitor. Caroline's Myspace page came up, and she said in a low, strangled voice, "No!" She now knew the source of her daughter's tears. *How could he have done that to El? Dear Lord, how could he have done that?*

David heard his wife's voice and turned toward her. He saw the pictures, and he wanted to smash the computer. He wanted to rip it from the wall. He wanted to beat Richard to a pulp. Roark spoke to him again, *None of that would help Elizabeth. None of that would change anything, and you would hate yourself if you did those things. Give this to God. Richard needs you, David. You're his pastor, too. He and his parents are dealing with this now, and they need their pastor.*

David released Elizabeth and moved to his desk while Lynne stepped aside so that David could see the screen. As he clicked through the images and read the comments, Xander and Lynne held a quieted Elizabeth. Finally, David clicked out of Myspace, shut down the computer, and faced his wife and daughter. He was himself again. "Let's pray about this together."

The little family joined hands as David led them in prayer, the three guardians grouped around them, heads bowed, with their large, angelic hands covering the clasped human hands of their charges.

After they had finished praying, David picked up his phone and called Jim Williams.

~~~~~~~~

Richard raced into his house, fully expecting to delete the comments from his page before his parents could see them. He intended to tell them what had happened, but the idea of his mother and father reading what was on his page and asking to see the graphic images made him physically ill. *I will never feel clean again. I wish that I could bleach my brain and wash away the memories. I hate myself.*

Richard's parents were sitting in the den watching television, Raymond and Sacha standing by them, when he burst into the room, Garnet nearly running behind him. Taking in their surprised faces, Richard slowed down and tried to walk past them. He was nearly to his room when he heard his father's voice calling him. *I should have known better. They know me too well.*

"Richard? What's wrong, son? Come back and talk to us."

Richard groaned. He knew that they would still love him, but he could not stand to hurt them again. He hated for them to know that he had lied to them before he had left for church. *They will be so disappointed in me.*

He trudged back into the den to face them. "I have to tell you something. It's really bad."

His mother's face was so trusting, so loving, that he had to look away. He could not look her in the eyes and rip her heart out.

Richard began to cry, and his sobs wracked his body. "I'm so sorry. I'm sorry for everything." Garnet put his hand on Richard's back. *Tell them, Richard. They will help you.*

Jim stood and pulled his son to him. "Just tell us what you've done, Richard. We'll get through this together."

His mother rose and put her hand on his back. "We'll always be here for you, son."

"Come to my room with me," he said through his tears.

The Williams family and their guardians gathered in Richard's room; he sat down heavily in the chair at his desk and booted up his computer. When Richard pulled up Caroline's Myspace page, his mother nearly fainted. She held her hands tightly to her mouth to stop herself from crying aloud. Raymond stroked her arm as she prayed, *That wicked, wicked girl! She finally trapped him. Oh, why didn't I tell him to come home last night? Why didn't I go and get him? Dear God, forgive me for failing my son. Forgive him for being weak. Please take this hatred for Caroline out of my heart. Lord, please help my family.*

Jim Williams, seeing his wife's distress, folded her in his arms and kissed her hair. The tears ran down his face, and he struggled to make no sound.

Sacha touched his mind with his thoughts. *Jim, Richard needs your forgiveness. He needs your guidance.*

After some minutes had passed, Jim released his wife, and they both turned to their son. He had put his head on his desk and was sobbing into his folded arms, feeling fully the weight of his actions.

"Richard, let's talk about this. Tell us what happened." Jim's voice was soft and kind.

He took Richard's hand and led him to the bed. Richard sat on the edge with a parent on either side of him as he told them everything that had happened. The story flowed from him in a flood of words and tears. When he was finished, Jim knelt in front of his son and his wife with their guardians hovering over them, and the small family held hands as Jim talked to God. He poured out his heart to his Father, and God spoke healing to his family. Following his father's example, Richard prayed and asked God to forgive him. He called his sins by name and admitted what he had done. Delores finished the prayers, quoting and claiming I John 1:9, "If we confess our sins, He is faithful and righteous to forgive us our sins and to cleanse us from all unrighteousness."

The Williams family had just finished praying when the phone rang. It was David. After they talked for a few minutes, Jim hung up and turned to his wife and son. "The pastor's on his way over here. We have some things to discuss."

Richard's eyes widened. "No, Dad. Please don't make me face him. He must despise me for what I've done and for how I've hurt, El. Please, Dad," Richard begged.

"Richard, I think you have it wrong. The pastor doesn't hate you. He wants to help you. You're going to have to man up to what you've done. There are consequences to our actions, and you have to accept your part in all of this. Pastor David is going to counsel all of us. I think it's a mark of his love for us, and for you, Richard. This is something he wants to do, and I don't think he's asking too much of us."

Within a few minutes, David was knocking on their door. Roark, grim-faced, was by his side.

By the time David had finished talking with Richard and his parents, Jim and Delores had agreed on a course of action. Jim called Mrs. Miles, the principal of Peniel Christian Academy. She asked that Jim, Delores, and Richard meet her at the school in an hour. They agreed, and she proceeded to call each member of the school board to come to the school for a special meeting.

~~~~~~~

"Do not be deceived, God is not mocked; for whatever a man sows, this he will also reap." Galatians 6:7

During third period the next day at Peniel, the intercom squawked calling Caroline, Grant, and Lydia to the office. When they arrived, the office secretary directed them to the chapel. They were not worried at all. What they had done was off campus. It wasn't anyone's business but theirs. All three of the teens were absolutely certain that their parents would take up for them against the school administration. After all, they always had before. Besides that, they were seniors, and they would graduate in a few weeks. Nobody could stop that.

As they opened the doors to the chapel, it became obvious why the meeting had not been held in the principal's office. There was not room enough in there to hold all the people present in the meeting. Their parents were all there, as well as Mrs. Miles, the school board members, Jim and Delores Williams, and Richard. The guardians stood somberly near their charges. They knew that they were about to witness Psalm 7:14-18 in action. "Behold, he travails with wickedness, and he conceives mischief, and brings forth falsehood. He has dug a pit and hollowed it out, and has fallen into the hole which he made. His mischief will return upon his own head, and his violence will descend upon his own pate."

Mrs. Miles stood at the front of the middle row of pews at a podium, her guardian Alik beside her. She had a computer behind her on a table, already booted up and opened to Richard's Myspace page. His parents and Mrs. Miles had asked him to wait a day to take down the comments and block his erstwhile friends, and though it meant exposing himself and his sin to this entire group of people, he had agreed to their request. He quickly navigated from his page to Caroline's page, then to Lydia's, and finally to Grant's.

Caroline stood, open-mouthed, before her parents, and all those present could see that they looked seriously displeased. Ros, on the other hand, wore a look that was very like hope. *This might be exactly what she needs to bring her back to God.* Caroline had finally overstepped her parents' limits for her. Even they were shocked at the pictures, and they were in no mood to defend her behavior.

In the meeting that had taken place earlier that morning with the school board and Mrs. Miles, Donald Bingley had tried everything in his arsenal to prevent his daughter from having to receive the full consequences of her actions. He had threatened the school with a lawsuit and called his lawyer, only to be told that because he had no chance of winning, it would be better not to expose Caroline further by showing the pictures of her in open court. He was also told that Richard could possibly countersue him and his family for invading his privacy by taking and publishing pictures of him without his consent; he could possibly win a huge judgment. Had the attorney known that Caroline had drugged Richard, he would have further warned Donald to avoid a rape charge at all costs, but Caroline had kept that secret well hidden. Frustrated, Donald had offered the school fifty thousand dollars to make the problem go away. There had never been any time in his adult life that neither his power nor his money could solve his difficulties, but the school board would not be moved. Donald Bingley was angry, and as no other target was available, his daughter would have to answer for what she had done.

Grant's parents were no happier with him. He had used their home for the party, and for Caroline's scheme to set up Richard. He had called Delores Williams and deceived her so that Richard's parents would not look for him. Their country club circle would all know of their son's behavior; their own children had probably been at the party as well. It was likely that the Willoughbys would lose some of their friends in the aftermath of this episode. Grant's use of their home for a party with underage drinking and sexual activity could open them up to legal difficulties. The Willoughbys had known there would be trouble as soon as they had arrived home Sunday night. The house had been strewn with bottles, cans, and filth, and even their own bed had been used. While they sat in the degrading meeting, a professional cleaning crew was hard at work in their home, and they had seen from Donald Bingley's antics that there was no buying or threatening their way out of the problem.

Lydia's parents would not even look at her. Her comments on Richard's page, along with her pride in taking the disgusting pictures and posting them on her wall, made them ashamed of her. Though they were not church people, they had tried to rear her with moral standards and had placed her at Peniel at great personal sacrifice. The Hendersons, unlike the Bingleys and the Willoughbys, were not wealthy people. Lydia's mother and father both worked extra hours to pay her tuition, and she had greatly disappointed them.

Mrs. Miles cleared her throat. "Caroline, Grant, Lydia, do you have anything to say for yourselves?"

Caroline spoke quickly. "Mrs. Miles, I really don't see how this is any of your business. It happened on a weekend off this campus." Ros looked expectantly toward Mrs. Miles. He had confidence in her.

Her father spoke brusquely, "Caroline, shut up and sit down."

"But, Daddy!" she whined.

"I said, shut your mouth, sit down, and listen for once. You aren't getting out of this, young lady. If my money was not enough, what makes you think that acting like a spoiled brat will work?"

Ros actually smiled. *Finally! There may be a chance for her yet.*

The three teens all sat, wondering what the school could possibly do to them. Detention? That was a joke.

Mrs. Miles spoke in a moderated tone. "Caroline has raised a legitimate question. Richard, would you please go back to Caroline's page?" Richard clicked on her name from his page. Her page came up.

"Caroline, do you see the school name that's listed in your information?"

"Yes. It says 'Peniel Christian Academy.' What's the problem?"

"The problem, Caroline, is that you've linked the name of this school with your lewd, illegal activities and pictures. As distasteful as it has been for all of us present at this meeting, we have looked at your pictures and read the comments. If you will refer to your student handbook, you will find that using the name of this school in any way that reflects badly on its reputation before this community is grounds for immediate expulsion. Myspace has been named specifically in this section. Here is a handbook," Mrs. Miles said, handing her a book opened to the correct page with the pertinent text highlighted. "Read it for yourself. Everyone else in this meeting has already read it. Remember that you signed the back page of the handbook, as did your parents, at the beginning of the year, promising to abide by the rules stated in the book. Here are the signed pages for you, Grant, and Lydia. In the state of South Carolina, this is a legally binding contract." The principal held up the three pages as she spoke. "You are all equally guilty. The same things are on all of your pages.

"I certainly take no pleasure in these proceedings. I have loved all three of you for many years, and it breaks my heart to have to do this, but you are seniors – leaders – in this school. If there is no punishment for your behavior, or if the consequences are not severe enough, it will encourage others to follow your example. We must think of what is best for everyone involved. The testimony of the school is at stake. Allowing you to graduate after what you've done would severely hamper our ability to minister in this town. People place their children with us to avoid the type of influence that you are exhibiting. I hope that you will allow God to use this in your lives to bring you closer to Him. I will be praying for you and your families." Mrs. Miles spoke kindly but firmly.

"But, we're supposed to graduate in a few weeks! We've been coming here since kindergarten! You can't do this!" cried Lydia.

"The board has already voted, Lydia. This is not a negotiation. We are simply letting you know the decision that has been reached. This is a private school; you have no other agency to which you can appeal. Your parents are in agreement with the decision of the board. All three of you should be expelled; however, we have offered your parents the opportunity to withdraw you so that an expulsion will not be on your records. All of your parents have accepted the offer. While you have been in here, your teachers have packed up your belongings and sent them to the office."

"But how are we supposed to finish school and go to college?" Grant asked.

"We are willing to help your parents homeschool you for the last few weeks of your courses by providing copies of the teachers' lesson plans and your tests and quizzes should your parents choose to join a homeschool association, but you will not receive a diploma with the name of this school on it. Your diploma would be issued by the homeschool association, if you choose to go that route. We will submit a transcript to the college of your choice with your grades through the first semester of your senior year. For the second semester, your transcript will simply say, "Withdrawn." Some colleges will accept that. Some may require that you pass the GED exam. Your parents will need to contact the college of your choice and talk to the admissions department. I recommend the local junior college for your first two years. They will be more likely to work with you. This meeting is adjourned."

"But, Mrs. Miles!" began Caroline, wailing.

Mr. Bingley stood quickly to his feet. "Caroline, shut up for once in your life. Wait for us in the car. We'll pick up your things," her father said sharply, his irritation evident.

"I'll just take my car," she sniffed.

"What car? You don't have a car. I have a car. I paid for it, and my name is on the title. Actually, you don't own anything, because you've never worked a day in your life. That's about to change, Caroline. Life as you knew it is over. Tell your *friends* 'goodbye' here and now. You won't be seeing them again. While you're at it, hand me your cell phone. You won't need it, because you won't be talking to anyone for a long while. Now go!" Caroline's father was a large, tall man, and he was very angry. She wisely backed away and joined her family as they began to walk out.

"Excuse me, Mr. Bingley," Richard said.

"Yes, Richard?" said the older man, stopping in the aisle and turning to face the teen. Everyone in the chapel looked toward Richard.

"I have a request before you all leave."

"We will be happy to do whatever we can for you, Richard. What do you want?" asked Mr. Bingley, thinking of his lawyer's advice and his family's connections. He had not forgotten that Chance was married to Janna, the sister of Richard's girlfriend, and that it would be Caroline's fault if Elizabeth broke up with the boy. Donald Bingley did not yet know how the Bennets would view his family after this debacle, but he wanted to do whatever was possible to salvage the acquaintance. He also realized that there was still a very real possibility that the Williamses would file a lawsuit against his family. After all, that is what he would do if the situation were reversed.

Alik, Garnet, and the other guardians were disgusted with his self-serving thoughts. Ros said, *It has ever been so, since the first moment I have been with Caroline's family.*

"I want these albums and comments to be deleted right now, here, before anyone leaves," said Richard evenly, looking at Caroline, Lydia, and Grant by turn. Garnet stood staunchly by his charge.

"Caroline will be *very* happy to do that, won't you, Caroline?" her father said, looking at her pointedly. *If the evidence is deleted, there will be less chance of the Williams family winning in court.*

Richard logged out and stood beside the computer.

Caroline scowled, but made her way back up the aisle. She logged in to Myspace and pulled up her profile. With a perfectly manicured nail, she hit the delete button for the album and it disappeared. Then she removed each comment on her page and logged out. She turned up her nose at Richard and rejoined her parents. Her secret was safe.

"Grant, Lydia?" Richard asked.

Their parents glared at them, and they also went to the computer, logged in, and removed the albums and comments from their pages. Grant looked up at Richard. "I'm sorry, man. That was really a stupid thing to do." Lydia nodded her agreement. Hanging their heads, they followed their parents out of the chapel.

Richard joined his parents, their three protectors shadowing them.

Anne Bingley, Caroline's mother, had wept silently through the proceedings, but she now approached the Williams family. "I'm very sorry for all of the trouble Caroline has caused you, Richard."

Richard squared his shoulders. "I should have said 'no' in the first place. If I hadn't gone to the party, I wouldn't have gotten into trouble. Sure, Caroline set me up, but she couldn't have done it without my cooperation." Garnet smiled. *He has learned much from this. It came at great cost, but it will stand him in good stead throughout his life.*

"That's very generous of you, Richard. What will you do now?" asked Mrs. Bingley.

"I plan to enter the military as soon as I can after graduation. My parents are already helping me with the paperwork. I want to be a Marine, like my father," Richard said, looking at his dad with pride. His father put his arm around Richard's shoulders and smiled a little sadly.

"Richard will be fine. Thanks for your concern, Mrs. Bingley. He has to get back to school now, but I'm sure we'll see you sometime when Chance and Janna are in town. I hope everything works out well for you."

Mrs. Williams and Raymond returned to her classroom while Richard and his dad thanked Mrs. Miles and the school board members for their time. Afterward, father and son walked out together, Sacha and Garnet trailing silently behind them.

Chapter 20

"And no wonder, for even Satan disguises himself as an angel of light." II Corinthians 11:14

September, 2006

The Dark Lord and his son descended slowly into the warehouse, their guards close on their heels. As they settled to the floor, their black satin capes gently swirled around their feet with a muted swishing sound. Father and son walked side-by-side, boots clicking on the wooden floor. Upon reaching the dais, they stepped up and seated themselves, Gregory at the right hand of his father. On a third throne to his left, Lucifer placed a gargantuan rattlesnake which immediately coiled tightly, its tail twitching malevolently and its head raised to view the proceedings with cold, unnaturally intelligent eyes. The serpent hissed and turned its gaze to Lucifer who stroked the snake with his long, beautifully tapered fingers.

The assembled demons each knelt silently on one knee, heads bowed inconspicuously, peeking at the animal with trepidation from under their hoods. This was the first time that Dark Spirit had attended a meeting; it was significant.

Lucifer regally surveyed his underprinces and captains; then he nodded to the Dark Son. Gregory scanned the room unhurriedly and, finding those he sought, spoke in a voice that was rich and melodic.

"Ryu, Tala, step forward," he called.

The hulking demons obeyed instantly, striding quickly to the front of the crowded space and kneeling before the thrones.

"Remove your hoods."

This was an unusual command, but the underprince and his captain showed no surprise. With rapid movements, they raised their hands and pushed their hoods back.

"Look at me."

The dragon, his fiery red hair flowing down his back, and the wolf, with a closely-shorn head of dark-brown waves, looked up expectantly into Gregory's beautiful face. He was smiling; they were stunned.

"You have served me well. The boy, Richard, is no longer an impediment to our plans. My friendship with the girl, Elizabeth, progresses. I seek to ruin her, as we did the human boy. Killing her at this time is unnecessary. It will be more effective to destroy her reputation; I can always dispose of her later. As of this moment, all attacks on Elizabeth and her family will cease until further notice."

A murmur of surprise rippled through the ranks.

"Silence! I will not be questioned or doubted." Gregory's eyes flashed crimson. His smile evaporated. He spoke harshly, in a commanding tone.

"We will never get past Xander by continuing a frontal assault on Elizabeth. Xander expects that, and he is prepared for it. He is now wearing the armor of a warrior." His voice became softer, modulated almost as if he was talking to imbeciles.

"The time has not yet come. Let us lull Xander into complacency. When his guard is down, when he no longer expects it, I will take her. If she is willing, he cannot interfere, and I assure you that I will not have to force her into anything. Even Xander cannot protect a human against her own free will. Did you learn nothing from the success of my plan with Richard and Caroline?"

Gregory waited for his words to take effect. "Every day I grow more powerful. With each earth year that passes, I am stronger. I have mastered the dark arts. In two earth years, even the great Xander will not be able to defeat me," he said with absolute confidence.

Lucifer stood, raising his son with him and holding their joined hands in the air. The poisonous snake slithered up his other arm and draped himself across their shoulders.

"This is my only begotten son. Hear him!"

A roar began in the ranks and swelled until it shook the building. Applause and cheers erupted as the dark ones stood and stomped their feet in rhythm.

The unholy trinity basked in the adulation of their servants, and Lucifer's pride grew to proportions unseen since the rebellion in heaven. The thick darkness swelled and grew, expanding exponentially until it sucked in the very moonlight that surrounded the building. Evil rolled from the building in waves and crept silently through the streets, its stench permeating the area, blotting out the moon and the stars. All was pitch black within and without.

In heaven, the Creator of All heard the words of the abomination called Gregory and read the familiar thoughts in the mind of Lucifer. It would soon be time to put more of His own plan into action.

~~~~~~~~~

Xander and Edward walked beside Elizabeth and Charlotte as they headed toward the dining hall at Converse. It was the first day of the fall semester, and Gregory and Elizabeth had seen each other in a class that morning. He had invited her and Charlotte to meet him for lunch, and he had promised them a special treat. As they hurried along the sidewalk, they encountered a group of students from India who were visiting the campus. One of the girls tapped Elizabeth's shoulder and asked her directions. Elizabeth stopped to answer her, and they exchanged a few pleasantries before Elizabeth turned back to Charlotte so that they could continue to the dining hall.

"Hold up," said Charlotte.

"What?"

"When did you learn to understand Hindi?" asked Charlotte with great curiosity. She had done quite a bit of research on the history of India in the previous semester and recognized the major language of the country, though she could not speak it.

"What are you babbling about, Char?" Elizabeth looked at her friend with a quizzical expression. "I don't speak Hindi. You know that I speak Spanish, Portuguese, and French rather well, but no other languages except for English."

"I'm not crazy, El. That girl spoke to you in Hindi, you understood her and answered in English, and somehow the girl knew what you were saying and continued the conversation. She kept speaking Hindi, and you kept replying." Charlotte was very emphatic about what she had witnessed.

"Char, you seriously need a long rest or something." Elizabeth laughed.

"Wait here," Charlotte said as she turned back to the foreign students.

"Do you speak English?" Charlotte asked the girl who had been talking with Elizabeth.

The girl looked at Charlotte, puzzled, then glanced at Elizabeth, who shrugged and repeated Charlotte's question.

The Indian girl smiled and shook her head. She replied to Elizabeth, "It is good that you speak my language."

Now thoroughly confused, Elizabeth said a word of farewell to the girl as she and Charlotte walked away.

"Well?" queried Charlotte, eyebrows raised.

"Well, what?" returned Elizabeth.

"What is going on, Elizabeth?"

"I haven't got a clue, Char. If I knew, I would certainly tell you." Exasperated, Elizabeth tugged on the straps of her backpack and kept walking. Charlotte sighed and caught up with her. She determined that she would solve the mystery, with or without Elizabeth's help.

Edward gave Xander a questioning look, and Xander replied aloud, *I think that she has the gift of tongues as it was given on the Day of Pentecost. It appears that she understands all languages, and everyone hears her in his own tongue. She does not know this as of yet.*

Edward was astonished. *Extraordinary.*

Nearly everything about Elizabeth is beyond the norm. She is exceptionally gifted in many ways. Xander's statement was matter-of-fact. Edward had seen Elizabeth only when she was with Charlotte. He knew that she was a musical genius and extremely intelligent, but he had not observed her other gifts. He did not realize the depth of her intellect or spirituality.

The group arrived at the dining hall to find a table laid with china and stemware. Gregory was elegant as usual, dressed immaculately in black slacks, a light blue button-down shirt, and a dark blue V-necked sleeveless pullover sweater, showing his athletic build to advantage. He smiled lazily at Charlotte and Elizabeth and stood to receive them as they entered the room. He was every inch the perfect gentleman.

Both girls exclaimed over the lavish spread.

"How did you know that Wasabi is my favorite restaurant?" asked Elizabeth with delight.

"Oh, I have my ways," he answered with a wink at her. "I make it my business to know what you like, El. My spies are everywhere." He gave her a crooked smile and held her chair for her as she sat at the table.

Who are these 'spies' that he commands? Do demons do his bidding in addition to guarding him? Xander looked at Gregory, trying to read his oddly silent mind. *Why is his mind closed to me?*

"Char, I hope you like Japanese as well?"

"Love it!" returned Charlotte, smiling as he pulled out her chair.

Gregory's guards no longer appeared in human form.

Xander thought, *If he knows the demons are there, he probably wants to be less conspicuous and to lull Elizabeth into believing that they are alone. He may have sensed that the guards made her uncomfortable. What is his plan?*

Xander and Edward, however, were very much aware of the two fiends standing behind Gregory, looking at them with disdain, chins raised in hauteur. *In whatever form, the foul odor is still the same,* thought Xander. He and Edward assumed protective positions behind their charges, faces set in impassive stares. Xander waited for any sign of a challenge; he would welcome it. *In the immortal words of Clint Eastwood, 'Go ahead. Make my day.'* His thought was private, and Edward did not hear it, though Niall picked up on it from his place by Lynne in the tutoring lab. He shook his head and smiled.

Both girls bowed their heads for silent prayers of thanks; Gregory permitted himself a small frown which immediately vanished as they looked up.

"What's the occasion, Gregory? This is bit extravagant for a school lunch," said Elizabeth as she made her selections.

"We never celebrated our birthdays this past summer. I thought we deserved a little party. Don't you?" Gregory asked, taking a seat across from the girls. Sitting between them would have meant turning his back to Charlotte in order to talk to Elizabeth. Gregory was far too intelligent to make such an error.

Everything that he does has an ulterior motive, said Xander to Edward.

"Ah, yes! Sweet sixteen." Elizabeth laughed.

"And never been kissed?" queried Gregory. His amber eyes held hers until she looked back down at her plate.

"Maybe a few times, but not in a while." Elizabeth was somber, pain evident in her voice.

"Anytime you wish to remedy that situation, just let me know," Gregory said playfully.

Over my dead body, thought Xander, clenching his fists. He placed his hands on Elizabeth's shoulders.

Elizabeth glanced at Charlotte with a silent plea.

"Gregory, you haven't visited us at Tabernacle yet. We have a terrific Life Group for people in college. It's only about a half hour's drive from here," Charlotte interjected quickly.

"Ah, yes. Your church. I'm of a different denomination, I think. My place of worship is in Charlotte, and I often return there for meetings."

"Well, just know that you're always welcome," continued Charlotte.

But you would have to leave your pets outside, added Xander, looking at the dark ones behind Gregory.

"I'm positive that I would be." Gregory's eyes glittered, and he almost succeeded in keeping the irony out of his voice.

His guards smirked and snorted, their amusement obvious.

"Where are your bodyguards, Gregory? I thought you didn't go anywhere without them?" Charlotte asked.

"Haven't you noticed? I'm a big boy now," Gregory replied with a wicked glint in his eyes. "My father has agreed that I'm perfectly capable of defending myself in this situation. I believe that I could handle both of you girls if you were to attack me."

So does he know that the demons are there, or not? Xander looked at the evil ones. *Did he know that that they were demons when they were in human form?*

With practiced ease, Gregory changed the direction of the conversation to one which suited his tastes.

"El, are you ready for Saturday?" he asked.

Oh, yes. Saturday. I will certainly be ready for whatever you might have in mind. Xander crossed his arms over his chest.

Elizabeth and he would be presenting a joint concert in the Twichell Auditorium to open the performance schedule for the semester. Having the two most exceptional young musicians in the country give a concert together was a stroke of genius. The event was highly anticipated and had been sold out for months. Gregory and Elizabeth had discussed the program by phone at the beginning of August and had been practicing separately since that time. They had agreed on a practice schedule, to begin rehearsals after classes ended for the day and to continue to meet daily until the concert. The two nine-foot Steinway grand pianos were already situated in Twichell, and the times for their rehearsals were blocked out through the music department. Though there would be a few solo numbers, most of the selections were duets, including Rachmaninoff's Piano Concerto No. 2 to end the program. They were using the two piano arrangement with Gregory playing the symphonic part.

"Yes, I think so, though I'm looking forward to our rehearsals. I'm very curious about your solos. What have you selected?"

"You like surprises don't you? I wouldn't want to spoil it for you by telling." Gregory smiled impishly.

"Now I *am* curious. Not even a hint?" Elizabeth asked teasingly.

"Not even the smallest clue," he replied smugly.

"Aren't you a devil! You're such a tease, Gregory." Elizabeth laughed aloud.

Gregory smiled sardonically. "You have no idea, my innocent little angel."

Xander looked at him sharply. For the second time, he had the oddest feeling that Gregory could see him. *He is far too smooth for a sixteen-year-old boy. His choice of words was no accident.*

Charlotte was following the exchange with interest, her brows knitted together. *There is an undercurrent of something here. I can't quite put my finger on it, but there is definitely more to what he's saying than the obvious meaning of the words. What game is Gregory playing?*

What game indeed! agreed Xander.

Elizabeth was just getting over the heartbreak with Richard. She had prayed that God would take away her love for him, and He had answered her prayer, but her wound was still healing. She had confided in Charlotte throughout the ordeal, and Charlotte was fiercely defensive of her friend. She liked Gregory, but she would not allow him to hurt Elizabeth if she could help it.

Charlotte is a wonderful young woman, Xander said to Edward, who replied, *She is, my chief.*

"El, it's about time for us to go. Our next class is about to begin, and we don't want to be late on the first day," said Charlotte, glancing at her friend. Edward and Xander read her mind. *There's something about him I don't like. He creeps me out.*

She has excellent instincts, said Xander. Edward nodded his agreement.

Elizabeth knew what the look meant; she and Charlotte had been best friends for nearly two years now. She would think about the "why" later. Right now, Charlotte was signaling her that she was ready to leave, and Elizabeth responded to her cue. Both girls pushed back their chairs and stood.

"Wow! Where has the time gone? Thanks so much for lunch, Gregory. It was spectacular. I'll see you at rehearsal this afternoon?" Elizabeth smiled at him with a question in her eyes.

"I'll be the one at the piano waiting for you." Gregory grinned in response.

"Thanks, Gregory. I'll see you later," said Charlotte.

"I'll be looking forward to it, Char," Gregory said as he watched her leave with Elizabeth.

Xander and Edward walked closely behind their charges.

Gregory's smile had been replaced with a speculative expression. He sat for a moment, thinking, and then looked around. The dining hall was empty, and he and his guards were alone. Gregory focused on the leftover food and dishes on the table for a second. When he looked away, the table was completely cleared. He stood to his full height, now well over six and a half feet, quickly assumed demonic form, and flew through the roof of the building. Gregory wanted to clear his mind with the freedom and speed of flight. He and his guards headed in the opposite direction of the campus to avoid detection by Xander. Gregory had at least an hour to kill before his next class followed by his practice session with Elizabeth. He could scout the entire southeastern dominion in that amount of time.

~~~~~~~~

Xander stood behind Elizabeth as she performed Debussy's "*Reflets dans l'eau* (Reflections in the Water)" to open the concert. Her music washed over him like a gentle wave; it was as soothing to him as the sweet balm of Gilead. She was dressed in a flowing dress of white chiffon, off one shoulder, cut in a classic Greek style. Her dark hair fell in curls to her shoulders from a knot caught up in the back with pearls which were threaded through the cascade. Her brilliance and beauty nearly distracted him, but thousands of years of discipline stood him in good stead. Thinking of Gregory and those that accompanied him soon focused him upon his duties. His guards had stationed themselves in the wings and were visible to Xander at all times.

As the evening progressed, the pianists played original duets as well as those arranged for two pianos, interspersed with several solo pieces. When the curtains opened after the intermission, the audience, as well as Elizabeth, was surprised to see a portion of the stage curtained off. A microphone on a stand was set just offstage in the wing. Gregory strode onto the stage for a solo, magnificent in his Armani black tail tuxedo, with a Stradivarius in his hand. A stagehand moved the microphone to the center of the stage, and Gregory stepped up to speak.

"Good evening. I hope you have enjoyed yourselves. As you can see by the program, I am supposed to be playing Beethoven's Sonata No. 23, more commonly known as the 'Appassionata.' However, before I perform that tempestuous piece for your pleasure, I have planned a small diversion, a little surprise for you. Are you willing to be amused by something not quite so . . . formal?" Gregory asked with a blinding smile.

The applause was deafening. They were happy to be entertained by anything the amazingly handsome young man proposed.

He turned to several stage hands in the wing to his left and nodded. The curtain was removed to reveal several types of guitars on stands, amplifiers, a drum set, three microphones, and a double bass. Musicians and backup singers came to the stage from the audience.

As soon as his band was in place, Gregory stepped up to the mike and launched into a spirited rendition of "The Devil Went Down to Georgia," a song made popular by The Charlie Daniels Band. He played the fiddle parts and sang the lead while dueling with a professional electric guitar player.

After he had finished to a standing ovation, Gregory called Elizabeth to the stage. She was reluctant to answer his summons, but she had little choice. He asked the audience to help him, and they called her name until she appeared, Xander by her side.

"You've heard Elizabeth play better than anyone else on the planet, but did you know that she sings as well? In fact, I've heard her sing a song that I'd like for her to do for you tonight. Elizabeth, you can accompany yourself, and I'll join you on the violin. Can you guess which song I want you to do?"

"Gregory, I'm not sure about this." She looked at the audience uncomfortably.

He turned to them and smiled. They would do anything for him.

"Do you want to hear her sing?"

Thunderous applause was her answer.

Sighing, she went graciously to the piano and settled herself. Xander towered over her. A microphone on a piano stand had been placed there for her while she and Gregory were in front of the audience.

She began to play the quiet, simple opening bars, and the crowd stilled. When she started to sing "Angel" by Sarah McLachlan, every heart was touched by the sweetness of her voice. As the melody soared, Gregory added a plaintive violin obliggato that pierced the souls of those who listened.

From his place behind her, Xander placed his hand on her back between her delicate shoulder blades. He had heard Elizabeth sing the song before, but he wondered at Gregory's selection of it. "The Devil Went Down to Georgia" was obviously some little private joke of Gregory's, but why would he choose a song featuring an angel for Elizabeth? *Does he see me? Does he see all of us? Who is he? **What** is he?*

The final notes faded away, and Xander was pulled from his reverie.

The audience remained silent, unwilling to break the spell she and Gregory had woven. After a moment, Gregory smiled and gestured for Elizabeth to join him. Her white flowing dress made a stark contrast against his black tux. They were beautiful together, a study in dark and light.

"Isn't she marvelous?" he asked a bit possessively, his arm around her shoulders. The audience roared its approval, and Elizabeth bowed before she left the stage.

Xander growled his disapproval and stepped closer to Elizabeth. *Would you like to keep that arm?* Niall and Roark smiled from their places in the audience.

Standing on the opposite side of Elizabeth from Gregory, Xander looked over her head at him in surprise. *He is nearly as tall as I am now.* The guardian warrior scrutinized the boy. *It is not normal for a boy so young to be so large. He looks strong and fit as well. He would be a formidable opponent if he were a dark being.*

The program continued as planned, with Gregory's virtuoso performance of the Beethoven sonata followed by their concerto. After the final performance, Elizabeth and Gregory bowed before another standing ovation. There were cries for an encore, but Gregory begged off for them, citing the lateness of the hour and their two unscheduled musical offerings. The evening was hailed as a great success; everyone raved about the extraordinary talents of the two young performers.

After the Bennets had traveled home with the guardians flying low overhead, and a weary Elizabeth was safely in bed, Xander started to wonder why he was so on edge. He began to pace in her room, his head down and his fingers raking his dark hair back from his forehead. The guardian could not quite isolate what was bothering him. He should be profoundly relieved. All had been quiet since May, and Elizabeth was nearly always happy again. *So what is bothering me? Why do I feel so unsettled?* Then, it hit him, and he stopped dead still. The words in his head were ominous. *All has been quiet since May, and there has been no attempt on Elizabeth's life since well before that. Things are so normal that it is abnormal. What are they planning now, and what part will that boy play in the plan?*

Chapter 21

"Even though I walk through the valley of the shadow of death, I fear no evil; for Thou art with me; Thy rod and Thy staff, they comfort me." Psalm 23:4

Xander was still moving restlessly about Elizabeth's room the next morning as the clear, beautiful Sunday dawned. As her mind began to leave its dream state and form thoughts, he stopped by her bed to watch her awaken. It was his favorite part of each day; he had her to himself and could gaze at her with his feelings undisguised. There was no need to school his features or stop himself from speaking aloud. He tried to control his thoughts, for Niall and Roark were nearby with their charges, but these few moments were always the time that he felt the most freedom to admit to himself his growing feelings for Elizabeth. His flawless face reflected the tenderness in his heart for his charge as his expression softened into one of longing. He felt vulnerable and weak before this human girl.

He recognized that it was an impossible situation. He was a holy angel, and would never follow the ways of the foul Nephilim; he would never leave the service of His Master. *Elizabeth cannot ever have a relationship with me – not even a friendship. If she ever did know me for what I really am, what would she think of me? Surely she would be terrified if she ever saw me in my true form. Even if she learned to be unafraid, how could she accept that she was my assignment? I know everything about her; I have seen her most private moments and heard all of her most intimate thoughts. She would feel violated, and she would never understand.*

He caught his breath in a near sob. *One day, she will truly fall in love. She will marry, have children, and grow old with someone else. That is how it should be. Father, please let her husband be deserving of her.*

As he watched her, greedily devouring every detail of her face, she suddenly smiled, her eyes still closed. He "saw" the remnants of her pleasant dream fade away as she came closer to full consciousness. *She is so unbelievably beautiful.* Her eyes slowly opened, still heavy with sleep, and he was pierced to the soul. *I cannot bear it.* He clenched his fists. *I cannot watch her fall in love with someone else and give herself to him, yet I will not leave her. The very thought of being separated from her is painful; I think it would kill me to live the reality. Beyond that, how could I explain myself? What would I say?*

Elizabeth sat up and stretched, deciding what she would wear to church, and Xander covered his face with his hands. *I will not become what is anathema to Jehovah-Sabaoth. I will not leave my first estate or abandon my proper abode. Jude 1:6 records the Lord's condemnation of the fallen angels who have behaved in that way. 'And angels who did not keep their own domain, but abandoned their proper abode, He has kept in eternal bonds under darkness for the judgment of the great day.' I will not become a byword, a whisper, to my brothers. I shall conquer this!*

Xander heard Niall gently question, *Xander, are you well?*

He stiffened, realizing that his inner struggles were not secret. *I shall be, Niall.*

But you are not happy.

No, Xander agreed. *I am not. But there are more important things at stake than my happiness.*

Both Niall and Roark knew what Xander had not yet admitted to himself – their chief loved Elizabeth, not as a brother or a father, not as a friend, but in the way of a man for a woman. They would not speak to him of it as yet, but they were very concerned. Roark had approached Niall a few days earlier while Xander was gone with Elizabeth to her Aunt Grace's house.

I am anxious for Xander. Have you not noticed his growing love for his charge? Roark had asked.

I have, but I have confidence that Xander will do what is right in the sight of Jehovah-Elyon. He is honorable, and his strict sense of duty will not allow him to do what is wrong. Our brother suffers, and we must help him when we can do so, Niall had answered with conviction.

Roark had agreed.

~~~~~~~~

Xander walked by Elizabeth's side as she left home Sunday morning to attend her Life Group at Tabernacle Church. He trailed her as she entered the room, where Charlotte rose from her chair and hurried to meet her, Edward walking beside her.

"It's so exciting, El! You must be thrilled!" her friend exclaimed happily.

Elizabeth's forehead creased as she drew her brows together. "What are you talking about, Char?"

"You mean you don't know? That's rich. The entire world is watching you, and you don't have the faintest idea." Charlotte laughed at Elizabeth's puzzled expression.

"Okay, Char. Spill it. What is 'the whole world' watching?"

"YouTube, silly. You and Gregory have gone viral." Charlotte was nearly giddy with excitement.

Xander's jaw tightened. *Elizabeth and Gregory.*

"YouTube? Gregory and I are on YouTube? Doing what?" Elizabeth asked incredulously.

Yes, please tell us all about it. He ground his teeth together. Edward looked at him with curiosity.

226

"The film crew put up several videos of your concert last night, and it's going crazy. There's one of you singing 'Angel' with Gregory playing the violin, another of his 'The Devil Went Down to Georgia,' and several of the solos and duets. You, my friend, are the latest YouTube sensation. And I must say, both of you are gorgeous as well as supremely talented. It's unreal. The comments are wonderful. Some of them are in foreign languages. Everyone appears to understand what you were singing. It reminded me of those people you talked to from India last week."

Ah. Her gift will soon be recognized. The Master's plan progresses.

"That's so bizarre," Elizabeth replied thoughtfully. "I do remember that the people filming asked us to sign releases for publicity purposes, but I had no idea that it would be put on YouTube. How did you find out about it so soon?"

"It was on the local news this morning. Everyone is talking about it. El, you are famous! I googled 'Elizabeth Bennet,' and you came up as the top choice. There are about a zillion hits on your name."

"Wow! I'm speechless. I wonder what Gregory will say about it."

"Ha! Gregory won't mind at all. He lives for attention, especially yours."

Xander's blue eyes narrowed. *She does not return his attentions. He is her friend. That is all.*

As if on cue, Elizabeth's cell phone buzzed. It was a text from Gregory. "Hey beautiful! How does it feel to know the world is watching u? Ur awesome!"

She replied, "Weird, huh? I'm at church. Talk to you later."

I do not think modern technology is of great benefit. It is very intrusive. And texting encourages poor language skills. He had spoken aloud. Edward and the other guardians turned their heads toward him.

You disapprove of cell phones, my chief? Edward questioned.

Not really. I just think that people should avoid interrupting church with calls and texts. It is very distracting to those who are trying to listen.

Edward considered his answer. It was reasonable. He nodded.

The class was ready to start, so the girls took their seats in the circle, and Elizabeth began to lead the discussion of the day's lesson. She was in her senior year at Converse and had completed over half of her classes online for her degree in theology from Liberty, so she had been asked to team teach with an adult. Her knowledge of the Bible was vast; she had been taught the Scriptures from the time of her birth, and her mind was like a gigantic filing system. She never forgot anything she saw or heard; it was all stored away for future reference. In addition, her understanding of the Word had grown through her theology classes. Her own father marveled at her grasp of the things of God and enjoyed having regular discussions with her. His wisdom tempered her knowledge.

~~~~~~~~~~

Spring, 2007, Midnight

Xander stood rigidly in the small pool of moonlight by Elizabeth's bed. He was unaccountably anxious. She had been sleeping peacefully for at least an hour, turned toward him on her side with one leg bent and her hands by her face on the pillow. The light danced in her long hair, tangled and spread out behind her.

He felt the tension in the air, and thunder sounded in the distance. A storm was coming. The wind had been blowing steadily for the last hour and now was gaining strength. Xander saw the light flash; then the clouds drifted over the moon, blocking the moonlight and darkening the room.

The wind began to howl mournfully outside, and he suddenly noticed that something was not right. The massive angel lifted his head and sniffed the air. *What is that stench?* He detected the same offensive odor that he had found in her room during the previous year. His every sense was heightened as he examined the room with his eyes, never leaving Elizabeth's side.

Xander found the object of his search perched in a corner of the ceiling about eight feet beyond the foot of Elizabeth's bed. His blood ran cold as he recognized the source of the putrid smell. Gregory.

My first instinct was correct. Gregory Wickham is Nephilim. Who is his father? Who has challenged Jehovah-Bara?

Gregory was alone, having instructed his four guards to wait in the trees outside Elizabeth's bedroom window. He was confident that he would need no help, as he did not intend to fight.

Gregory smirked at Xander, winking at him, teasing him, issuing a dare.

Come down from your hiding place, Nephilim, Xander said to him softly as the wind picked up outside, whistling through the trees. The first raindrops began to pelt the windows, and thunder rumbled as the storm moved in.

Elizabeth began to stir, shivering and tossing in her bed. Her dreams had become nightmares; she was running as hard as she could in the darkness, but she could not escape. She panted, looking behind her, hearing something monstrous crashing through the trees, coming closer and closer to her. She could feel the heat radiating from its twisted body and smell its foul breath. The dream seemed to be happening in slow motion. She started trying to run again though she was not able to move more than a few feet. Her chest was exploding with the pain and the awful weight of the effort of escaping through the thick night, and she fell.

Elizabeth, all is well. Sleep, my little one. Nothing will harm you, Xander whispered to her, never moving his eyes from the halfling.

Elizabeth's body jerked when she fell in her dream, and she awoke to a sense of pervading evil. Her eyes were wide with fear, her pupils dilated until she seemed to have no irises. She trembled, too frozen in dread to reach out and turn on her bedside lamp.

Gregory laughed at him from his place up in the corner. *How can you promise her that nothing will harm her? How can you lie to her? You are worse than I am, Xander. At least I know that I am lying. You actually believe that you can protect her from me. I am an arm's length from her every day. One day, she will come to me willingly. You will not be able to stop her.*

The darkness of her room seemed thick and airless. The lightning flashed, and she could make out the distorted shapes of familiar things: her dresser, a bookcase, the clock on her nightstand, the windows – but she found no comfort. The shapes became sinister in her mind, and she was terrified. Her beloved room seemed to be haunted, and though she refused to believe in ghosts in the light of day, anything seemed to be possible in this black, shifting world.

Xander fought to keep himself under control. Gregory's wicked avowal to seduce Elizabeth ignited his anger, but he knew that he must remain calm to defeat the abomination. If he allowed his feelings for Elizabeth to rule his temper, he would lose the battle, and Gregory would achieve his goals. *Gregory has a smooth tongue, but can he hold his anger when insulted?* Xander asked himself. The guardian had to have just cause in order to attack the fiend, and they both knew it.

Come down here, little halfling, Xander mocked him. *You are nearly as tall as I. We are evenly matched. Do you fight as well as you talk? Do you fear me? You should.*

The thunder drew closer; flashes of lightning were accented by the booming sounds. The rain came down in a cloudburst, hitting her windows heavily and pounding on the roof. Elizabeth caught her breath in a little, frightened gasp. She knew that something vile was in her room, come to take her, perhaps to kill her. Her rational mind said that it could not be true, but her spiritual self knew that it was so. She was too afraid to speak aloud. *What if it answers me? It hates me.* She held her breath, not wanting to make a sound, and closed her eyes tightly.

Gregory rose to the bait and drifted to the floor. He had eschewed his regal robes in favor of a black tunic very much like Xander's white one. He faced the imposing guardian, his contempt evident in his sneer.

I fear no one. I am the Dark Son. Already Elizabeth is fascinated by me. Do you think she will be able to resist me? Women fall all over me even when I do not try to attract them. They cannot wait to give themselves to me. Do you think Elizabeth will refuse me if I make an effort to secure her affections?

She began to recite Scripture in her mind, and then she sang every song about God that she could remember. After she sang in her mind, she prayed continually, pleading for protection from the wickedness that had invaded her sanctuary. The hours dragged on minute by minute. The storm grew fiercer, and the branches of the trees whipping in the wind hit against her windows and made eerie patterns in the lightning flashes.

The Dark Son? Xander could not believe he had not seen it before. The amber eyes and black hair, the feeling that he had seen Gregory before – Gregory was a younger version of Lucifer! *You are the spawn of Satan!* He spat the words.

Niall and Roark, following the exchange through Xander's mind, were horrified. They could not leave their charges, but they could ask them for help.

Niall woke Lynne as Roark roused David. *Pray,* the angels whispered. *Pray for Elizabeth.*

Husband and wife looked at each other, each surprised to see the other awake.

"Why are you awake in the middle of the night, David?" Lynne asked.

"I just had an overwhelming impression that I should pray for El. How about you?" queried David.

"That's exactly what has just happened to me," she answered. "Should we go check on her?"

"That's not what we were told to do. We were told to pray for her. I would have heard if anyone were climbing the stairs outside our door. This is a spiritual battle, not a physical one. We need to obey the Holy Spirit," said David; they held hands and began to pray for their daughter, interceding on her behalf. It had not been the first time that David and Lynne had been awakened from their sleep with an impression to pray for someone or about something, but they had never before been awakened together. Neither

Lynne nor David believed in coincidences. Something was not right with Elizabeth.

I cannot believe you have not realized who I am before this time, Xander. I thought you were known for your intelligence and discernment. You seem a little slow to me.

I am more than fast enough for you, boy. Draw your sword and test me.

Look at her, Xander. She is frightened out of her senses. That is what my presence can do to her. How I look forward to her pain as I pleasure myself with her.

Xander turned his head to glance at Elizabeth. In that second, Gregory could not resist exploiting the guardian's weakness. The Dark Son lunged forward, unsheathed his sword, and swung it with all his might in an arc aimed at Xander's unprotected throat.

The house shook with the crashes of thunder, and the explosive lightning hit a nearby tree, ripping it to shreds as it spiraled around the tree and into the ground. By turns moaning and whistling, the wind ripped its way through the woods and around the buildings.

Xander heard the metallic shriek of Gregory's weapon being drawn and he turned, raising his left arm to block the blow. As Gregory's sword hit Xander's armor, Xander drew his own sword with his right hand and swung it in a half circle at his enemy's abdomen. Gregory leapt backwards in an attempt to avoid Xander's sword, but he was not fast enough. Xander almost severed the Dark Son's upper torso from his hips, slicing him nearly in half with one motion. Gregory's wound was a mortal one, but he did not dissolve. For a moment, Xander stood confused over Gregory's form, splayed out over Elizabeth's floor, waiting for him to disintegrate, but he did not.

As fast as the strike of a snake, two of Gregory's guards flew through the walls, scooped up his body, and sped into the night, leaving Xander with more questions than answers.

How could he survive that cut? Demons have died from wounds that were much less severe. Why did the guards take his body?

GUARDIAN

The storm abated, turning into a gentle rain, and the thunder sounded in the distance as it moved away. The danger had passed.

After a few seconds of reflection, Xander remembered that Elizabeth was still very much afraid. She was shivering as he went to her and knelt by her bed, stretching his upper body over her and breathing the peace of the Lord into her. His strong heart was over her fluttering, human heart; his brawny arms encased her fragile mortal form; his dark hair mingled with hers on her pillow; his lips spoke words of comfort into her ear. He began to quote Psalm 3:1-5 to her. *'Many are rising up against me. Many are saying of my soul, 'There is no deliverance for him in God.' But Thou, O Lord, art a shield about me, my glory, and the One who lifts my head. I was crying to the Lord with my voice, and He answered me from His holy mountain. I lay down and slept; I awoke, for the Lord sustains me.'*

Elizabeth, I am God's shield for you. He is your Jehovah-Magen, your God Shield. Elizabeth, I love you, and I will never allow you to be hurt while I draw breath. I will always watch over you as God has charged me to do. I will never leave you, no matter how difficult it becomes for me. Please, Elizabeth, my little one, be at peace. Sleep. You are safe.

Xander spoke softly to her until she calmed and relaxed. Somehow, she knew the threat was gone; she felt safe, her breathing slowed, and she slept. The massive angel did not move from her for the rest of the night.

Downstairs, directly under her room, her parents drifted off to sleep.

~~~~~~~~~

Xander lifted his head the next morning as the sun's rays broke over the horizon. The alarm clock by her bed sounded all too soon, and Elizabeth's eyes opened wearily to face the school day. Xander stood to his feet, and Elizabeth sat up.

*Now **that** was a strange dream I had last night. It all seemed so real, but it couldn't have been. I must have let my imagination run away with my good sense.*

233

She dressed and rushed down the stairs, convinced that all she had lived through the previous night had been a terrible nightmare.

Xander followed her closely. *Think that if it gives you peace. Let me handle the demons for you.*

As she hurried into the kitchen for a quick breakfast, Lynne stopped her. She touched her daughter's arm and asked, "What happened to you last night? God woke your father and me in the night, and we prayed for you for hours."

Concerned by the shocked look on her daughter's face, Lynne questioned her further. "Are you all right, El? What happened?"

Niall and Xander exchanged dark looks. *They will never know the battle that was fought for her*, thought Niall.

They do not need to know. If humans ever saw what was happening all around them, they would be paralyzed with fear. They would never sleep.

Elizabeth could not speak immediately to answer her mother's question, but she now knew that she had not dreamed or imagined what had happened. She was in danger of choking on the fear that had returned full force. She had not dreamed what had happened. She had lived it. Her mind screamed, *It was real! It was all real! There was something horrible in my room last night!*

She began to tremble, and Xander stepped up behind her and wrapped his arms around her shoulders as Lynne embraced her from the front. *Yes, evil was there, but I was there as well.* He quoted Numbers 6:24-26 into her mind. *'The Lord bless you and keep you; the Lord make His face shine on you, and be gracious to you; the Lord lift up His countenance on you, and give you peace.'* After a few minutes, Elizabeth calmed and was able to tell her mother everything she could remember about her terror the night before.

Lynne never questioned the veracity of her daughter's story. She knew the power of evil only too well. Every night for the next week, David and Lynne put a sleeping bag for Elizabeth at the foot of their bed, and she slept there on the floor. Elizabeth was glad to revert to her childhood habit and have a "sleepover" with her parents each night that week. It took that long for her to enter her room without feeling as if someone was looking over her shoulder, watching her.

Chapter 22

"And I saw one of his heads as if it had been slain, and his fatal wound was healed. And the whole earth was amazed and followed after the beast." Revelation 13:3

As two dark guards raced through the night sky carrying Gregory, a third guard was on a mission to awaken a doctor, a servant of Satan who had cared for Gregory since his infancy, and the fourth was flying ahead at flash speed to give instructions to Cathy and George Wickham.

Lucifer was indulging his appetites when Gregory's guard flew through the ceiling at the Wickham home, interrupting his master's pleasure. Lucifer's eyes flashed a warning red as he glared at the demon; the young actress he was using pulled a sheet around herself and ran to the adjoining room. It was well-known that Lucifer was particularly likely to inflict pain when he was distressed, and she did not care to be the object of even more of his abuse than usual. An extra measure of his sadism was a high price to pay for her career.

"There had better be a most pressing reason for this unprecedented intrusion, Crevan."

The dark one went immediately to his knees, bowing low before Satan. "My lord, the reason is grave indeed. Your son is severely injured, perhaps unto death. Jolon and Braeden are even now speeding with him to Dr. Brone's office. Duglas is with the doctor, making certain that he is ready to care for the young lord and preparing a place for his recovery. Dr. Brone will likely need to call another surgeon to assist him."

The Prince of the Power of the Air fixed the huge demon with a cold stare and spoke distinctly, clipping his words. "Exactly what were *you guards* doing when my son was injured?"

The guard cleared his throat. "The four of us were in a tree outside of Elizabeth Bennet's bedroom."

Lucifer's voice grew deceptively softer. "And where was Gregory?"

"He was in her room in demonic form, my prince."

"Alone with Xander?" The soft voice rose a quarter step in pitch.

"Yes, my lord. The young prince ordered us to stay outside. He assured us that he would not engage Xander in battle."

"Obviously, all did not go according to his plan. Did Xander attack without provocation? Did he break the rules of engagement?"

The demon heard the warning in his master's voice, but he knew that a lie would not save him. Beelzebub wanted him to blame Xander, but to do so would be unwise. If Lucifer went before God to accuse Xander, the truth would be shown. No matter how he answered, his master would be angry, and Lucifer always needed a target for his wrath.

The guard cringed and kept his head bowed. "No, my sovereign. Xander's sword was still sheathed when the young lord struck at him. Xander taunted Prince Gregory, but he did not attack him."

Apollyon stood, imperiously raised a brow, and asked with contempt, "Give me one reason why I should not send you to the pit this instant."

The demon kept his head bowed in submission, thinking quickly. His chances of survival had been nearly nil since the moment he had entered the house, finding Lucifer instead of the Wickhams. His only, very slim, hope of avoiding oblivion was to tell the truth.

"Because I was obeying you, my master."

Lucifer exploded in rage, his eyes fiery, roaring, "When did I ever tell you to allow my son to face Xander alone? When did I ever instruct you to leave him?"

The guard spoke with great respect and caution, his voice barely above a whisper. "You told the assembled congregation to obey your son as if it were you speaking. You told us to follow all of his commands as if they came from your mouth, my lord. The young prince told us to wait in the trees for him. He wanted to go in alone." Crevan held his breath and waited for the Dark Lord's strike.

Beelzebub, the ruler of the demons, did not speak for a long moment. The only sound was his accelerated, forced breathing as he considered the words of one of his most trusted guards.

"Come with me to Dr. Brone's office. Let us see what Gregory has to say about this. However, should he die, nothing will save any of you," he said malevolently, turning and taking flight, followed by Crevan and the rest of his attendants.

~~~~~~~~

Xander and Edward walked with Elizabeth and Charlotte to the Converse dining hall on Monday. The guardians watched as the girls went through the line making their selections, and then made their way to sit at their usual table.

"Have you seen Gregory today, El? I expected him to be flying high after all the attention you two are getting on YouTube." Charlotte picked up an apple and began to munch.

Elizabeth picked at her salad, lost in thought. "No, he's missed every class we have together. It's really weird. We texted a few times last night before I went to bed, and he said he'd see me today. Everyone's been asking me where he is."

238

I would like to know where he is as well. He should be in the abyss. Something is definitely odd about this.

"That is strange. He loves to be the center of attention, and he's missing it all," answered Charlotte.

"Yeah. He hasn't answered any of my texts today, and he usually replies right away. I hope he's okay," Elizabeth said a little sadly.

Only you would be concerned about the well-being of the son of Satan, thought Xander. *Spare him no sympathy, for he will hurt you in any way that he can, and the perverse delight he will take in your pain will be great.*

~~~~~~~~

A month later, Gregory suddenly reappeared at Converse as if he had never been absent. Elizabeth was surprised to see him in their first hour class and took her seat beside him.

Xander watched his guards with interest. *How did they survive the wrath of Lucifer? I am shocked that he did not kill them himself.*

"Gregory! It's great to see you again. Where in the world have you been hiding yourself? What happened? You didn't answer any of my texts or calls." Her eyes expressed her genuine concern.

"Hi, El. It's so good to be missed. I've had a few health issues, but nothing to be overly concerned about. I had to have some surgery, but everything is fine now." He smiled at her, glancing over her shoulder and up at Xander with a malicious glint in his eyes.

Nothing to be overly concerned about? You come back from the dead and act as if it were nothing?

Xander crossed his arms over his chest and moved even closer to Elizabeth. Gregory's guards stepped up behind him.

"Surgery? That sounds serious, Gregory. What about your classes? Aren't you behind?"

"Don't worry about me, El. I had tutors while I was recovering. They got my assignments from my professors, and my absences have been excused. It's as if I was never gone at all. Nothing has changed. I'll pick back up right where I left off."

When the professor began his lecture, Elizabeth turned her head away from Gregory to look toward the front of the room. Gregory rested his elbow on his desk and held the side of his face with his hand, tilting his head to look directly into Xander's eyes. The guardian warrior held his stare and returned a look that issued a challenge of his own. Gregory's guards muttered, unhappy with the situation.

Finally, seeing in her peripheral vision that Gregory's face was turned in her direction, Elizabeth glanced at him, and his gaze was redirected toward the professor.

Xander placed his hands protectively on Elizabeth's shoulders. *There are no lengths to which I would not go to protect you, my Elizabeth. He will never harm you as long as I exist in this world.*

~~~~~~~~~

Fall, 2007

Xander stood in his usual silent vigil by Elizabeth's bed, listening to her mind still praying until she drifted off to sleep. Michael flew quietly through the bedroom wall and approached Xander. He wore the tunic of a guardian.

Xander was not surprised to see him, but he waited for Michael to speak, never removing his eyes from Elizabeth.

My brother, you have been summoned, said Michael softly, a crease forming between his eyes. *I will guard Elizabeth until you return.*

I have long been expecting this, Michael. Do not be anxious for me. Had I not been summoned, I would soon have asked for an audience. Xander squared his shoulders and looked at Michael. *I am sorry that I have failed you. If I do not return, I know that you will keep her safe.*

240

Michael put his hand on Xander's shoulder. *You have not failed anyone. She is well protected and happy. She daily increases in wisdom and in favor with God. You have fought and won battles for her. I know that all will be well, Xander.*

You do not know my heart, Michael, but nothing is hidden from Jehovah-'Uzam. I would rather be unbodied than to grieve our Maker. Xander's eyes glistened, but he held his tears.

I may not know all of your heart, Xander, but I know the boundless love of Elohim. Go to Him. You need the rest that only He can give to you.

Xander gazed solemnly into Michael's kind, green eyes. The archangel faced the chief guardian and grasped his shoulders, speaking forcefully. *He has a plan, Xander. I know that all things have happened for a reason. Trust Him.*

With his voice breaking, Xander lowered his eyes and replied, *I trust Jehovah-Bara, but I no longer trust myself.*

He turned and fled the room, speeding away as if fleeing his own personal demons.

~~~~~~~~~

The cleansing, beautiful light of Jehovah-Hoshe'ah was in the throne room awaiting Xander as he walked dejectedly through the arched entryway.

Xander sank to his knees and covered himself with his wings before Elohim.

"Xander." The most beautiful voice in the universes caressed his name. It broke his heart, and he wept, great sobs that wracked his body. He fell prostrate before his Maker, arms and hands laid straight out from his torso.

"Xander, tell me what troubles you."

Xander rose to his knees with his head bowed and began to quote Psalm 69, "Save me, O God, for the waters have come up to my soul. I have sunk in deep mire, and there is no foothold; I have come into deep waters, and a flood overflows me. I am weary with my crying; my throat is parched; my eyes fail while I wait for my God. O God, it is Thou who dost know my folly, and my wrongs are not hidden from Thee. May those who wait for Thee not be ashamed through me, O Lord God of hosts; may those who seek Thee not be dishonored through me, O God of Israel. I have become estranged from my brothers."

"Xander, what have you done that distresses you so? Have I dealt harshly with you? Have I been displeased?"

With his head in his hands and his shoulders shaking with his grief, Xander exclaimed, "Oh, my God! I have failed in my duties. I do not deserve Your mercy. I am unworthy to be in Your presence."

The voice continued to speak gently to the immense angel. "Xander, I know all things. I know of nothing in which you have failed Me. Tell Me of your tears."

Xander could barely speak. In a voice choked with emotion, he said, "I love Elizabeth. I am no better than the fallen ones. I have been jealous and proud. I have been angry. I have sinned."

"Did you think that I did not know that you love Elizabeth, Xander? Did you suppose that you had hidden your anger and jealousy from Me?" God's voice was tender and loving.

Xander was silent. He had realized long before this time that the Almighty had known his innermost thoughts. *Why has He not destroyed me for my sin?*

"Xander, if you could have anything that you desired, what would you ask of Me?"

He was surprised by the question. "I want more than anything to serve you well, my Master. I do not know what to ask for. My love for Elizabeth is a part of me. To remove it would kill me now. I cannot ask for that, but I would do anything to be able to serve you and to love her without sinning." Xander paused for a moment as he collected his thoughts. "What I would ask would be impossible."

The voice laughed gently, and the wondrous sound caught the attention of every holy angel, both in heaven and on earth. They listened to His plan unfold. "Impossible? Nothing is impossible for Me. 'Behold, I Am the Lord, the God of all flesh; is anything too difficult for Me?'"

Xander raised his head a little, an awareness dawning as he recognized the words of Jeremiah 32:27. "Could I become human?"

"You would want that? You would take a lower position, give up the powers that you have, live a mortal life, grow old, and die for Elizabeth? You would sacrifice everything for the love of her?"

The chief guardian answered without hesitation and with great conviction, "I would."

"You have pleased Me greatly, Xander. You could have asked for more power, for worlds to rule, for wealth and honor – yet you request to sacrifice yourself for the one you love. What if I grant your request and she does not return your love? You know I will not force Elizabeth to love you against her will."

Xander bit his lip. *I thought that she could not love me as an angel, but I never considered that she may not love me as a human, either.* "I am willing to risk that, my Lord. It is the only chance I have to win her favor and gain her love. At least I would be able to love her openly, without guilt and without sinning."

Xander was truly stunned when God Almighty laughed aloud. It was a beautiful sound, pure and wonderful, and the holy angels radiated His light and joy throughout heaven and earth. Every light being had heard Jehovah's astonishing questions and Xander's amazing answer. Creation reflected the laughter of its Maker. Birds ceased their singing; wolves did not howl; no dog barked – all animals were silent, listening to the joyous voice of their Creator. The sun burst forth through every cloud, and the moonlight grew in brilliance until believers everywhere looked to the heavens in wonder, praising His name for the sheer power and beauty of His creation.

"Xander, I Am so delighted with your request that I will give you what you asked and more, just as I did with Solomon. From this moment, you will possess a dual nature. You will be fully human, yet fully angel. You will have all the attributes of a human man as well as all that is angelic. You will still be Elizabeth's guardian, but I have an addition to your assignment, My guardian warrior in whom I am well pleased."

Xander was so overwhelmed that he struggled to form words. "I will do whatever You ask of me, my Lord and my God."

Elohim spoke from the light. "When you were given this charge, I gave you the capacity to love Elizabeth and experience human emotions. Though you have had free will in this, Elizabeth was formed to be the perfect mate for you, and it would have been extremely difficult for you not to love her. It was in My will for you to love her, and you have not sinned in that. You fear that you are like the Nephilim; you are not. The fallen ones never loved the women they took nor the children they created from the satisfaction of their lust. Their motives were completely selfish, and their actions were abhorrent to Me.

"I want you to continue to guard her, but I also want for you to strive to gain her love in return. Xander, this will not be an easy task. You are an ancient being, but you have never had to win a woman's affections. If you follow the precepts of love as I have directed in I Corinthians 13, she will love you in return. Meditate on that chapter and on Ephesians 5:25 – 28. I want you to win her love and marry her.

"You now know who Gregory really is, but there is even more to know about Lucifer and his son. He plans to use Gregory to thwart My will for Elizabeth. She is in great danger from Gregory. You must do all that is in your power to separate them and to protect her when she is in his presence. Satan has a greater plan for Gregory after he eliminates Elizabeth; however, the time is not full. He cannot be allowed to force My hand.

"I have gifted you in the same manner in which I have gifted Elizabeth. Use those gifts to draw her to yourself so that you can serve Me together. As a couple, you will be capable of such great and wonderful things that heaven and earth will rejoice in your success. You will bring glory and honor to My name.

"Do you have any questions for Me, Xander?"

Xander thought for a moment, and then asked, "How can I live as a human? I have no identity, no education, nowhere to live."

A deep, loving chuckle came from within the light, and the angelic realm knew the sound heralded something wondrous. The host rejoiced in the plans of their Creator and in His wisdom, and every angel listened in great awe and with avid curiosity. All of heaven was silent, and all light beings held their breath in anticipation of Elohim's answer to the guardian.

"Xander, those are the easiest things you will face as a human. When you leave My presence, go to Asim. All has been arranged. Your identity has been established with a few strokes on a computer, and there is a bank account that will always have whatever you need in the way of funds. After all, I own the cattle on a thousand hills, and I have servants everywhere. You may not have a college degree, but I think you will find that you are well-equipped to earn one very quickly. You do, after all, speak every known language as well as the ancient ones that are no longer used. Your mind is perfect, and you will remember everything that you have ever heard or seen. Asim will also provide you with the paperwork that you need to enroll at Converse so that you can get to know Elizabeth. Major in music. You will be amazed at what you have the ability to do. In addition, Liberty University will grant you a graduate degree in theology. You have only to take the required tests. As you have a complete and perfect knowledge of the Scriptures and the history of the church, there will be no difficulty. Asim will give you all the details."

There was a pause as Xander absorbed all that Jehovah-Eli had said.

The Lord then spoke again, very tenderly. "There is one more point that must be discussed, Xander."

"Yes, my Adonai?"

"As you said, you have sinned. Loving Elizabeth was not a sin, but anger and jealousy are. Sinless angels do not need a Redeemer, but sinful humans do." The voice was loving and persuasive.

Xander raised his head for the first time, hope alight in his clear blue eyes as they focused on the floor beneath the holy light. "I can be forgiven? I can be Your child?"

"Do you wish to be My child?"

"More than anything, Jehovah-Go'el. To receive salvation would be beyond anything I could ask, beyond any hope I could harbor. It is the greatest gift of all."

Jesus, the Son of God, stepped from the light and approached the dual being. He held out His hands to the kneeling Xander.

"These scars in My hands, in My side, and on My feet were for you, Alexander Darcy. They are the marks of My love for you. Do you accept My sacrifice to cover your sin?"

Xander took the hands of the Son and drew them to his lips, gently kissing them as his tears fell to the scars left by the Roman nails. He released the hands of his Savior and knelt farther to kiss His tortured feet. Then he looked up into the face of his Redeemer. "Please forgive me for wounding You with my sin. Please live in me and be the Lord of my life."

Jesus took Xander's hands, drew him up from his kneeling position, and walked with him to the river of life that flowed from the throne of God. There, the Lamb of God, the Living Water, the Bread of Life baptized a new child into His family.

"Xander, your armor is complete. You now have use of the helmet of salvation, and your feet are shod with the preparation of the gospel of peace. Feed My sheep."

Xander was amazed as the sounds of great rejoicing rang through the halls of heaven. *They are celebrating my salvation! Many times have I done this for the children of God, but I never thought there would be happiness on my account.*

The laughter and joyful shouts of the host echoed through the streets, and the Light of the World that was Elohim grew until astronomers on the earth were sure that they had discovered a new star. Jesus shielded Xander's eyes with His own hands and led him from the room. He then turned, walked back to the Father and the Spirit, and disappeared into the light.

Xander remembered that he was to meet with Asim before he could return to Elizabeth, and he hurried to their meeting where he found the heavenly scheduler ready to receive him. After listening carefully to his instructions and going through the procedures necessary to complete the paperwork for his human life, he flew the familiar route to the Bennet home, taking a moment every few seconds to flip and spiral in the air, as joyous as a child with a new toy at Christmas. He was nearly giddy with relief and excitement, and he could hardly contain himself; the exhilaration of his heart was almost too much to bear.

Xander smiled widely in exuberance as he fully extended his wings and raced back to his love. His heart seemed to swell within his chest, nearly bursting with the lightness of being forgiven. He knew that many dangers lay before him and his charge, but he wanted to enjoy the happiness as long as he could. For now, he would not worry about how to win her love, he would not be anxious over all that would await him as a human, and he would not think of Gregory and the coming battles. He would instead bask in the joy of his salvation and in the wonder of the gift of love he had been given.

He was free to admit to the world that he loved Elizabeth with his whole heart, mind, and body. He wanted to shout it to the masses and write it across the skies.

It was truly a night of miracles.

The End

The story continues in ***The Guardian Trilogy: SoulFire, Book 2***.

Keep reading for an excerpt from *SoulFire*.

SoulFire

Chapter One

"Do not neglect to show hospitality to strangers, for by this some have entertained angels without knowing it."Hebrews 13:2

January, 2008

Xander, Niall, and Roark flew above Lynne's Honda as David drove Elizabeth and his wife to the airport early Friday morning. Since the concert which unintentionally had become her worldwide debut a few months prior, resulting in the creation of her reputation as a widely renowned pianist and vocalist, she had received numerous offers to perform, and she had decided to accept an engagement in Toronto after making it clear that she wished to perform sacred as well as classical music. Lynne would be traveling with her; they planned to spend the weekend as there would be a rehearsal Friday evening and the performance on Saturday night.

David had insisted on leaving well before the time that was necessary. It was an hour's drive to the airport, and he hoped to miss the morning rush hour in Greenville. Any hope of avoiding traffic problems evaporated as a car sped off of a ramp in front of a semi-truck several cars ahead in the lane to the right of them. To their horror, the truck was unable to stop and could not pull into the adjoining lane without hitting other vehicles. The driver had nowhere to go. Everything seemed to move in slow motion as they watched the scene of the accident unfold. The driver of the car realized, too late, that the truck was going to hit her. She attempted to merge with the cars in the next lane, but the truck clipped her from the rear, sending her into a spin across three lanes of traffic. Her Toyota Camry was hit by four cars as the truck jackknifed and slid down the road sideways. The terrible screeching of tires skidding and metal impacting metal seemed to go on and on; then suddenly everything was eerily quiet for a moment. All traffic came to a complete standstill in the wake of the multiple wrecks.

The Camry was crushed and twisted, and several other cars were also badly damaged. The truck driver opened his door and began to walk back down the road to survey the damage and await the police. He was already on his cell phone calling 911. Lynne and Elizabeth bowed their heads to pray for the people involved in the crash as David left the car to see if he could be of assistance to anyone. Roark walked beside him.

Xander already knew that praying for the woman in the Camry was unnecessary. Seconds before the collision, he had seen her guardian flying over the car with a tall, slender angel dressed in flowing, shimmering robes of blinding white. The angel's eyes were large and violet, and his long, white hair was held back with a silken cord. His blue-white wings were not created for speed, unlike those of a guardian or a warrior, but they were large and beautiful. Xander had seen death angels many times before when Jehovah-Shalom was ready to call one of His children home. The presence of such a light being signaled to the protector that the battle was over, and the reward for the saint was at hand. He was always filled with awe and reverence for his Master each time he witnessed the escorting of a child of God to heaven. It was never a time of sadness, for Jehovah-Rohi's timing was always perfect. The believer simply closed his eyes in one world, and opened them in the arms of an angel. Xander watched in peace as the eternal spirit of the woman left her lifeless mortal shell and went to her escort. The death angel held her close in his embrace and spread his wings, lifting her into the air as he flew with her from one world to the next, followed by her guardian.

David had gone directly to the Camry, and, seeing that the woman had not survived the accident, he had hurried to another car to comfort a crying infant whose mother was unconscious. A few other people had also approached the wrecked cars to stay with the injured until the ambulances had time to arrive. Before long, the wailing sirens were heard, signaling the arrival of the police, medical personnel, and wreckers. David returned to the car, but did not tell Elizabeth and Lynne that the woman had died. He saw no need to further upset his wife and daughter when there was nothing they could do. Roark and Niall knew that he would tell Lynne later, apart from Elizabeth.

Well more than an hour had passed before the road was cleared enough for a single line of cars to begin the painfully slow process of breaking up the traffic jam. Even though the Bennets were near the front of the congestion, by the time they reached the airport, checked their bags at the curb, and wended their way through security, Lynne and Elizabeth had missed boarding their plane. Followed closely by their guardians, they hurried to the ticket counter. Lynne explained what had happened, and they were put on another flight that would be departing in another hour, but, unfortunately, their luggage had already been loaded on their original flight and was on its way to Toronto via Pittsburg, while they had a layover in Philadelphia before changing to a different airline for the remainder of the trip. Since both flights were to arrive at Toronto International Airport, Lynne thought there would be no problem retrieving their bags. She had been assured by the customer service agent that their luggage would be kept safely for them during the one hour time difference between the flights. Lynne used her cell phone to call their contact in Toronto and apprise him of the problem. Because David had left them at the airport curb thinking that they had made it in time, she also called him to let him know about the delay.

As they sat down to wait, Elizabeth, already upset after witnessing the pileup on the freeway, started to worry that she might miss her rehearsal. *I need that time with the orchestra for my vocal pieces, and I want to be able to spend several hours becoming familiar with the piano I will be playing. We need to do sound checks with the technicians, too.* Xander, behind her, stepped closer, rubbing her shoulders and whispering in her ear. *Be anxious for nothing, my beloved. It will be well. Our Father will supply all your needs according to His riches in glory.* Xander's blue eyes twinkled in merriment. *I will fly you there myself if need be.* Elizabeth pulled a book from her bag and began to read.

Beside him, Niall rolled his eyes. *Xander, being with you now is like enduring a lovesick human male. You have not yet introduced yourself to the lady, you know.*

Xander squirmed a little uncomfortably. *Niall, I have been preparing myself for that by closely observing the ways of men with women, and there were other things I had to accomplish as well. You know that I am now registered at Converse and ready to start my classes when the term resumes. I had to take all those CLEP tests, and qualify for my degree at Liberty. Michael has been helping me by guarding Elizabeth when I have had to be gone and is now prepared to step in when needed. There has been much to arrange, and everything had to be done to my satisfaction. I cannot just appear and start talking to Elizabeth. She will ask questions, and I have had to think about the answers.*

Niall laughed at him. *Admit it, Xander. You are afraid. You are as nervous as a moonstruck teenager asking for his first date.*

There was silence between the brothers for a few minutes. Xander, his hands resting on Elizabeth's shoulders, turned his head to look at his brother.

What if she does not ever love me, Niall? Xander's voice was low and strained.

Niall looked at his brother, and his expression was serious. *Of course she will love you.* Then he grinned. *What woman could resist a tall, handsome fellow like you?*

Xander released his breath slowly in obvious frustration. *I know that human women find my physical form to be attractive, Niall, but what if she does not like the way I am? I am not witty and, even in the angelic realm, I do not converse easily with those whom I do not know well. I fear that I am boring, Niall. Elizabeth loved the human boy, Richard, and I am nothing like him. It is safer to love her from a distance than to reveal myself and risk her rejection.* Xander looked at the floor morosely.

'Faint heart never won fair lady,' Xander. You said that our Master told you that you were formed for each other. As Shakespeare said, 'Screw your courage to the sticking place.' If you accidentally bump into Elizabeth when Lynne is there, I will be with you to whisper hints into your ear if you become tongue-tied. I am fluent in the Song of Solomon.

But you have no more experience with human women than I do! Xander exclaimed aloud. A few guardians passing by with their charges glanced at him in wonder. He took a deep breath and calmed himself.

Niall chuckled. *I am witty and the essence of charm.* He smiled roguishly. *The material point is that I am not in love, and I will be able to think of interesting things to say. I guarded one of Solomon's closest advisors, and you are well aware that Solomon had seven hundred wives and three hundred concubines. I know a few things about wooing a woman.*

I have always wondered about that. Solomon was the wisest human who ever lived. Why did he have so many women? If it is difficult to keep one woman happy, why would he choose to multiply the effort by one thousand? It does not seem very wise to me, Xander interjected.

That is exactly the sort of thing you should not say to a woman. You are definitely going to need me. Niall let out an exaggerated sigh.

I will know when the time is right, insisted Xander, crossing his arms over his chest.

Try to make it before her child-bearing years are past, returned Niall with just a hint of sarcasm.

Do not quit your day job. Stand-up comedians have a short shelf life.

Ouch. Am I leaking light from that wound?

Xander snorted, but resumed his usual stoic mien as several more guardians passed by with a group leaving on a mission trip. He was silent as he contemplated Niall's words. As much as he hated to admit it, his brother was correct on two points: he needed to make Elizabeth's acquaintance very soon, and he was gripped by fear at the very thought of it. Elizabeth had reached her full height of five feet nine inches – not short for a human woman, but much smaller than he was. How could such a little person cause such anxiety in him? He knew the answer; she held his heart in her small hands. Her rejection would crush him, and his failure to win her would have far-reaching consequences for the rest of humanity. Xander set his jaw with determination. He must win her love, and he must start that process as soon as possible. He would conquer his fear by facing it.

After what seemed to be an eternity, an airline employee stepped to the counter and announced that boarding would commence for Lynne and Elizabeth's flight. Mother and daughter gathered their belongings and joined the line, Niall and Xander on either side of them. They found their seats in coach, and in due course, they arrived in Pittsburgh and disembarked, crossing the terminal to get to the gates for the other airline. Lynne was mystified to find no one at that desk, and she and Elizabeth went in search of the ticket counter for their original airline. Lynne approached a ticket agent and handed her their tickets.

"Hello. My name is Lynne Bennet. We have just arrived from Greenville, South Carolina, on your airline and were supposed to connect with a flight to Toronto. There is no one at that airline counter. Could you possibly help us?"

The woman looked at their tickets with a puzzled expression. "Mrs. Bennet, I'm sorry to have to tell you that the airline you are booked on is not flying today."

Niall and Xander flanked Elizabeth who stood behind her mother.

"Excuse me? There must be some mistake. Your airline booked us on that flight," Lynne said with exasperation.

The ticket agent turned to her computer and typed in some information. "Mrs. Bennet, you are correct. I have no idea why they set it up this way in Greenville."

"You don't understand. We have to be in Toronto tonight. My daughter is performing at Roy Thomson Hall tomorrow night and she has a rehearsal with the orchestra this evening. She has to be there."

The woman looked around Lynne at Elizabeth and recognition lit up her face. "Didn't I see you on YouTube?"

Elizabeth nodded shyly.

"Have a seat over there, ladies, and let me see what I can find. It doesn't look very promising, but I'll do my best."

Lynne and Elizabeth trudged to the seats indicated by the agent and sat down heavily. Elizabeth bowed her head. *Father, you know we need to be in Toronto in just a few hours, and it doesn't seem that we have a way to get there. Please help us, dear Lord. In Jesus' name.*

Elizabeth thought, *Amen*, and then opened her eyes to see a pair of feet in low heels directly in front of her. She lifted her head to see the lady from the ticket counter looking at her, smiling.

"It's not wonderful, but it's the best I could do. I have booked you both on an Air Jamaica flight flying stand-by. They're ready to board, so you need to get to that gate as quickly as possible."

"Thank you so much," said Lynne, accepting the tickets from her. The woman quickly gave them directions, and the group of humans and angels jogged to the Air Jamaica terminal and found the correct gate. Lynne approached the agent there and presented their tickets. The last passengers had just finished boarding the plane.

The agent smiled at them. "This is your lucky day. You are in the last row on the flight. We have room for three."

Xander glanced at Niall. *Watch them both for a second. I will be back immediately.*

Niall raised an eyebrow at him, and then turned to follow Lynne and Elizabeth.

Xander stepped into the men's room beside the gate, changed to human form, and emerged carrying a small bag and wearing a long-sleeved charcoal Henley, a black sports coat, jeans, and boots. He walked up to the agent and handed her his ticket. She looked up at one of the tallest men she had ever seen, and briefly lost her ability to speak as she took in his angelic face and powerful physique in one up-and-down glance.

"Did I make it in time? I am on stand-by for this flight," he asked, flashing his most devastating smile at her, dimples on full display. He heard her heart accelerate and read her jumbled thoughts. *If only I could be assured of this response from Elizabeth! But Elizabeth looks beyond outward appearance. She is more concerned with the heart.* When the woman made no response, he cleared his throat. *I need to get back to Elizabeth – today if possible.* The sound jolted her back to coherence.

"Uh, yes. There's one more seat. In the back. In the last row." *I sound like a complete fool. I wonder if I could sneak a picture of him with my cell phone. No one will believe me when I describe this man.*

"Thank you. Have a wonderful day." He smiled again, and she stared at him, dumbfounded.

Xander boarded the plane and made his way to the very back of it, heads turning toward him in a wave as he walked. All chatter ceased as he walked down the aisle, and the men and women gave him their full attention. He could hear their thoughts – the men noticed his musculature and wondered about his work-out regimen, and the women absorbed his physical beauty while their minds turned to images of intimacy. Xander felt naked, and he was embarrassed as the sound of his boots tapping on the floor seemed to grow louder with each step. *They are all looking at me. I am now a spectacle for humans instead of them being a spectacle for me. I Corinthians 4:9 now applies to me, 'We have become a spectacle to the world, both to angels and to men.'* He tried unsuccessfully to make less noise.

Xander drew no less attention from the few other guardians onboard the flight. The entire angelic realm was aware of their chief's dual nature and of his love for Elizabeth. To see him in his human form approaching the object of his interest raised their curiosity to unheard of heights.

I am a spectacle for the angels, too. Maybe meeting her publicly on a plane was not the best idea, after all. If it goes badly, I will be trapped for the entire flight.

It will be well. You can do this, thought Niall. *You cannot back out now. The course is set.*

Lynne sat by the window, and Elizabeth was in the middle seat. They were probably the only two beings on the plane who not noticed him. *Perfect,* thought Xander with great relief, smiling at Niall a little smugly.

Niall smirked in response and nodded toward the seat by Elizabeth. Xander's smile rapidly faded, and his muscles bulged as he lifted his bag to put it in the overhead compartment. His head nearly touched the roof of the cabin.

Good thing I am in the aisle seat. Otherwise, there would no place to put my legs. He straightened his shoulders. *This is the time. Now or never.*

He glanced at Niall once more before turning toward Elizabeth and Lynne. Leaning over slightly, he asked, "Do you ladies need for me to put anything up here for you before I take my seat?"

Both Elizabeth and her mother had been looking out of the window. At the sound of a low, masculine voice, they turned their heads toward him. Immediately, Lynne went back in her memory to the time her four-year-old El was lost at Tabernacle. *This young man looks like the same man who brought El back to me, though his hair is shorter. But, it's not possible that they are the same. That was almost fourteen years ago, and this guy can't be older than twenty or twenty-one. The man that found El would be between thirty-five and forty now. I guess it's true that everyone has a doppelganger, even Hercules.* Niall rolled his eyes.

Elizabeth stared, transfixed, into Xander's eyes. *I've seen those eyes before. There could not be another clear blue pair like those in the world. Those wonderful, kind eyes reassured me when I was a lost child, and they comforted me when we were in the wreck with Janna.* She looked down to her lap at her hands. *It can't be him. He's not old enough.*

He cleared his throat. *I seem to be doing this quite a bit today.* He was pleased that they had come up with their own explanations for his reappearance. His effort to look a little younger by wearing his hair in a modern style and dressing in clothes that were popular with college students had been successful. He had just turned twenty-one years old according to his identification papers.

Lynne was the first to leave her reverie. "No, thank you. We've already put our things away." She started reading her magazine.

Xander sat down by Elizabeth, trying unsuccessfully not to crowd her. His frame was too big for the seat, even when he scooted as far as he could toward the aisle. *Maybe meeting her on a plane was not the best idea.*

Elizabeth started giggling. *He's trying so hard not to touch me.*

She is laughing at me. I am dying here, Niall.

Give her a moment. It is not every day that a giant appears, you know. It will be well. Relax.

She turned her head to tell him not to be concerned about taking some of her space, but she was struck dumb by his perfect profile. She had been so caught up in his eyes, that she had completely missed seeing the rest of him. *I thought Gregory was beautiful, but even he isn't as gorgeous to me as this guy. There's something . . . a little too smooth about Gregory that makes me uncomfortable sometimes, but I feel completely the opposite about this man. It's almost like I know him, but surely I would remember meeting a guy who looks like this. Everything Gregory does, or says, or wears seems very studied, but this man appears to be genuine.*

Xander, reading her thoughts, could not help but smile. *She already prefers me to Gregory.* He also heard Niall's response. *Humph!*

He slowly turned his face toward hers, and she forgot everything she was going to say. Xander decided that helping her express what she had been thinking about telling him might be a good way to start a conversation. He had spent hours daydreaming of this moment, and the idea of talking to her made his palms sweaty. *That has never happened before*, he thought with surprise. He took a deep breath and forged ahead. *It was easier to close the mouths of the lions in the den with Daniel.*

"I am sorry that I take up so much room. These seats are not made for someone like me."

She bit her bottom lip to keep from laughing. "You are rather, uh, large, but don't worry about it. We were just glad to get on the plane. We were afraid that we'd be stuck in Philadelphia." She smiled a little shyly at him. She had never been so aware of a man's presence before. He seemed to fill the space around her. Even his scent was powerfully appealing to her. *What cologne is he wearing?*

"Me, too. I am flying stand-by. Last minute trip on family business," he said. It was difficult for Xander to think clearly as she leaned a little closer to him and breathed in, trying not to be obvious about it.

He smells heavenly.

Lord, please help me not to sound like a blithering idiot. Being human around her has heightened all my senses, and I cannot think well.

The flight attendant's voice came over the speakers instructing them to buckle their seat belts and prepare for take-off. They complied with her request automatically.

His voice is musical. She struggled to think of a response. *This is ridiculous. Stop thinking about the way he sounds, and looks, and smells. That's three of my five senses he has overwhelmed in one shot.*

Xander could not suppress a small smile. *The Acqua Di Gio was a good idea.*

Niall smirked behind him. *You are welcome.*

After another moment's pause, she answered, "So are we. Flying stand-by, I mean. We missed our flight in Greenville, and somehow we were booked onto a connecting flight on an airline that wasn't flying today. It's been crazy."

Xander looked out the window past Elizabeth and Lynne, spotting two demons riding the wing of the plane. *Niall, do you see them?* he asked with a small frown.

Yes, they have been there a few seconds, observing you and Elizabeth.

With an effort, Xander replaced his slight scowl with a more pleasant mien and returned his attention to his companion.

"May I ask why you are going to Toronto?" he queried.

"I'm giving a concert tomorrow night at Roy Thomson Hall," she answered, lowering her eyes.

She is so beautiful. I would love to touch her face. I remember how soft her skin was when I held her close and flew her to the hospital. Patience, Xander, patience. He forced himself to concentrate on making a sensible reply.

"Really? How interesting. What sort of concert?"

"I play the piano and sing."

"Have I heard of you? What is your name?"

"Probably not. Elizabeth Bennet. Everyone calls me El."

"I have heard of you! I have just enrolled at Converse for the spring semester. I, too, am a pianist and a vocalist, though not of your caliber, I am sure."

"That's amazing! What a small world. What's your name?"

"Alexander Darcy."

Niall rolled his eyes. *Nobody gives their full name.*

You are right. Xander cringed inwardly.

Do not worry. It was a small error.

Elizabeth chuckled, her brown eyes full of amusement. "That's quite a mouthful. What should I call you?"

Whatever you want to. Just call me, please.

Focus! Niall thought, smiling behind his hand.

He fought his way through his mental fog. "Most of my friends call me Xander, though my name is Alexander. Do you like Xander?"

"Yes, I do. It's unusual, but it fits you. I'll call you Xander, then." *I hope I won't be like everyone else to you.*

That would not be possible, Elizabeth.

"May I call you Elizabeth? You seem more like an 'Elizabeth' to me than an 'El.'" *I do not think I could call you anything else. You have consumed my thoughts as 'Elizabeth.'*

"You'll be the only one that calls me that, but that's okay." *Just call me whatever you want to.*

"I would like to come to your concert tomorrow night, if that is all right with you."

"I wish I could invite you, but it's been sold out for a while now. I can't get a ticket for you." *What if I never see him again?*

He smiled widely, showing his dimples. "I am not entirely without connections. I may be able to get a ticket myself. If I can come, would you and your mother like to go to dinner afterwards?"

Dimples! How is it possible that he could be even more breathtaking? Elizabeth tore her eyes away from his face and looked at her mother, a question in her eyes.

Lynne had been following the conversation carefully, though she had not looked up from her magazine. She caught Elizabeth's glance in her peripheral vision and raised her head to see El's eyes pleading with her. Niall whispered to her, *This is a good man. You can trust him.*

Lynne reflected a moment. *She hasn't shown any interest in a boy since Richard broke her heart last year. Perhaps we should get to know this young man a little better.*

"What did you have in mind, Fitzwilliam?" she asked, directing her gaze toward him.

Niall remembered Lynne's telephone conversations with the booking agent. *They are staying at the Intercontinental Toronto Centre which is within walking distance of the Roy Thomson Hall. The Azure Restaurant there has a reputation for being classy and romantic.*

Xander smiled at Lynne. "The Azure Restaurant is located in the InterContinental Toronto Centre near Roy Thomson Hall, and it is very good. I would love to treat you, ladies."

"I think it might be good for you two to be friends, since you'll be going to school together in a couple of weeks, and the location is perfect. We are actually staying in the hotel," Lynne replied.

Thanks for the help, Niall.

Actually, you are doing quite well on your own. I am pleasantly shocked.

"Excellent. I will meet you backstage after the concert."

"But what if you can't get a ticket?" asked Elizabeth.

"I promise you that I will be there. You can trust me on this. I would not miss it for anything," said Xander, looking rather seriously at her.

He is very self-possessed for such a young man. Very mature, Lynne mused.

You have no idea, thought Niall.

Xander, quite pleased with his progress, continued to chat with Elizabeth and Lynne until they landed in Toronto.

After they retrieved their items from the overhead compartment and exited the plane, he joined them as they walked to the baggage claim area. They waited until all the passengers had retrieved their luggage, but there was no sign of theirs. Together they approached the customer service area.

Lynne explained the entire ordeal to the agent, and he checked his computer. "Ah!" he exclaimed. "Air Jamaica passengers are already in Canada when they leave the plane. The flight from Pittsburgh was on a different airline and left your bags in their area. Your bags have not yet cleared customs, and you can't go get them because you are already through. Let me see what I can do."

"But we're in a hurry," Lynne said.

From behind them, Xander had scanned the large area and had seen their luggage, actually sitting some distance away at the other airline's baggage area. He stepped outside the small office. *Niall, get their luggage. I will stay with them.*

Niall flew at flash speed to the men's room on the other side of the customs area. After he had morphed into human form, he walked to the other baggage area and picked up the luggage. Niall telepathed with the guardian standing by a customs agent, and the agent's protector stepped into an office and came back out in human form, dressed as an agent. Niall approached him, produced a passport, and was quickly cleared through customs. Then he casually walked by Xander, left the luggage behind him, and walked quickly away, returning seconds later in angelic form.

"Mrs. Bennet, Elizabeth," Xander called from the door. "Look what I found."

Lynne was delighted. "How did you do that?"

"I told you that I had a few connections," he replied, winking saucily at Elizabeth.

Elizabeth blinked. *Is he flirting with me?*

Lynne turned back to the office and called to the young man who was still busily typing away at his computer. "Never mind. Everything's fine."

He looked surprised as he glanced up to see the Bennet ladies walking away with a towering man carrying several large pieces of luggage, along with his own small bag, as if they were of no weight at all. *Is there an American pro basketball team in town?*

Xander waited with Lynne and Elizabeth at the curb while Lynne hailed a cab. While the cabbie stowed their bags in the trunk, Xander had a chance to say a few words privately to Elizabeth.

"I will look forward to your performance tomorrow night, Elizabeth. Do not forget our dinner engagement," he said, smiling into her deep brown eyes.

She looked up at him in wonder. *There are very few boys my age who treat me this way. He's huge, but I like it. Rather than feeling threatened, I feel protected and safe.*

"There is absolutely no chance that I will forget it." She turned from him and slid into the cab with her mother.

He stood watching as the car drove away. *Look back at me. Please, Elizabeth, my love. I want to see your face looking at me.*

As if she had heard him, she turned to look out the rear window at him, and lifted her hand to wave goodbye.

Xander smiled widely and waved back. Then he quickly stepped into a crowd of people and changed into angelic form. In less than a second, he had caught up to the cab and flew over it with Niall.

You are grinning like a lovesick teenager.

Xander could not find it in himself to care whether or not he looked foolish. His heart was light and filled with hope. *This may not be as difficult as I thought it would be.*

Then he remembered the demons on the wing. *There will be complications.*

We will deal with them, answered Niall with confidence.

I look forward to it, said Michael appearing suddenly on Xander's other side, flying with them in formation.

ABOUT THE AUTHOR

Robin Helm's books reflect her love of music, as well as her fascination with the paranormal and science fiction.

Published works include The Guardian Trilogy: *Guardian, SoulFire,* and *Legacy*), the Yours by Design series: *Accidentally Yours, Sincerely Yours,* and *Forever Yours* (Fitzwilliam Darcy switches places in time with his descendant, Will Darcy), and Understanding Elizabeth (Regency romance).

She contributed to *A Very Austen Christmas: Austen Anthologies, Book 1*, an anthology featuring like-minded authors, in 2017, and *A Very Austen Valentine: Austen Anthologies, Book 2* which was released on December 29, 2018.

New releases for 2019 include *More to Love,* a standalone historical sweet romance dealing with body image; *Lawfully Innocent,* a historical U.S. Marshal romance book in the Lawkeepers series; *Maestro,* a historical sweet romance featuring a brilliant musician and his student; and *A Very Austen Romance: Austen Anthologies, Book 3.*

She lives in sunny South Carolina where she teaches piano and adores her one husband, two married daughters, and three grandchildren.

For updates on new releases, follow Robin Helm on her Amazon Author page at https://www.amazon.com/Robin-Helm/e/B005MLFMTG/

Robin Helm recommends books by Wendi Sotis,
Laura Hile, and Mandy Cook.

Our latest book -

A Very Austen Valentine: Austen Anthologies, Book 2

Six beloved authors deliver romantic Valentine novellas set in Jane Austen's Regency world. Robin Helm, Laura Hile, Wendi Sotis, and Barbara Cornthwaite, together with Susan Kaye and Mandy Cook, share variations of Pride and Prejudice, Persuasion, and Sense and Sensibility, featuring your favorite characters in sequels, adaptations, and spinoffs of Austen's adored novels.

Experience uplifting romance, laugh-out-loud humor, and poignant regret as these authors deftly tug on your heartstrings this Valentine's Day.

A Very Austen Valentine, the second book in the Austen Anthologies series, features six authors, all friends, who wished to share Austenesque variations, prequels, and sequels with their readers. Working together to produce the first book in the series (*A Very Austen Christmas*) was such an enjoyable experience, and the book was so well received, that we knew we had to do another one. Our four original authors invited two more to join us in the follow-up, and we plan to do at least five books in the series.

Most of our stories feature our own original characters, as well as the favorite characters of Austen. We strive to keep Austen's heroes and heroines within the confines she set for them herself. In other words, we do not have the characters act in ways she would not have written. The good guys remain good guys, and the bad guys remain bad guys. We also believe in happily-ever-afters. We want you to be happy at the end of each story.

All six of us are experienced writers with previously published books. I hope you enjoy this introduction to six authors, some of whom may be new to you. If you loved *Pride and Prejudice, Persuasion, Sense and Sensibility, Emma, Northanger Abbey, or Mansfield Park*, you will enjoy their books.

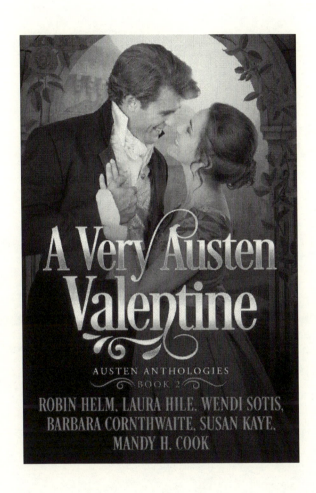

Made in the USA
Columbia, SC
19 March 2023

14027229R00164